THREE WISHES

T0283114

What Reviewers Say About Anne Shade's Work

Love and Lotus Blossoms

"Shade imbues this optimistic story of lifelong self-discovery with a refreshing amount of emotional complexity, delivering a queer romance that leans into affection as much as drama, and values friendship and familial love as deeply as romantic connection. ...Shade's well-drawn Black cast and sophistication in presenting a variety of relationship styles—including open relationships and connections that shift between romance and friendship—creates a rich, affirming, and love-filled setting... (Starred review)" —*Publishers Weekly*

Masquerade

"Shade has some moments of genius in this novel where her use of language, descriptions and characters were magnificent." —*Lesbian Review*

"The atmosphere is brilliant. The way Anne Shade describes the places, the clothes, the vocabulary and turns of phrases she uses carried me easily to Harlem in the 1920s. Some scenes were so vivid in my mind that it was almost like watching a movie. ...*Masquerade* is an unexpectedly wild ride, in turns thrilling and chilling. There's nothing more exciting than a woman's quest for freedom and self-discovery."—*Jude in the Stars*

"Heartbreakingly beautiful. This story made me happy and at the same time broke my heart! It was filled with passion and drama that made for an exciting story, packed with emotions that take the reader on quite the ride. It was everything I had expected and so much more. The story was dramatic, and I just couldn't put it down. I had no idea how the story was going to go, and at times I was worried it would all end in a dramatic gangster ending, but that just added to the thrill."—*LezBiReviewed*

Femme Tales

"If you're a sucker for fairy tales, this trio of racy lesbian retellings is for you. Bringing a modern sensibility to classics like *Beauty and the Beast*, *Sleeping Beauty*, and *Cinderella*, Shade puts a sapphic spin on them that manages to feel realistic."—Rachel Kramer Bussel, *BuzzFeed: 20 Super Sexy Novels Full of Taboo, Kink, Toys, and More*

"Shade twines together three sensual novellas, each based on a classic fairy tale and centering black lesbian love. ...The fairy tale connections put a fun, creative spin on these quick outings. Readers looking for sweet and spicy lesbian romance will be pleased." —*Publishers Weekly*

"All three novellas are quick and easy reads with lovely characters, beautiful settings and some very steamy romances. They are the perfect stories if you want to sit and escape from the real world for a while, and enjoy a bit of fairy tale magic with your romance. I thoroughly enjoyed all three stories."—*Rainbow Reflections*

"I sped through this queer book because the stories were so juicy and sweet, with contemporary storylines that place these characters in Chicago. Each story is packed with tension and smouldering desire with adorably sweet endings. If you're looking for some lesbian romance with B/F dynamic, then these stories are a cute contemporary take on the bedtime stories you loved as a kid, featuring stories exclusively about women of colour."—*Minka Guides*

"Who doesn't love the swagger of a butch or the strength and sass of a femme? All of these characters have depth and are not cardboard cut outs at all. The sense of family is strong through each story and it is probably one of the things I enjoyed most. *Femme Tales* is for every little girl who has grown up wishing for a happy ever after with the Princess not the Prince."—*Lesbian Review*

"All of these characters have depth and are not cardboard cut outs at all. The sense of family is strong through each story and it is probably one of the things I enjoyed most."—*Les Rêveur*

Visit us at www.boldstrokesbooks.com

By the Author

Femme Tales

Masquerade

Love and Lotus Blossoms

Her Heart's Desire

My Secret Valentine

Securing Ava

Three Wishes

THREE WISHES

by

Anne Shade

2023

THREE WISHES

© 2023 By Anne Shade. All Rights Reserved.

ISBN 13: 978-1-63679-349-8

This Trade Paperback Original Is Published By
Bold Strokes Books, Inc.
P.O. Box 249
Valley Falls, NY 12185

First Edition: May 2023

This is a work of fiction. Names, characters, places, and incidents are the product of the author's imagination or are used fictitiously. Any resemblance to actual persons, living or dead, business establishments, events, or locales is entirely coincidental.

This book, or parts thereof, may not be reproduced in any form without permission.

Credits
Editor: Cindy Cresap
Production Design: Susan Ramundo
Cover Design By Jeanine Henning

Acknowledgments

I would like to acknowledge Princess Akeem McDowell who unwittingly became the muse for this story when she revealed her love for the Aladdin tale and her wish to see someone write a sapphic version of said tale. Well, Princess, challenge accepted! I hope you learn to love this story as much as the original. Thank you for the inspiration.

PROLOGUE

Long ago in a Faraway Land

Once upon a time, on an island off the coast of Madagascar, Adnan Fadel arrived on the shores of Akiba from Africa after leading a revolt against a cruel king who profited off enslaving his own people. They were attempting to sail to Madagascar, but their boats were caught in a storm and thrown off course. When they landed onto the shores of what they thought was a deserted island, they were approached by a small group of tall, beautiful, elegantly dressed people whose leader, called Chirag, offered them a home on the island. Adnan was wary of the stranger, but as their boats were destroyed and fortune had not only saved their lives but brought them all safely ashore, he convinced his people to accept Chirag's offer.

Chirag revealed that his people had inhabited the island for over half a millennium and were a society of spirits called jinn who chose to find a home where they could live in peace and light. The jinn were spiritual beings who only revealed themselves if they chose to, in any form they chose. Human form was the most common one Chirag and his jinn used. They were happy but had grown bored with their quiet existence and hadn't realized what was missing until Adnan and his people arrived on their shores. The jinn saw it as a gift from the heavens and the chance to be a part of the human existence once again but without all the strife the outside world brought with it. The jinn had been touched by the humans' story and their brave escape. Chirag knew from looking into the thoughts and minds of the newcomers that all they wanted was the same thing that Chirag and his people had wanted when they created their little island, peace.

The jinn chose to live amongst the people of Akiba in human form, becoming a part of their daily life. Like humans, jinn lived in similar societies, ate, drank, and practiced whatever ideology they chose. But, while both humans and jinn died, the jinn's mortal lives could last for thousands of years. Through the centuries, some of the jinn had even married and raised families of their own within Akiba. The jinn became so enmeshed with the Akiba kingdom over time that humans were treated as equals by the jinn. With the integration of humans and jinn living in Akiba, Chirag, who had become Anand's vizier, formed a council of jinn to assist in maintaining peace and order.

That was the world in which Princess Aliya Fadel had grown up and one she would never imagine having to leave. Aliya was the descendant of Akiba's first human leader, Adnan Fadel, and the twin sister of the crown prince and future king of Akiba, Adnan the Second, named after their forefather. Aliya was glad she entered the world just moments after her brother or she would be the one being pricked and prodded while being fitted for coronation robes right now. She giggled as Adnan sucked in a breath as the seamstress stuck him with another pin.

"Is all of this truly necessary?" Adnan complained.

"Yes, Your Royal Highness. You are much broader than your father, so new robes are required," the seamstress said.

"How can you stand this?" Adnan asked Aliya.

"I'm used to it, dear brother. Besides, me having to be poked and prodded by a seamstress means I'll be getting a lovely new garment to add to my wardrobe."

"You mean a new garment to catch Naima's eye," Adnan said with a grin.

Aliya smiled. "I don't need a garment to do that."

Adnan chuckled, causing his shoulders to shake, which brought another prick from the seamstress. He quirked an eye at her. "I'm beginning to think you're doing that on purpose."

Her eyes widened in fear. "No, Your Royal Highness, I would never do that!"

Adnan smiled softly down at her and gently grasped her chin. "I know, Fulani. I was just teasing."

Aliya shook her head as Fulani blushed prettily and bashfully looked away. "I believe I am finished, Prince Adnan."

Adnan sighed with relief. Aliya stood and helped him to carefully remove the heavy robe then handed it to Fulani.

"Why don't we do my fitting first thing after breakfast in the morning, Fulani, so that you can get right to work on Adnan's robe. His attire is far more important and complicated than mine."

"Yes, Princess Aliya. Thank you." Fulani gave them both a slight bow then gave Adnan a shy grin before hurrying out of his chambers.

Adnan sunk onto a pile of pillows. He picked up a date from a bowl and popped it into his mouth, chewing thoughtfully.

"Aliya, do you think I'm ready for this? Father still has plenty of good years ahead of him. Maybe we can hold this off until next year."

Aliya sat beside him. "Adnan, you have been preparing for this since you were a boy. You are more than ready to lead us. Our people love you almost as much, if not more, than Father. Besides, he was ready to pass the crown on to you in your eighteenth year but chose to give you a couple of years to travel, see the world outside of Akiba, and enjoy a bit of freedom. That is more than I could ever dream of and I'm not the future king."

"You know you can leave on your own adventures any time."

Aliya sighed. "Yes, but I would have to take Malik and half the royal guard with me. Do you know how difficult it would be to roam freely with a contingent of guards with me? I trained right alongside you, Malik, and Naima growing up. I can defend myself. I don't know why Father insists that I must be guarded at all times."

"Because you are the heart and soul of your kingdom, your people adore you, and they couldn't bear to lose you," a feminine voice said.

"Naima!" Aliya turned, scrambled up off the pillows as gracefully as she could, threw herself into Naima's open arms, and peppered her face with kisses. "My love, when did you return? Why didn't you send word?"

Naima laughed. "I just returned and came here as soon as I found out where you were."

Aliya hadn't realized how worried she had been these past few weeks that Naima had been gone. After Adnan's coronation, Naima would become his vizier, and part of her duties would be regular visits to Akiba's trade routes to ensure that there were no issues. The trip she had just returned from was a tour with their current trade council to introduce her to those routes and their representatives. It was the longest Naima had ever been away from Akiba and the longest she and Aliya had been separated since they were children. As daughter of the current vizier, Naima had practically grown up in the castle with Aliya and Adnan so the three were close. While Adnan looked at Naima as another sister, Aliya had developed stronger feelings for the beautiful girl that had turned into a stunningly beautiful woman. Though it had been five years since they admitted their feelings to one another, Aliya still couldn't believe Naima felt the same way.

Adnan walked up and stood beside them. "Sister, you do realize that even though you will be married, Naima is still my vizier, and you will have to share her."

"Yes, but until the coronation, she is all mine." She gave Naima one last kiss and stepped away to allow her brother to greet her.

Aliya watched them chatting and thought how much of an imposing pair they made. Adnan had inherited their father's height and broad frame. She only stood to his shoulders, a gift from her mother. She had also inherited her mother's curves, which gave the seamstresses a devil of a time fitting her properly. Naima, being a jinni and a descendent of the first jinn of Akiba, was just as tall as Adnan with a smooth glowing copper complexion, eyes that were dark as the night sky yet still had an otherworldly glow about them, and thick, long black hair that she wore in a braided loop style at the back of her head. Except when she was alone with Aliya when she would let it hang loose and free. Naima also regularly trained with the jinn royal guard, so beneath her generous curves was hardened and toned muscle. Aliya thought the contrast was very alluring.

"As much as I would love for this visit to be a social one, I must discuss an important matter with both of you," Naima was saying as Aliya woke from her trance of absorbing her beloved with her eyes.

"What is it?" Adnan asked.

"Why don't we sit." Naima directed them toward seating on Adnan's terrace.

"What's wrong?" Aliya asked as soon as they settled.

Naima sighed. "It's Malik. There is word that he is stirring up trouble among the younger jinn."

Adnan frowned. "What kind of trouble?"

"That he's tired of pretending that humans and jinn are equal. That because the jinn have magic that they should be the ones in power and humans should be serving them," Naima said.

Aliya gasped in surprise. "But Malik is head of the royal guard, a position his father and their fathers before held since Akiba came to be four hundred years ago. Just as you, he has practically grown up in this castle with us. Why would he be trying to start an uprising?"

Adnan frowned and pulled at the end of his beard the way he did when he was worried. "Malik has not been happy since the day you and Naima announced your betrothal. He has been in love with you, Aliya, since we were children. I think he held out hope you would return his feelings someday. He had also hoped that with my coronation I would name him my vizier, despite how the position was one inherited by the previous vizier's heir if they chose to take it."

"I don't think Malik expected me to step forward when my brother Hakeem chose to be part of the royal guard instead of following in our father's footsteps. As you know, if the previous vizier's heir does not take the position, the incoming king has the right to elect one of his choosing," Naima said.

"Malik assumed that would be him because he has been my friend and personal guard for so long. I never gave him any reason to believe that I would choose him. From the moment Hakeem turned it down I had determined I would choose Naima," Adnan said.

Aliya looked from her brother to Naima. "Has his talk brought any trouble? I haven't heard of any issues from the jinn council."

Naima shook her head. "Thankfully, not yet, but we need to put an end to it before it does. I wanted to speak with you two first before bringing it to the jinn council's attention, although, I would not be surprised if they had not heard something already."

Aliya reached over and took Naima's hand. "You know I have never given him any reason to believe I returned his feelings? I was always courteous and friendly to him, but that is all."

Naima gave Aliya a smile of reassurance. "I know, my love. Malik misconstrued your kind and generous heart for love and Adnan's friendship to gain power. Now he seeks to hurt those who he thinks have hurt and betrayed him."

"As Father is still king until my coronation in a few days, I will speak with him and the four of us will go together to speak with the jinn council. Maybe we can find a way to make his punishment more lenient. After all, he has laid his life on the line for me on several occasions during our travels."

By the time Naima and the royal family met with the Akiba jinn council, word of Malik's attempted uprising had already reached them, and they were determined to give him the fullest extent of punishment required for such an offense. They exiled Malik not only from the kingdom but the entire island. No amount of his own magic could break the exile placed on him. Aliya was heartbroken that their pleas for leniency to the council had no effect on their decision. Malik railed against the decision and his parents wept as the council performed the exile spell and Malik disappeared in a cloud of silver smoke. Aliya prayed that Malik would someday see the error of his ways and be able to return to Akiba.

10 Years Later

Naima loved the way Aliya watched her as she dressed, amazed that after ten years of marriage, she could still feel even more love and attraction for her wife as she did the day they were married.

"Do you have to go so early? Another few moments in bed won't hurt," Aliya said, posing seductively.

Naima looked at her skeptically. "A few minutes with you could turn into an hour. How would it look for the king's vizier to show up an hour late to a council meeting?"

Aliya sighed in resignation. "You're right. Just remember, you promised to escort me to the mountain villages later."

Naima sat on the side of the bed and brushed a thick curl of hair from Aliya's face. "I remember and I will be there. Now, give me a kiss to sustain me until then."

Aliya grabbed Naima's face for a kiss that could sustain her for years to come. "There, now begone before I start undressing you," she said, releasing Naima with a teasing grin.

An hour later, Naima sat beside Adnan trying to calm her racing heart.

"What do you mean Malik is back in Akiba? I thought the council exiled him?" Adnan's voice was filled with confusion and concern.

"We did, Your Highness, but it seems Malik has found a way to override our spell. He was first spotted a few days ago by some of the fishermen walking along the shore. When one tried to follow him, the fisherman said he simply disappeared. He was seen again a day later walking along the edge of the village and once again disappeared."

"He's traveling through the realms," Naima said angrily.

"For what purpose?" Adnan asked.

No one on the council spoke for a moment. They looked as if they were afraid to continue. As if by not speaking it aloud, they could keep whatever was happening from being true.

"He has found help from a dark jinn," Naima said.

Adnan looked over at her in confusion. "Once again, for what purpose?"

"Revenge, Your Highness. Word from the Imaginal realm is that Malik had joined with a very powerful black jinn, to seek revenge for his exile," Aman, a senior council member, said.

Adnan stroked his beard. "Do you know who the jinn is?"

Aman looked at the only two other senior members who had been there since the days of Chirag. "Yes, Your Highness. His name is Jahir. He had sought to live among us long ago but was turned away due to his belief that jinn and humans were not equal. He has been very outspoken over the millennia about Chirag's betrayal of their friendship by turning him away. They have not communicated since then so he may not be aware of Chirag's ascension. We believe his and Malik's feelings of betrayal by Akiba have brought them together."

There were few things that scared Naima, the first and foremost was losing Aliya and her home and being helpless to do anything about it. A feeling of foreboding turned her blood cold as she realized what could happen if the council wasn't able to fight Jahir and Malik. Malik's magic was not as strong as it could have been if he had chosen to use it more often, but he wanted so much to appear human for Aliya that he shut away that part of him. Jahir, on the other hand, was widely known throughout the realms for his dark magic and that few jinn or even demons had survived a battle with him. Despite the number of powerful jinn on the council, they had been living simple lives within the kingdom, and Naima wasn't sure if Akiba would survive such a battle. Especially the humans who would be caught in the middle.

"There must be something we can do," she said.

"Until Malik or Jahir reveal themselves or their plan, there is nothing we can do but wait. They have not revealed themselves to jinn, only to humans, which means they may be testing us to see how we'll respond."

"For them to sneak up on the island rather than announcing themselves outright and act so clandestinely with their appearances could only mean they are up to nothing but trouble. We must protect our people," Adnan commanded.

Naima agreed with him and knew, as vizier, she had to help him find a way to protect the humans of Akiba and leave the welfare of the jinn in the council's hands. Naima was a direct descendent of Chirag, the original and most powerful jinn of Akiba and practiced her magical skills just as much as she practiced her combat skills, but defeating a powerful jinn like Jahir gave her doubt in her abilities. If Malik were back for revenge, Aliya was probably at the top of his list, and Naima had a sick feeling they would be finding out what he had planned soon enough.

As Aliya made her way to the jinn council hall to meet Naima, she felt the remnants of Naima's worry filling her with a cold dread. They had a psychic bond, not much different than what she shared with her twin brother. She was suddenly anxious and found herself nervously looking around her surroundings. She had a guard with her, but something told her she needed to hurry and get to the council hall. She picked up her pace and was relieved to see her guard do the same. He must have felt her anxiety because he too began looking around. They were just a few buildings away from the hall when she stopped and stared wide-eyed at the sight of Malik standing between two stalls. Her mind told her it couldn't be him, he was exiled, but there he stood smiling at her as if it were just another day.

She looked back at her guard. "Rahim."

"Yes, Your Highness."

"Tell me, do you see a man dressed in black robes and turban with a braided beard standing between the stalls ahead of us?"

"No, Your Highness. Is there something wrong?"

She gazed from his look of concern back to where she had seen Malik. There was no one there. "I could have sworn I saw someone." Her brow furrowed in confusion.

She shook her head and continued when movement out the corner of her eye made her turn back to her guard who was no longer there. In his place stood Malik with a dark look on his face. "Good morning, Princess."

Aliya looked around for her guard, but he was nowhere to be found.

"Don't worry, he's safe. I've sent him back to the palace. Since when does the royal family have human guards escorting them outside the palace?"

Aliya attempted to use her connection to Naima for help, but something blocked her. Malik gave her a smug grin and shook his head.

"Can't have you calling for help now, can we?"

Aliya looked at the people passing by, but for some reason they looked right through her. She looked down at her hands and could see that she was still a solid form, but no one even acknowledged her gaze. She reached out, but they walked around her like she was some unseen obstacle.

"How are you here, Malik? What is this about?" she asked.

"Your questions will be answered in due time, Princess. For now, we're going to need you to come along willingly. We really don't want to hurt you," Malik said.

Aliya considered what her options were. She was combat trained, but Malik had been a royal guard, his training far outweighed hers. He was also a jinn. He hadn't used his power often while he was here but judging by how easily he had sent her guard away and was controlling what the people in the marketplace saw, it was obvious his skills had strengthened since being exiled. She was no match for him. She could only hope her guard had informed the royal guard of them being separated and that Naima would immediately be notified. She tried once more to reach out to Naima but was blocked. Malik gave her a knowing grin.

"Princess, if we have to force you, others may get hurt." He waved his hand indicating the people swirling around them in the marketplace.

"No, please, don't hurt anyone. I will go with you willingly."

"Excellent." Malik snapped his fingers, the marketplace flashed away, and they now stood in the throne room.

Malik's eyes shone with an eerie red light and Aliya knew that this wasn't the Malik she had grown up with. There was something, or someone else, behind that light that frightened her.

"What has happened to you, Malik?" she asked warily.

Suddenly, the light dimmed, and he was now the man she recognized. "Now you show concern. You and Adnan allowed the council to send me from the only home I have known, causing shame upon my family and the legacy my father lay before me without a word of defense." His voice rose angrily as he spoke.

"We did speak on your behalf. When the council informed us of your sentence, Adnan and I asked for mercy. We knew, in some way, we held some responsibility for why you had turned to treason. That we unintentionally misled you to believe things that weren't true. Adnan was devastated after your exile. He blamed himself for the longest time, and we are both truly sorry that we couldn't sway the council's decision." Aliya hesitantly approached Malik and took his hand. "There was nothing we could do. You know as well as we do, since Chirag and Adnan the First, that the royal family and jinn council work together and may not always agree, but when either has made a decision for what they feel is best for their own people, we may try and sway, but we are not allowed to interfere in the action taken," Aliya said.

There was a momentary look of doubt in Malik's eyes, but it was replaced by that eerie light. He snatched his hand away and sneered at Aliya.

"Do not try to sway us from our path with your lies."

Malik walked past her toward the two thrones on a dais behind her and sat in the more ornate one designated for the king. The second was usually occupied by her until Adnan took a bride. He stroked the head of the golden phoenix statue at the end of the armrest. Adnan the First had chosen a phoenix as the symbol for Akiba because like the mythical bird, his people overcame adversity through aggression. They had fought their way to freedom and like the phoenix, transformed themselves with an undefeatable spirit.

"Why is it that you humans worship beings far more powerful than you? Is it because you are weak and envious of that power? Because by worshiping something greater than you it gives you the power to control them by tying them to your wishes and whims? The jinn were once some of the most powerful and intelligent beings in existence. We were here before your Adam was molded from the clay on which we stood. We were here before your precious Muhammed, Jesus, or Buddha." Malik stared off as if seeing the unseen. "Before humans, the jinn enjoyed God's favor, reigning supreme, and building great cities to rule as we saw fit." He looked back at Aliya with eyes alight with fire. "Then God created Adam and wanted jinn and angel alike to kneel before him. We were all-powerful, yet he raised that weak, pathetic human above us. But a jinn named Iblis defied God and refused to kneel before Adam, and what did God do? He did what the humans and jinn of Akiba tried to do to us, exiled him. Iblis vowed to lead Adam and his kind to hell as revenge for what had been done to him." Malik leaned forward and a wicked grin spread across his face as he looked at Aliya. "Do you think we shall provide Akiba with the same revenge?"

Aliya shook with fear, not for herself but for her people. "No, please, I will do anything you ask as long as you leave my people unharmed."

Malik relaxed back into the throne and smoothed his braided beard in contemplation. "Call to your wife. You are free to reach out to her now. I want her and Adnan here immediately."

As if a veil had been lifted allowing in sound, Naima's voice rose in Aliya's head calling her name. "I'm at the palace in the throne room. Hurry and bring Adnan," she answered wordlessly.

The words had barely finished leaving her thoughts when a cloud of purple smoke appeared, and Naima and Adnan stood before her in its remnants. Aliya ran into Naima's arms. After a brief embrace, Naima pulled back and gently took Aliya's face in her hands.

"What happened?" Naima frantically looked her over in concern. "One of the palace jinn guards came to us at the hall and told us your guard had suddenly appeared out of nowhere without you. When my calls to you were met by a wall, we frantically searched the marketplace for you, but no one had remembered seeing you or your guard all morning."

"Malik is here," Aliya answered Naima telepathically and gazed toward the throne.

Naima's whole body stiffened. As she turned around, she placed Aliya protectively behind her.

Adnan watched them in confusion then turned as well, his eyes widening in surprise.

"Malik."

"Ah, such a wonderful reunion," Malik said sarcastically.

The doors to the palace room banged open and Aliya turned to see a contingent of royal guards running into the room, but they were just as quickly thrown back out by an invisible force. The doors slammed shut leaving the sound of the guards banging and shouting from the other side. Aliya turned and looked past Naima at Malik whose eyes were dimming from the glow that shone when he used his powers.

"I'd prefer not to have an audience. Let's keep this between old friends, shall we?"

"Why are you here, Malik?" Adnan asked.

"Well, Your Royal Highness," Malik said in a tone that belied the respect the title deserved. "We are here to right a wrong that has been done to us. One that was instigated by Jinn Naima and went unmitigated by you and your sister."

"None of us have wronged you. You wrought what you sowed when you committed treason. You tried to cause strife and upheaval within a fair and inclusive society that took centuries to build," Adnan said, bravely walking toward the foot of the dais to stand before Malik.

Aliya feared her brother's bravery would be the death of him someday. She prayed that today would not be that day. She moved to stand beside Naima who took her hand.

"We did nothing but tell the truth. The jinn were not meant to be ruled by humans. Humans should be bowing down to us and the power we were given by the Almighty. You are weak, pathetic fools to think you are equal to the jinn." Malik stood and looked down on Adnan. "Foolish to believe that you should be sitting on this throne instead of us. We are here not only for revenge for your exiling us but also to raise up the true ruling class of Akiba, the mighty jinn."

"The jinn council will not allow you to do that, and why are you speaking as if there are more than one of you here?" Adnan asked, looking around the room.

Malik sneered and looked at Naima. "Ask your vizier. She sees the truth."

Aliya looked to Naima. "What is he talking about, Naima?"

A muscle in Naima's jaw flinched, a tic that occurred during the rare moments Aliya had seen her truly angry, and her eyes shone with a bright light. "Because Malik is not the only one there. Jahir, a black jinni, has joined with him. That is how he was able to overcome the exile spell."

Aliya felt her blood run cold with fear. Black jinn were some of the most powerful jinn that existed. They were also the jinn most associated with evil and practicing black magic.

"What wrong have we done this Jahir that he would seek revenge with you?" Adnan asked Malik.

Malik walked down the steps of the dais toward Naima and Aliya. He stood directly before Naima as his lips curled in disdain. "Tell them," he commanded in a voice that was quiet yet reverberated around the room.

Naima looked directly into the red glow of Malik's eyes to show she did not fear him or Jahir. She felt Aliya grip her arm and saw

Adnan, out of the corner of her eye, move to stand on her other side, as if they were the anchor she needed before the storm that was about to strike. She wordlessly reached out to both, letting them know that whatever happened, she would protect them with her life.

"Jahir came to Akiba centuries ago seeking refuge and was turned away by a jinni he had thought was his friend, my grandfather, Chirag."

"Yes, my dear friend Chirag who, unlike most of your jinn in Akiba, was a black jinni who lost all taste for the black arts when he lost his mate during a battle with angels who had been sent to hunt us down for the trouble we had wrought. He sought out Buddha himself and became a jinni of peace, understanding, and forgiveness. I came to him for refuge and his teachings were suddenly forgotten. He turned me away with no cause to do so other than he wanted to remain the most powerful jinni on the island."

He was no longer identifying himself as *we* which Naima realized meant that he had pushed Malik out of the way to speak directly to them and not through Malik.

Naima shook her head. "You weave lies just as easily as Chirag said you did. He and the council had good cause to turn you away. You sought to bring mischief and strife into the kingdom for your own entertainment. You had not changed, nor did you have any intention of doing so. It took Chirag years to undo the damage and distrust you had caused amongst the humans and jinn of Akiba. Because of you, the human descendants of the ones directly affected by your games are living in the mountains still distrustful of the jinn and the royal family of Akiba."

Chirag had welcomed Jahir, believing, like him, his old friend had changed and sought to live his remaining life in peace. But Jahir was a trickster and took advantage of Chirag's kind nature, almost causing a civil war between the jinn and the humans. Many humans fled the island, fearful of the jinn they had known for a lifetime turning on them or their descendants to enslave them. Chirag had tried to convince them that the treaty they had signed in magic and blood would hold true, that the jinn had been tricked just as the humans had been by Jahir, but fear of enslavement was a strong factor from a people who had barely brought up one generation as freedmen. Many of the ones who chose to stay moved into the mountains. Isolating themselves from the kingdom and the jinn. The longer they stayed away, the more distrustful they had become. They accepted the kindnesses of the royal family, but they tended their own lands by hand without, as far as they knew, jinn magic. What they didn't realize was that the island was created by jinn magic so the fact that their crops bore fruit season after season had more to do with that magic than how well they tended them. It helped to have good caretakers, but the crops would thrive with or without them.

Chirag exiled Jahir from the island promising that for as long as he held breath, Jahir was forbidden to return. With Jahir sharing a human form with Malik, they were able to override both of their exiles because, technically, they were no longer truly Jahir or Malik. Combined, they were something dark and dangerous. Naima hoped the more senior members of the council who had been the original jinn with Chirag were able to stop them. They were all blue jinn so their individual magic wasn't as strong, but together they might be able to end this without destroying Akiba.

Malik shrugged. "They are not worth our efforts. It is the jinn and the humans of this city who are the ones that betrayed us. The ones that have let you and the royals trick them into believing jinn and humans are equal." He looked at Aliya and Adnan with bitter resentment. "As Iblis did with Adam, we refuse to bow to you, and when we make the jinn see how weak these humans are by removing their precious royals and Chirag's legacy, they will learn how truly powerful we are."

"Malik, you can't let him use you this way. These are your people and your home. Your parents are still here. They still plead with the council after all these years to allow you to come back home. If you allow Jahir to do this, you will put them in the middle of a war," Aliya said.

Malik looked unsure. Naima realized the true Malik had stepped forward and that Aliya's words were getting through to him. She looked over at Adnan who acknowledged her with a nod that he also noticed.

Adnan spoke up as well. "We met with the council this morning. They had been considering your parents' plea, as they felt enough time had passed for your punishment, then word got back to them that you had been spotted on the island. Doing this, allowing Jahir to bring you here to seek revenge, only gives them cause to believe they were right in sending you away. Stop this now, before anyone gets hurt, and you can come back home, my friend."

Malik frowned. "Your friend?"

Adnan nodded and placed a hand on Malik's shoulder. "I blame myself for what happened, and I will always consider you my friend."

It appeared to Naima that Aliya and Adnan might have gotten through to Malik. She chose to stay quiet as their friendship with Malik went far deeper than hers. Her interfering would only cause trouble seeing as the anger toward her came more from Jahir's feelings toward Chirag.

Malik's eyes shone with moisture. "They will truly let me come home?"

Adnan gave him an encouraging smile. "Yes, just let this need for revenge go."

Malik looked confused again, as if he were battling with something. Naima knew it had to be Jahir trying to wrest control back. "Jahir," he said, grimacing as if in pain.

"Let the council help you. They can deal with Jahir," Adnan said.

Too late, Naima realized that was the wrong thing to say. She could only pull Aliya into her arms as Malik's eyes blazed like a white-hot fire and an unseen force threw them across the room. Naima made sure to keep her back to Malik to take the brunt of it to protect Aliya, who had automatically wrapped her arms around Naima and held on as they slid across the marble floor.

"You dare threaten US with the council!" Malik's voice echoed and reverberated through the room in a near-deafening sound.

Naima and Aliya looked back toward Malik. He towered over Adnan, the glow from his eyes now surrounding his body, his robes floating about his ankles as he levitated inches above the floor. Adnan held his arm close to his body; his hand was a broken jumble of flesh and bone. Naima realized it was the hand he'd had on Malik's shoulder.

"ADNAN!" Aliya screamed, holding her own arm.

Naima knew, that as twins, Aliya and Adnan shared a bond that no other brother or sister who had not shared the same womb did. They could feel each other's pain and emotions but only if they were extreme.

"Jahir!" Naima called as she stood and blocked Aliya from view. "It is me you seek to hurt, not them. Let them go and you and I can settle whatever wrong Chirag has done you."

"Naima, no," Aliya said in a pained whisper.

Malik floated toward her and sneered down at her with a gleeful madness. She knew then that Malik was gone, at least for now. "Oh, my jinn child, believe me, I have something special planned for you. In the meantime, I have an agreement with Malik that I must fulfill."

He made his way back toward Adnan and Naima called up her magic and threw it at him with everything she had. She might not be the powerful black jinni Chirag was, but she was a high-ranking blue jinni and she hoped it would be enough to keep Malik busy until the council was able to breach the doors. The explosive sound of magical blasts had been going on for several minutes, so she knew they were trying to get past Jahir's black magic. Her blast had barely caught Malik's attention. He smiled maliciously over his shoulder at her before pinning her against the wall with a flick of his wrist. She struggled against the magical bonds that held her, to no avail. Naima could only watch as Malik lifted Adnan from the ground by his neck and squeezed. Aliya screamed and Naima did the only thing she could think to do for the woman she loved as she watched and felt her brother dying, she entered her mind and told her to sleep. Aliya's screams stopped as she collapsed back onto the floor unconscious.

Naima struggled in vain against her bonds then she heard a sickening snap and looked up to see Adnan go limp. She shook her head in disbelief as Adnan's bright soul rose from his body and looked in confusion around the throne room until his eyes landed on Aliya lying unconscious on the floor. He floated over to her and stroked her cheek lovingly before pressing a kiss upon her brow. Adnan then looked up at Naima.

"I'm sorry, my friend," she said, tears streaming down her cheeks.

"Keep her safe, Naima," Adnan's spirit said.

Naima nodded and the room grew dark as shadowed figures rose from the floor and surrounded Adnan's spirit.

"Did you think I would let you go so easily?" Malik said, looking down upon Adnan.

"No...No...NO!" Naima screamed.

Adnan's spirit tried to fight off the shadows as they pulled him back down into the floor with them.

"You will suffer as we have, exiled from your home. Your spirit will not have the pleasure of walking this island as your ancestors had before they moved on. This is our revenge upon you, Adnan Fadel," Malik said gleefully.

Malik's expression turned to one of horror as he witnessed Adnan screaming and struggling against his fate.

"No, this isn't what I wanted. You've gone too far," Malik said. "I'm done, no more, please." Malik looked toward Naima.

"Help him...help me," he pleaded.

Naima shook her head. "I can't. You must fight him, Malik, before he takes full control."

When Malik's expression turned to one of angry disgust, Naima knew Jahir had taken over once again.

"I give you power beyond your wildest imagination, and you shy away from it like a frightened child. Look away if you must, but I will still have my revenge," Malik said, seeming to speak to himself.

Adnan stared at Naima in fright as he was pulled completely down into the floor. Naima stared at the spot willing him to come back, but she didn't have that power. Then her gaze fell on Malik as he knelt beside Aliya. Naima began her struggles anew.

"Don't you touch her! She had nothing to do with this. She's innocent!" Naima shouted.

Malik cocked his head at her. "She spurned Malik's love, and she didn't succeed at speaking up for him at his hearing before the council. I see nothing but guilt within her mind over these things."

"Jahir, please, do what you will to me, but don't harm her." Naima pleaded directly to Jahir since he was the one in complete control now.

He looked back down at Aliya and gently stroked her face. "Malik may be weak, but his feelings for this human are strong. That may be the only thing that saves her." He looked back up at Naima with a sneer. "Not your pitiful pleas. You still must pay for Chirag's betrayal."

Naima watched in fear as he slowly strolled toward her with an evil grin on his face. "There is a part of the story Chirag did not tell you. His mate was my mate as well. When we lost her, I was just as devastated, but instead of staying and sharing our grief, Chirag left me alone to mourn not only her loss but his as well. He took what little light I had left within me. The darkness almost swallowed me whole until I heard all he had done with this little island. While I had been wallowing in grief and despair, he had been creating a life of light and love." Malik frowned. "He had done all of that without reaching out to ask me to join him. We had shared a millennium together, and it was as if none of that ever happened. I wanted to know why so I came here and asked to join his paradise, but he treated me as if he didn't know me. He loved his little humans more than he loved me and I grew jealous. I thought that if I could show him the flaw in his plan, he would give it up and we could be together again." Malik's eyes burned bright with anger as he looked back at Naima. "But he chose those weak mortals over me."

"Chirag didn't choose the mortals as much as he chose a life of peace and to share that peace with human and jinn alike. To live in a world where fear and distrust no longer existed among the two beings and that, despite our powers, jinn and humans shared more in common than any other beings in the realms. You came in and tried to destroy that peace, that is why he sent you away."

"The reason why does not matter. All that matters is that he did it. What we shared should have outweighed what he built here," Malik growled angrily into Naima's face.

If Naima weren't pinned to the wall, she would have backed away from the madness in his eyes. Malik gathered his composure and backed away from her just as the doors to the throne room crashed open and the council stood in the doorway, hands raised in a defensive spell. Aman's gaze landed on Adnan's lifeless body, the awkward way his head lay on his broken neck, and then back at Malik in horror.

"What have you done?" Aman said in despair.

"I eliminated the only barrier to my throne," Malik said, looking smugly at the council.

Jinn council member Aman looked at Aliya's still form.

"She is alive," Naima said.

Aman looked at Naima with relief and nodded. He turned back toward Malik, watching him warily as he walked toward him.

"Who are we in the presence of?" Aman asked.

Malik smirked. "Someone far more powerful than you, Jinni Aman. Do you really think your council can stop me? I am the most powerful black jinn in the realms. I have molded dark magic to my will over millenniums."

"We sense Malik is still with us. We would like to speak with him," Aman said.

"I will speak on behalf of Malik. Have you come to bargain with us?" Malik asked.

"What could we possibly have to bargain with a jinn as powerful as you?" Aman responded.

Malik turned his back on the council and soldiers now crowding the room and walked toward the throne. Once he was seated, he looked at Aman as if he were seriously considering the question.

"I want Akiba to rule as I see fit. After all"—his gaze briefly landed on Adnan's body then back on Aman—"you are without a ruler."

"A bargain calls for an exchange of something. What would the people of Akiba get in return?" Aman asked.

Malik shrugged. "Your lives. There would be no need of a council as I have the only say in what happens so the jinn would be free to do as they please. The humans will be allowed to continue to stay with the understanding that jinn and human equality will be no more. They are here out of the kindness of my heart and will learn that their place is beneath that of the jinn."

"That is no bargain, and we will not allow you to take Akiba," Aman said, standing bravely before Malik with no defensive spell to protect him.

Malik raised his hand, snapped his finger, and turned Aman into a pile of blue ash. There was a moment of stunned silence before chaos erupted. The rest of the council and the jinn guards threw everything they had at Malik. With his powers focused elsewhere, Naima was able to break her invisible bonds and pull Aliya out of harm's way, forming a protective bubble around them as the sound of bones snapping, blood-curdling screams, and scurrying feet resounded throughout the room. The scurrying feet were the human guards trying to escape, but Malik wiped them all out with a flick of his wrist. When the slaughter ended, Malik raised his hand and forced both Naima and Aliya forward, to their knees before him.

❖

Aliya looked at the monster before her, remembered what he had done to her brother, watched as he destroyed the most powerful jinn in Akiba with a snap of his fingers, and her blood ran cold with fear. Naima had awoken her just as the battle had begun and dragged her away or she would have been lying right in the middle of it. She knew Malik was no longer occupying his human body, but she hoped there was something good left of him that could stop Jahir from destroying Akiba. Malik's eyes looked down at her, but there was no sign of the young man she once knew in them. The thing that looked out of them now was gazing at her as if she were a tempting morsel ready for his taking.

"What shall I do with you, Princess?" Malik asked, tapping his chin in contemplation.

"Just let her go, Jahir. You have what you wanted. You've taken the throne and destroyed the council. What more could the princess give you?" Naima said.

Aliya reached over and took her hand. "Please, let us both go. We won't fight you."

Malik looked down at their clasped hands and back up at her with a slow grin. "Ah, but, Princess, I have one last act of revenge and you are going to help me complete it."

Aliya shook her head defiantly. "I will not fight you, but I also will not help you."

"You already have."

Aliya looked at him in confusion and he turned his gaze on Naima. She realized what he meant to do. He was going to use her to exact his revenge on Naima. She gripped Naima's hand harder and moved closer to her. Naima wrapped her arm around Aliya's shoulder in comfort.

"Isn't love an amazing thing," Malik said with a mocking pout. "It has been known to heal the most broken of beings, but it has also been known to bring down the strongest of them. Let's use your human history as an example. God had placed Adam in a position of great power with angels and jinn kneeling at his feet. Yet Eve, the woman he loved, managed to get him to betray the Almighty for a taste of forbidden fruit. With one bite, Adam lost favor and was banished from the garden. Can you imagine how strong their love must have been for Adam to do such a foolish thing?"

"Is this what this is all about? Love?" Naima said, causing Malik to look at her in annoyance.

"In a way, yes. You see, I loved Chirag and our mate just as passionately as Adam loved Eve. Like Adam, I would have done anything they asked. But unlike Adam, my banishment for loving so passionately was spent abandoned and alone. I had no Eve to ease the pain, thanks to Chirag, who lived his life as if I never existed. Since he is not here to pay for the part he played in my heartbreak, you will have to do so in his place. I have such a delicious plan for you, dear Naima."

Malik lifted his hand and magically snatched a bejeweled lamp from a nearby shelf. He held it up, twisting and turning it before his face, admiring the large opal stone on the side. Aliya couldn't fathom how the lamp played in all of this until she felt Naima tense beside her. Malik smiled knowingly as Naima gazed at the lamp in fear.

"Naima, what is it?" Aliya had never seen Naima afraid of anything, let alone a simple lamp.

"Do you remember when we were children and my father told us stories about jinn being imprisoned in rings or vessels?" Naima's voice shook as she spoke.

"Yes. They are only freed by someone who finds the object and..." Aliya's blood ran cold as she remembered the stories.

She looked back at Malik who stroked the lamp almost seductively. That still didn't explain how he was going to use her.

"I will tell you, Princess," he said, answering her unspoken thought. "Your dear Naima will be tied to this lamp granting wishes until she is found by her one true love. Only then, once she grants her true love's final wish will she be free."

Aliya saw a flaw in his plan. If she was Naima's one true love as Naima had always told her, all she had to do was find a way to get the lamp and have Naima grant her wishes.

"It is not that simple," Naima said, reading Aliya's thoughts. "Is it Jahir?"

Malik's lips curled up cruelly. "No, it is not. You see, Princess, the only way for that to happen is if you remember not only who Naima is but who you are as well."

Aliya was once again confused. "Why would I not remember who am I? Who Naima is?"

"Therein lies my final step. If I recall correctly, unlike jinn who live for thousands of years, you mere mortals live only one life at a time. As my final touch to this delicious portrait of revenge, I grant you a thousand lifetimes, your spirit traveling from one soul to the next, never knowing who you are until you find the lamp. Only then will you recognize who you truly are."

Aliya's eyes widened in alarm. "I'll live a thousand lifetimes not knowing who I am? Not knowing how to find the lamp unless I happen to come across it by chance?"

Malik looked at her with sadistic satisfaction. "Exactly."

"And if I don't find the lamp within those lifetimes?"

Malik smiled with an almost childlike glee. "Your soul will move on, and Naima will be left to a life of servitude at the bidding of anyone in possession of the lamp."

Aliya turned to Naima, reached up, and wiped a tear from her cheek. "I will find you. I don't care how long it takes, my love, I will find you," she said vehemently.

Naima began to fade, and Aliya screamed, "NOOO!" as she changed into a cloud of purple smoke slowly drifting into the lamp Malik held. She tried to lunge for it, but an invisible force held her in place. As Aliya pleaded and cried Naima's name, a voice whispered in her head, "I love you," before the last tendrils of purple smoke evaporated in the air. Malik tossed the lamp toward Aliya, and she was just able to touch it before it disappeared completely. That last heartless act was the final straw for Aliya.

What Malik, or anyone else, including Naima didn't know was that she'd been learning and practicing the magical arts for months with a witch who lived within Akiba's mountain tribes. She had begun the practice after the woman had offered to read Aliya's fortune and revealed that there was jinn blood within the Fadel ancestry. The witch told her that with practice, Aliya could be a powerful witch in her own right. With her brother wearing the mantle of king and her wife holding the powerful position of vizier, Aliya had felt the need to do more for her people than provide baskets of gifts or words of encouragement. She wanted to have the power to protect them just as Adnan and Naima were doing. Her abilities weren't enough to stop Malik, but her recent dabbling into the dark arts had given her skills that would not make his existence any easier than Naima's would be chained to that lamp.

She looked directly into Malik's eyes with an intensity she could feel throughout her body. "I curse you, Jinni Jahir, and Jinni Malik. I call forth the jinn and human ancestors of Akiba and curse you for what you've done here this day. I curse you both to that body for however long it takes me to find Naima and only when we both stand before you, freed from your curse will you be freed from mine."

Aliya meant it with every fiber of her being and could feel a power running through her that she'd never felt before. With satisfaction, she could see not only a look of fear in his eyes, but she could swear she saw the real Malik grinning within them as well. His hand raised, and everything went dark.

CHAPTER ONE

Present Day

"Did you enjoy your stay, Ms. Porter?"

Elise gave the young woman behind the front desk a pleasant smile. "Yes, Bindi, I did, thank you. Everyone was lovely."

"Excellent." Bindi slid her credit card back across the counter. "Will there be anything else?"

"Yes, may I store my luggage here while I take one last walk around the marketplace before I get the ferry to the mainland?"

"It would be our pleasure."

An hour later, Elise was heading back to the hotel feeling a strange sense of loss. Something she felt every year at the end of her annual trip to Nosy Be. She had first visited as a teenager during a family vacation to Africa. Part of the tour included a few days at a resort located on a small island off the coast of Madagascar. The moment she had stepped off the ferry she felt as if she were home. The feeling had deepened, and a sense of déjà vu had almost frightened her when she and her family visited the ruins of a past kingdom. When Elise told her mother, she had teased her, saying maybe she had lived there in another life. The day they left, Elise felt such an intense sadness and loss that she had cried as she stood on the ferry back to the mainland watching as they drifted farther away from the island. Her family had never gone back to Nosy Be, but Elise knew, someday she would. She never forgot that feeling through the years. Had even looked up the history of the island and had found nothing on the mysterious ruins there. There were no records of any society of the grand scale of the ruins found having inhabited the island. As a matter of fact, the first recorded inhabitants were Swahili and Indian traders in the fifteenth century. The ruins dated centuries before that, but Elise knew, deep within her soul, that there was more to the small island than anyone knew.

When Elise went off to college, her obsession with Nosy Be dimmed as she threw herself into her studies, campus life, and then building her career and starting her own interior design firm. It wasn't until five years ago, on her thirty-fifth birthday, that Nosy Be became a focus in her life again. Her parents were downsizing and selling the family home. Elise and her twin brother, Marcus, were helping them go through boxes in the attic when she found a small plastic genie lamp she had bought while in Nosy Be all those years ago. The vendor who'd sold it to her, a tall, elegant man with long white hair and beard dressed in brightly colored robes, told her that it was once rumored that an evil genie had been the downfall of the mysterious kingdom on the island. That it was believed that it would rise again one day when the kingdom's princess found her true love who had been trapped in a lamp by the genie. She had been charmed by the story and bought the lamp.

She returned to the marketplace to find the vendor the next day to hear more of the story, but he wasn't there. When she asked some of the other vendors about him, they had no idea who she was talking about. She held that lamp close to her heart as she cried upon leaving the island. Elise had stroked the lamp lovingly and felt a tear roll down her cheek. She had quickly wiped the tear away and tucked the lamp in a box of old toys to be tossed, but she couldn't toss away the renewed need to return to Nosy Be. So, the following spring, and every spring after that for the past five years, she made a sabbatical to the little island, always returning to the ruins with flowers and a prayer. For what, she didn't know, but the need to pay her respects was always there. She also looked for the mysterious vendor who had sold her the plastic lamp but never saw him again.

As Elise finished her stroll through the marketplace, something pulled at her. She turned to find the vendor from all those years ago smiling at her from an over-ladened cart she hadn't seen the whole week she had been there. She stared wide-eyed as he waved her over. He looked exactly as he did when she'd first encountered him so long ago. How was that possible? She walked over to him.

"You've grown into quite a beautiful woman, Elise," the vendor said.

"H-how do you know my name?"

"You told me when you bought the lamp all those years ago and I would never forget such a beautiful face," he said cheerfully.

Elise didn't remember that, but how else would he know her name?

"Come, I have something I've been saving just for you." He walked around to the back of the cart, out of sight of the other vendors. She was hesitant to follow.

He poked his head back out. "There is no need to fear me, child."

Elise looked around and noticed a few vendors smiling her way. Feeling a little better knowing that others saw her with the strange man, she followed him to the back of the cart. Without even looking, he reached into the cart and pulled out an oil lamp that was a larger, real-life replica of the plastic one he'd first sold her. Even under the layers of dust, the large opal on the side of the lamp caught the sunlight. There were a few other, smaller jewels decorating the top and base of the lamp, but the opal alone would be worth a fortune. The vendor held the lamp out to her.

"It's beautiful, but I couldn't possibly afford it." Her business was doing well but not enough to afford a lamp with a handful of precious stones.

The man gazed down at the lamp with a frown, then looked back up at her with a strange light to his eyes. "What would it be worth to you? Here, hold it. Look it over if you like."

Elise accepted the lamp from him. She was surprised to find the metal warm to her touch. She also felt that the lamp was meant to be hers, as if she'd been searching for it all her life. She rubbed some of the dust off the opal and a tingle ran from her fingers and up her arm. She pulled her hand back as if she'd been shocked.

"How much would you like for it?" She expected to hear some exorbitant price that he would want to haggle about, but Elise knew she would pay whatever he asked.

The vendor thoughtfully stroked one of his beard braids as he considered her question, then gave a ridiculously low price, which happened to be the exact amount of money she had in her wallet. After she paid him, he carefully wrapped the lamp in a beautiful, deep purple silk material and placed it in a velvet, satin-lined box.

"May you have the love and strength to do what you must do, Your Highness." He gave her a slight bow as he handed the box to her.

Elise looked at him in confusion. "Uh, thank you."

He gazed lovingly down at the box in her hands and back up at her looking as if he were about to cry. "No, Elise, thank you. Now you better hurry so you don't miss the ferry."

Elise was about to ask how he knew she was leaving, but the sound of the alarm on her phone reminding her of the ferry departure silenced her. She gave the man a nervous smile and thanked him before turning and rushing off. Something made her look back over her shoulder, and when she did the man and his cart were gone. She stopped and stared wide-eyed at the empty spot before the horn for the ferry docking jarred her out of her disbelief. She shook her head and headed back to the hotel for her luggage.

It took Elise almost a week to find the nerve to open the box with the lamp in it. Something about the whole experience with the pull toward it, the disappearing vendor, and the intensity of her loss when leaving Nosy Be spooked her. She wasn't a superstitious woman, but her grandmother believed in all that nonsense about spirits, people being called to things, and reincarnation. Ever since she'd told her grandmother about that first trip to Nosy Be, she had tried to convince Elise to meet with a past life regression therapist to see if there was a connection. Elise had refused, calling it all hoodoo, but now, as she opened the box and felt that same sense of belonging when she looked at the lamp, she wondered if there was something to all of that.

"Don't be ridiculous," she reprimanded herself.

She carefully removed the lamp from its satin bed, placed it on her kitchen counter, and removed the silk wrapping. Surprisingly, the silk wrapping hadn't removed any of the dust. She took the edge of the material and gently began cleaning the lamp. She saved the opal for last, and as she rubbed at the stone the lamp seemed to heat in her hand. It was soon too hot to hold, and Elise dropped it. As soon as it hit the floor the top popped off and a plume of purple smoke billowed out of the lamp. In a panic, Elise turned and filled a nearby glass with water, spun back around, and tossed the water in the direction of the lamp. She stared in shock at a scantily clad woman standing over the lamp, her hair dripping with the water she had thrown on her. The woman was dressed in a high-neck turquoise satin crop top with voluminous sleeves, a pair of matching harem pants, and bare feet. She knelt before Elise, raising her hands in supplication.

"Thou who hast summoned me from the lamp, it shall be my honor to grant you three wishes for whatever your heart desires," she said in an alluring voice.

Elise gazed down at the top of the woman's head in confusion trying to piece together what was going on. She had turned her back for just a moment, hadn't heard the beep from the security system from any of her doors or windows opening, and she hadn't left all morning, so how the hell did this woman get into her home? She slowly backed up toward the counter where the butcher block of knives sat and grabbed the largest one out of its slot.

"Who are you and how'd you get into my house?" She held the knife threateningly toward the woman who still knelt on the floor.

"You summoned me," she said, peeking up at Elise through long, dark lashes.

Her pupils were so dark not even light seemed to reflect off them. She stared at Elise for a moment before her eyes widened in shock and the darkness changed into a whirlpool of black with silver swirls, like pictures Elise had seen of the Milky Way.

"Aliya?" the woman whispered as she slowly stood.

Elise shook her head and thrust the knife forward.

"Stay back! I don't know you or an Aliya, but I will cut you if you come any closer."

"I can't believe, after so long, we have finally found each other," the woman said, tears streaming down her face. "I'm not going to hurt you. Please, put the knife down. I can explain everything."

Elise hesitated, looking the strange woman over. She was barely clothed so she probably didn't have any weapons on her, and something deep within her told her the woman was telling the truth, she wouldn't hurt her. Elise had always been good at listening to that little voice in her head because it always seemed to keep her out of trouble. She set the knife on the counter but kept it within reach. She also reached into the pocket of her robe and pulled out her cell phone with 911 on speed dial just in case.

"Start talking," Elise said.

It took everything Naima had not to run up and pull the woman who now carried Aliya's spirit into her arms. Somehow, they had finally found their way to each other, and her heart was nearly bursting with joy. The woman standing fearfully before her didn't look like Aliya, but she was just as beautiful with a darker, richer complexion, at least a foot taller, and had soft curves that weren't as generous. Her wide, frightened eyes were the same golden brown as Aliya's, as well as the slope of her nose and full mouth. Naima could feel Aliya's soul deep within the woman. Had their time to end this curse finally come?

"I had almost given up hope, but here you are, at last," Naima said tearfully.

"Lady, I don't know what you're going on about, but if you don't either leave or start talking in the next two minutes…" She held up an electronic device so that Naima could see the numbers 911 lit on the screen. "I'm calling the police."

Naima had to remind herself that the woman had no idea who Naima was or anything about the lamp. This was not going to be an easy task.

"My name is Naima. I know this is going to be difficult to believe, but you summoned me from the lamp." She pointed back toward the lamp lying on the floor. "I am what you would call a genie."

The woman looked at Naima as if she'd lost her mind. "That's it, I'm calling—" Naima used her magic to snatch the device away and gently lay it on the counter out of reach.

"H-How did you do that?" the woman asked, easing her hand toward the knife, which slid out of reach and landed back in the butcher block. "I'm dreaming. That's gotta be it. I'm dreaming."

Naima hated having to use magic without warning humans first, their fragile minds just couldn't handle it, but under the circumstances, she had no choice. "Maybe we should sit down and talk. What's your name?"

The woman gave her a skeptical look. "If you're really a genie, you tell me."

With a sigh, Naima searched the woman's thoughts. "It's Elise, correct? Please, let's sit and talk."

Elise hesitated then walked around the counter and sat on a stool. Naima stayed where she was, not wanting to spook her further. "I'm going to need you to just listen and try to have an open mind for what I am about to tell you. Can you do that?"

"I-I guess," Elise said, nervously fidgeting with the belt of her robe.

Naima nodded and tried giving her a reassuring smile as she slowly squatted to pick up the lamp. Even after all these centuries, the sight of what had become her home still made her angry. She took a deep, calming breath and set the lamp on the counter between them. Naima had gone over in her head thousands of times what she would say to Aliya when she saw her again, but each conversation had been with an Aliya who knew who she was. Even with the knowledge of what Jahir's spell entailed, Naima had convinced herself that Aliya would instantly recognize her if, and when, she found the lamp. The fear in Elise's eyes showed her that was not the case.

"Please be there, Aliya. I can't go on much longer like this," Naima said, trying to reach out to Aliya through their bond that seemed to have been severed that day so long ago.

Elise's brow furrowed as she cocked her head and looked at Naima curiously but still fearfully. "Why do I suddenly feel like I know you?"

Naima tried to tamp down the hope rising in her heart. Recognition didn't mean she'd heard her silent plea. "Because, in a way, you do. Long ago, in another lifetime, you and I were…" Naima hesitated, not knowing if Elise was a lover of women. "Friends," she said to be safe. All of this was going to be difficult enough for her to believe without revealing they were married. "An evil jinn, or genie as humans have called us, attacked our kingdom seeking revenge, and wrought death and destruction to our people. He trapped me within this lamp and cursed you to live through one thousand lifetimes, or until you found the lamp, not knowing who you truly are."

Seeing the disbelief on Elise's face and how she looked at Naima as if she were a crazed woman, she decided to pause to let that sink in and answer any questions Elise might have so far.

"So, you're trying to tell me that I've been reincarnated, and in a previous life you and I were friends until an evil genie trapped you in a lamp and pretty much cursed me to a life of immortality. Let me guess, rubbing the lamp made you appear," Elise said sarcastically.

"That pretty much sums it up," Naima said, holding back a grin. She could already see her wife's no-nonsense attitude show through.

Elise stared at her wide-eyed for a moment, then laughed. There was a little hysteria in the sound. "That's it...I'm definitely dreaming...or losing my mind," she said between breaths of air.

"Do you have a birthmark in the shape of a heart on your inner thigh?" Naima asked.

Sometimes physical traits or habits carried over into a person's next life.

Elise's laughter died as she stumbled off the stool and backed into the kitchen wall. "H-How do you know that?"

Naima gave her a sad smile. "Because it's the same birthmark Aliya had."

Elise shook her head and slid to the floor. "I'm not dreaming, am I?"

"No."

Raising a shaky finger, Elise pointed at the lamp on the counter. "So, I bought a magical lamp with a real-life genie in it like some Disney movie?"

Naima frowned. "That movie is an insult to jinn everywhere."

The last person who had possession of her lamp was a huge *Aladdin* fan which had led him to buy the lamp in the first place. At his insistence, she had watched the movie with him and had been offended by the portrayal of her kind. As a parting gift before his final wish, he had given her a book titled *The Arabian Nights*, she had felt a bit vindicated by the more realistic jinn stories the character of Shahrazad had told. Naima still had that book amongst the few possessions she carried with her into each summoning along with her and Aliya's wedding bands. Naima had managed to slip Aliya's off her hand just before she was sent to the lamp.

Elise's eyes widened. "Everywhere? There are more of you?"

Naima came around the corner and knelt before Elise who practically merged into the wall to get away from her. Naima's heart ached at the sight of her fear. She was the last person in the world Naima would hurt.

"The jinn have been around for thousands of years, but that is something we can discuss another time. For now, do you have any questions from what I've told you so far?"

Elise snorted. "There's more?"

"Yes, but I need to make sure you are in the frame of mind to hear it. Do you have questions?"

"So many." Elise closed her eyes, took a deep breath, held it for a few seconds, and let it out slowly to calm her racing heart and jumbled thoughts.

"How long has it been since this Aliya was…" She found it so unbelievable to say the words. "Cursed."

"What year is it?" Naima asked.

"How could you not know what year it is?"

Naima cocked her head toward the counter where the lamp still sat. The opal stone sparkled brightly from the sunlight shining through her kitchen window.

"Oh, yeah, guess you must have been in there for a while. It's 2022."

Naima frowned. "That means the last time I was out of the lamp was thirty years ago, which makes it almost six hundred years since we were cursed."

"Six…hundred…years?" Elise was overcome with a wave of nausea. "I think I'm going to be sick."

She scrambled to stand and ran to the bathroom to empty her stomach of everything she'd eaten last night and this morning. At some point, she felt her hair moved off her neck and something cool and damp replace it. After a few more moments of empty dry heaves, she looked over her shoulder to find Naima holding a cloth on her neck and watching her in concern.

"Are you all right?" Naima asked.

"I will be after I brush my teeth. Do you mind giving me a minute alone?"

Naima looked as if she would argue, then nodded. "I'll be right outside if you need me."

Elise gave her a tremulous smile of appreciation. "Thank you."

After Naima shut the door behind her, Elise pulled herself up to sit on the edge of the tub and shook her head vigorously in denial.

"This cannot be happening. A beautiful, possibly crazy woman is standing on the other side of that door claiming to be a genie… jinn…or whatever. Telling me I have a soul within me that has been living under a curse for six hundred years." Elise began to giggle uncontrollably.

There was a soft knock on the door. "Do you need assistance? Should I come in?"

"No!" Elise practically shouted. "I mean, I'm fine. Don't come in. I just need a few minutes to think."

"I understand. I will wait for you in the living room."

Elise heard the sadness in her voice and her heart ached to comfort her. "I don't even know her." She tried reasoning with herself to keep from running out the door and pulling the mysterious woman into her arms.

Staring at the door, it was as if she could feel Naima walking away. She closed her eyes and could almost sense her presence in the apartment. Was what Naima said true? She took her time putting the pieces together. She had been so drawn to the lamp. Had a sense of foreboding every time she thought about taking it out of its box when she returned home. Then the purple smoke that rose out of it as she rubbed the dust off, and suddenly Naima was there telling her that she'd summoned her. She wasn't dreaming, she wasn't high, and she wasn't crazy…yet…so the only option was that all of this was true and that maybe her grandmother's beliefs weren't a bunch of hoodoo. She still found this all to be too much, but she got up, brushed her teeth, rinsed with mouthwash for added insurance, then headed out to the living room almost afraid that maybe she had imagined everything and Naima wouldn't be there. She sighed aloud with relief when she found her sitting casually on the sofa flipping through a fashion magazine, then, within a flash, she was dressed in a pair of skinny jeans, black platform sneakers, and a black T-shirt with the quote "Reclaiming my time." It would've been funny if it wasn't so surreal.

Naima looked up as she walked into the room and a thoughtful smile curved her mouth. "How are you feeling?"

Elise was momentarily struck speechless by how full and sensual her lips were. "Uh, better, thank you. I have more questions."

"I figured you would. Come, sit." Naima patted the pillow on the sofa next to her.

Elise chose the armchair on the other side of the coffee table. She thought it was cute the way Naima's lips turned down into a pout of disappointment. She had an urge to run her thumb across her lips to smooth the frown away and kiss her until the smile came back.

"Down, girl," she told herself, closing her robe and tying the belt tightly around her waist.

She should have put some clothes on. With an attire of boy shorts, a tank top, and ankle socks, she was just as undressed as Naima had been before she poofed clothes out of thin air.

"Where are you from?" Elise asked.

"Aliya and I are from an island off the coast of Madagascar that was once known as Akiba. I believe, from what I found out during my last summoning, it is now known as Nosy Be."

Elise felt as if she had the wind knocked out of her. There was a flash then Naima was on the couch one moment and kneeling in front of her the next.

"Breathe, Elise, that's it. In…and out…in…and out," Naima said.

"You have to stop doing that. Wiggle your nose, blink your eyes, or snap your fingers, anything to warn me when you're about to do your magic," Elise said in annoyance.

Naima looked apologetic. "I will. I apologize if I frightened you."

"You didn't frighten me. It just takes some getting used to."

"Then what brought on such a reaction?"

Elise felt an odd mix of anxiety and desire having Naima so nearby. "It was the mention of Nosy Be. Uh, would you mind sitting back over there?" She pointed toward the sofa.

The look in Naima's eyes seemed to say she knew what Elise was feeling. Thankfully, she walked rather than poofed back to the sofa, giving Elise a generous view of her perfectly rounded backside.

"Are you familiar with the island?" Naima asked.

"Yes." Elise told Naima of her connection to Nosy Be and the feeling of belonging she always had when she visited.

"It was Aliya's spirit calling you home," Naima said excitedly. "Something must have happened to shift our fates for us to find each other after such a short time."

Elise snorted. "You think six hundred years is a short time?"

"In the lifetime of jinn, yes."

"How old are you?" Aliya couldn't imagine Naima was much older than her.

"I was thirty-five years of age when I was put in the lamp."

Elise couldn't hide her shock. "That would make you six hundred and thirty-five years old!"

"Yes, if you count in human years, I guess that may seem old."

"How old was Aliya?"

Naima's smile faded. "She was thirty."

The heartbroken look on Naima's face gave Elise the impression that the two women were more than friends. "Naima, if I'm going to believe all of this craziness, I need you to be honest with me."

"Of course."

"Were you and Aliya more than friends?"

Naima hesitated in answering, then sat up straight as if preparing for battle. "Aliya and I were married. Ten years at the time of our separation."

"She was your wife?" Elise slumped into the chair shaking her head. "Well, I'll be damned."

"Elise, please know that I don't expect anything from you. I just want to find a way for us to break the curses so that we may live the rest of our lives the way we choose."

Elise nodded, wondering if she should tell Naima that she was gay. "And how do we break them?"

"To break yours, we must find a way for you to remember who you are. Once you remember, you must make three wishes. After your third wish is completed, I will be free of the lamp."

Elise had forgotten all about the wishes Naima had mentioned after she was released from the lamp. She looked over at the clock above her mantle. Not even an hour had passed since that moment. She turned back to Naima who was gazing at her longingly. When they made eye contact, Naima quickly looked away, but not before she saw the same swirl of black and silver in her gaze from earlier.

"So, I can't make my wishes until I...Aliya...remembers who she is?" Elise asked to distract her from the way that look made her feel.

"I didn't say that." Naima sighed tiredly. "If I were like the mythical jinn in all the storybooks that I've read over the centuries, I would selfishly trick you by telling you that you can only make your wishes after you remember, just so that I could free myself. But I am not that kind of jinn. You could simply make your wishes now and be done with it."

"If I did that, what would happen to you once I made my final wish?"

"I would be sent back to the lamp. It would disappear until the next summoner finds it."

"In all this time, no one has thought to wish for your freedom?"

Naima smiled wistfully. "Only one. She was an Oxford professor on sabbatical in India when she found my lamp. Surprisingly, she didn't find having a jinn in a lamp as unbelievable as you would assume with her being of an analytical mind. Her wishes were also not for herself. Her first was for her mother who was dying of a very debilitating and painful sickness. She asked that she be taken out of her misery to slip into a peaceful death. The next was for a mysterious benefactor to pay for one of her student's tuition so that they wouldn't have to drop out of school. Before her last wish, she asked if she could take her time thinking about it."

She didn't know how, and it freaked her out a little, but Elise felt a mix of grief and happiness from Naima as if it were her own. "What happened?"

"She waited almost a year before making her wish. A year in which we became friends and companions. She wished that I were free of the lamp. That's when I told her about how I ended up in the lamp and the only thing that could free me. Devastated about having to banish me back to the lamp once her last wish was made, she chose a wish that would free me for a short time. She wished for me to be her companion for the rest of her lifetime." Tears sparkled in Naima's eyes.

Elise got up and sat beside her, taking one of her hands in her own. The contact caused a small shock, like when you touch a doorknob after walking on carpet, running from her fingers and up her arm. They gazed at each other for a moment and Elise could swear Naima wanted to kiss her, so she continued talking.

"You stayed with her?" Elise asked.

"Yes. We spent twenty years together. Her friends and family wondered about the mysterious woman who moved into her home. In the beginning, she told them that I was her assistant, then a few years passed, and she told them that we had become lovers and that I was her companion."

"You were lovers?" Elise didn't like the jealousy in her own tone.

Naima smirked knowingly. "No. I have always been faithful to Aliya, and she respected that. It was just a ruse to explain why I was with her for so long. She was in her sixties when she found the lamp and content with her life, which is why her first two wishes had been for other people. She never asked anything of me, and I made sure she lived happily and comfortably as she aged."

Elise felt relieved. She was going to have to have a talk with her literal soul mate Aliya because this roller coaster of feelings was not fun. "I assume she passed and that's how you ended up back in the lamp?"

Naima nodded. "We'd spent the evening with her family celebrating her birthday and she seemed more tired than usual. I could sense what was about to come and I think she could also because she thanked me for all I had done for her through the years and told me that she could move on knowing she had lived a good life with no regrets. In all our years together, she had kept the lamp locked away in a drawer, but that night she brought it out and placed it on her nightstand. She asked me to lay with her until she fell asleep. A few hours later, I awoke to find her no longer breathing, her spirit standing beside the bed smiling down at us, and then I was fading back into the lamp."

"I'm sorry for your loss," Elise said.

"She was a beautiful soul, and although I appreciated her keeping me from having to grant people's wishes for all that time, it also took away the chance of whoever carried Aliya's soul of finding the lamp in whatever lifetime she may have been living at that time."

Elise ran her hands through her hair and shook her head. "This is all just so unbelievable."

Naima nodded in understanding. "I imagine it is."

"I'm assuming, after what you just told me about the professor, that there's no particular timeline for making my wishes if I choose to do so?"

"No." Naima looked disappointed.

Elise felt bad for asking that instead of how they could go about getting her to remember who she was to help free Naima, but the thought of what that would mean for who she was now was too daunting to consider.

"Good, because I need time. If you don't mind, right now I'd like to at least shower and dress. Is there anything I can get you to eat or drink? Do jinn eat and drink?"

Until that moment, Elise hadn't even thought about whether, as a magical being, Naima required any human necessities. Did jinn use the bathroom, need nourishment, need to exercise to look that beautiful and fit? Naima smiled as if she knew what she was thinking, which she probably did, making Elise even more nervous at the thought of having her mind read.

"Yes, we eat and drink just like humans."

"Okay, well, please feel free to raid the fridge and pantry for anything you'd like. I shouldn't be more than a half hour."

"Thank you."

"You're welcome."

For a moment, Elise was once again lost in the tiny universe of Naima's strange eyes, then she forced herself to turn away and practically run from the room. When she reached her bedroom, she shut and locked the door, then had to laugh at herself because if Naima really was what she said, a locked door wouldn't keep her out if she wanted to get in. She felt overwhelmed with all that had happened that morning. Her mind raced with what Naima told her and what she had experienced since first setting foot on Nosy Be. It was as if it had all led up to this moment. Including the mysterious vendor who'd first sold her the fake lamp, as if to prepare her for the real one he sold her this last trip. She vigorously shook her head to clear it and headed for the bathroom.

"Focus on one thing at a time. All you have to think about at this moment is a shower," Elise told herself to battle the anxiety she felt coming on.

Naima could hear the thoughts in Elise's head clearly now. Clearer than she'd ever heard previous owners of the lamp. She had to force herself to place a mental barrier between them as she couldn't bear the anxiety Elise was feeling. She wasn't hungry, but she went into the kitchen to look for food to occupy herself while Elise showered. She found a container of dates in the refrigerator and smiled as she remembered that Aliya loved dates. It seemed that love passed on to this lifetime. Naima sat at the counter, popped a date in her mouth, and chewed thoughtfully. She wondered if every new lifetime brought Aliya's love of dates with it and what other traits or habits transferred as well. She also worried that too many lifetimes had passed and that Aliya's soul could be too ingrained in these lives to even remember who she was. Were there any other jinn she could find to assist her in discovering a way to help Aliya find herself? That question reminded her that she'd asked *when* she was but not *where* she was.

Naima stood and looked around the kitchen for anything that would give her a clue as to her geographic location. She spotted a takeout menu pinned to a corkboard next to the refrigerator. It was for a bakery located in New York. Naima's eyes widened in surprise. In all her years in the lamp, she had been across Africa, Asia, Europe, and South America, but she had never been to North America. Even though Elise had an American accent, there had been many Americans who'd possessed the lamp but lived in those various countries. She found Americans seemed more fascinated with what the lamp represented than people from the lands where the jinn originated. She wondered how long Aliya's soul had been here. Had their paths ever come close to crossing over the centuries? If not, why now?

Naima sat back down on the sofa to continue perusing the magazine she'd been reading. She remembered something Elise told her about how she'd gotten the lamp and her heart beat excitedly. It wasn't just fate that had finally brought them together. It seemed they had a little help. Naima happily popped another date into her mouth, then she heard jingling and was caught by surprise by the apartment door opening.

"Elise, are you ready yet?" an older woman said as she walked into the apartment. "Oh, hello. I didn't realize Elise had company." She didn't look the least bit surprised, just curious when she spotted Naima.

Naima stood. "Hello. I just dropped by to surprise Elise. She's getting dressed." She offered her hand in greeting. "I'm Naima."

She accepted Naima's hand. "What a beautiful name. I'm Colleen, Elise's grandmother."

"Her grandmother? I would've guessed mother or aunt but not grandmother."

Colleen smiled. "Thank you, you're sweet. I'm eighty years young and proud of it."

"Okay, now you're just teasing me," Naima said.

Colleen was just as tall as Elise with her same smooth, dark complexion. Her dark brown eyes perused Naima just as intently as she was looking at her. She showed off her slim figure in a yellow, green, and red African Kente fabric jumpsuit that cinched at the waist and a tailored red blazer. Her head was wrapped in a matching Kente headwrap giving her a regal appearance, and she wore a pair of red canvas shoes.

"So, how long have you known my granddaughter?" Colleen asked as she laid her purse on one of the stools and began taking items from the cabinet and refrigerator.

Naima didn't like lying so she tried her best to answer Colleen's questions without directly telling her the truth. "We met some time ago. Since I was in town, I thought I'd drop in."

"I see." Colleen looked at Naima doubtfully as she went about brewing a kettle of water on the stove and laying out three ceramic mugs with the word *Magic* painted onto them, spoons, honey, and milk on the kitchen island.

Naima sensed Colleen knew she wasn't wholly telling the truth and she squirmed in her seat the way she used to when she was a little girl and was about to be reprimanded from her grandfather for sneaking out with Aliya to venture outside the palace walls.

Colleen put a mixture of herbs and tea leaves into a tea satchel, tied it with a string, and placed it in the kettle. "I don't recognize your accent. Where are you from, Naima?"

"I'm from Madagascar." Something told Naima that if she would have said any other place Colleen would know she was lying.

Colleen nodded. "Ah, so you must have met Elise during one of her sabbaticals there."

"Yes." Naima looked toward the direction of Elise's bedroom hoping she would return soon. She was feeling more nervous around Colleen with each question asked. She considered sending her a telepathic message, but she knew Elise was uncomfortable with her in her head that way, so she just waited.

Colleen took her time pouring equal amounts of tea into each mug, placed a little top onto each of them, then pulled a stool to the other side of the counter directly across from Naima. Colleen then folded her hands in her lap and gave Naima a sweet, grandmotherly smile.

"Now, shall I wait until Elise comes out to hear the real story or will you volunteer the information?" Colleen said knowingly.

Naima gave her a nervous smile. "I'm not sure what you mean."

"I guess we're waiting for Elise then."

Colleen removed the lids from two of the mugs, slid one of them across the counter to Naima, and began adding honey and milk to hers. The scent of turmeric, ginger, licorice, and lemongrass, drifted up to Naima and took her back to waking up to a similar scent when Aliya would wake her the morning after a particularly rough training day with tea and a soothing massage balm made with aloe vera for cuts and bruises. She put a teaspoon of honey in her mug, took a sip, and gazed curiously up at Colleen.

"This is very good," Naima said.

"It's called sunrise tea and has turmeric, ginger, licorice root, lemongrass, orange peel, and lemon peel. It's a great natural energy booster and much better to start your day with than coffee."

Naima schooled her expression so that Colleen wouldn't see her surprise. It was the exact same tea Aliya used to bring her. This was all too much to simply be coincidence. Someone was guiding her and Elise's fate, and she had a pretty good idea who it might be, even though he had said his farewell to her while she was a young woman before he supposedly left the earthly plane for good.

CHAPTER TWO

G rammy, you're here!" Elise said as she walked into the kitchen and looked nervously from her grandmother to Naima, both calmly sipping a cup of tea.

Her grandmother turned to her with a quirked brow and slid one toward her. "Why do you seem surprised? We did have a date to go shopping today, didn't we?"

"Yes, I just wasn't expecting you for another hour."

Elise removed the top, brought it to her nose, and took a deep inhale of the fragrant tea. Then she added a teaspoon of honey, sipped, and smiled. She didn't know why, but this blend of tea always calmed and energized her at the same time, and something like a memory lost deep in her subconscious always tickled at the back of her mind. Then she happened to gaze up at Naima watching her intently and the tickling sensation came followed by a memory that played out in her mind like a movie.

She was walking toward a huge bed draped in beautiful colorful fabric carrying a tray ladened with a teapot, two teacups, a small bowl of honey, a bowl with a white, creamy substance that smelled like aloe vera, and a soft cloth. She looked up from the tray toward the bed and saw someone moving from beneath the covers. It was Naima, yawning and smoothing her long, disheveled hair away from her face causing the sheet covering her to slide down and reveal her beautiful and perky breasts.

Hot tea spilling over her hand brought Elise back from her memory to her grandmother taking the cup from her shaking hands and Naima quickly trying to dab up spilled tea from the countertop.

"Lord, child, are you all right?" Grammy said.

She accepted a paper towel from Naima but refused to meet her eyes. "It's just been a strange morning."

"I guess so. Why don't you sit down and tell me about it?" Grammy refilled her mug and placed it in front of the stool next to Naima.

Elise looked at her grandmother and concluded that she knew something was up and she wasn't going to settle for half-truths. She sighed in resignation and looked at Naima.

"I'm assuming you didn't tell her anything."

Naima gave her a nervous smile. "What's there to tell? I dropped in unexpectantly and here we are."

Elise walked over to sit on the stool next to Naima. "There's something you need to know about my grandmother. She's a claircognizant intuitive empath. She knows and can sense things others can't. For instance, she knows when someone is lying or not being completely open."

Naima's eyes widened. "She's a psychic?"

Grammy's face wrinkled in distaste. "Such a cheap and garish word that makes people think of those cheesy storefront fortune tellers. I prefer to be called an empath."

"I meant no disrespect, Colleen," Naima said, giving Grammy a seated bow before gazing back up at her with a look of respect. "To be gifted with the knowledge of foresight is truly a blessing."

Grammy looked amused. "You're definitely not from here, and I don't just mean this country, I mean this time. One of you should probably start talking or we'll be sitting here all day." She refilled her mug and looked from Naima to Elise expectantly.

Naima began to speak, but Elise placed her hand on her forearm to stop her. She did her best to ignore the possessiveness that ran through her from the contact. "It'll probably make more sense coming from me."

Naima gave her a soft smile and nodded in agreement.

Since Grammy knew everything that happened before this morning's magical experience with the lamp, Elise told her what happened from that point until she had gone and showered, unknowingly leaving Naima to greet Grammy upon her arrival. Aliya thought she'd had at least an hour before her grandmother was due to arrive. An hour in which she could've taken time to accept the craziness of what was happening before she sprung it on Grammy, who she found she couldn't keep secrets from no matter how hard she tried. To Grammy's credit, she didn't bat an eye at being told that her granddaughter was in the possession of a magical lamp that presented her with a jinn who offered to grant her three wishes and that due to a curse, she may also be metaphysically in possession of that jinn's wife's soul from a mysterious kingdom no one had ever heard of. When she finished, Grammy nodded in understanding then turned a knowing gaze toward Naima.

"I believe there's more," Grammy said.

Naima looked nervous. Elise had a feeling there wasn't much that could ruffle the jinni's feathers, but Grammy had that effect on people. She envisioned Naima dressed in military style attire from centuries ago. She had to squeeze her eyes shut and open them again to clear the vision before her. Fortunately, Naima wasn't paying her any attention as she looked like she was trying to figure out what to say to Grammy. A moment later, she nodded as if she'd made up her mind.

"I didn't have the opportunity to tell Elise all of this because she hadn't taken what I had already told her too well, so I wanted to give her time to let that settle in before I revealed the remainder of the story." Naima glanced at her briefly then turned back to Grammy. "In order for you to understand what happened, I need to start from the beginning."

"Hold on, I think we're going to need more tea." Grammy picked up the kettle, refilled it with water, set it on the stove, then sat back down looking like an excited child about to hear a bedtime story.

Elise felt the same way as Naima began her story.

"Many centuries ago, Aliya's forefather Adnan Fadel freed his people to escape a cruel slave master's kingdom in Africa and stole a ship only to be caught in a storm and stranded on what they thought was a deserted island off the coast of Madagascar, then known as the Malagasy Republic. Adnan was met by my grandfather, a powerful jinni named Chirag. He informed Adnan that the island wasn't deserted but in fact inhabited by a peaceful jinn tribe who had spelled the island preventing any human eyes to see it. Because of that he believed it was fate that allowed Adnan's stolen ship to find the island."

Naima smiled wistfully. "You see, my grandfather and the other jinn missed having human interaction and suddenly a ship full of humans looking for a home arrived on their shores. The jinn offered Adnan and his people a home if they were willing to live amongst the jinn as equals, and they continued to maintain the peace that the jinn had developed. The jinn helped them to build the Kingdom of Akiba and having led them from the cruel life they had been leading, the humans chose to make Adnan their king as they didn't fully trust the jinn. Adnan and Chirag decided that in addition to human advisors, a jinn council was needed to help not only maintain the peace amongst their own people but also amongst each other as well."

Elise was mesmerized by Naima's story. She also felt as if she'd heard it so many times, she could recite it herself. She realized it must be Aliya's spirit coming through. She wanted to tamp it back down, but something told her that to do that would cheat her of the memories Naima brought on.

Naima gazed at her as if she could feel what she was feeling and smiled hopefully. "The Fadels ruled Akiba with strength, compassion, and a stern but fair hand, and the kingdom prospered. They developed an army of human and jinn soldiers to help free other enslaved kingdoms and gave the people they freed an option to begin their lives of freedom some place far from their homeland or in the kingdom of Akiba which continued to be kept hidden from human eyes, particularly ones who had heard of the mysterious island's riches and would want it for themselves." Naima told them what happened if anyone chose to leave Akiba, if a new jinn wanted to join Chirag's tribe, and how they shared and bartered their prosperity with other needy kingdoms. "We thought Akiba would always be safe. That with my people, the magic of the jinn, and the army the royal family kept trained and at the ready that no one could ever end our peace."

With a pained expression, Naima closed her eyes and took a shuddering sigh. Grammy placed her hands over Naima's tightly clenched fists on the counter. Something, or should she say someone, within Elise ached to ease Naima's pain, despite having feelings almost as intense herself.

Naima opened her eyes, straightened her posture, and continued. "By the time Aliya and her brother, Adnan, came of age to begin ruling Akiba, many generations had passed since Adnan the First and Chirag had joined their human and jinn tribes. Akiba was one of the most powerful kingdoms many had heard of but few had seen. Aliya and Adnan were just as strong and compassionate leaders as their forefathers and foremothers. With my father being the vizier, I had the fortune of growing up in the palace with them. We played, ate, and trained together along with our other jinn companion, Malik."

Elise felt both a sense of loss and fear at that name and unconsciously began to reach for Naima's hand then quickly pulled back when she realized what she was doing.

Naima continued. "Aliya was much loved by her people. From the time she was ten years old and began her royal training, her focus was always the well-being of the Akiban people. Since she and Adnan were twins, they could have shared the throne equally, but Aliya chose to step aside and let her brother rule as he was a full minute older, and she could focus on her efforts to ensure Akibans never went without. Whether they were in the villages inside and just outside the palace walls or living in the mountains secluded away from the kingdom because of ongoing fear and doubt of the jinn, she would personally see to any issues they had. When the ships returned from their raids to free the enslaved or after a battle, she would be at the docks to greet them. She oversaw the building of homes, the school for jinn and human children, and brought a basket of food from the palace gardens and linen from the palace tailors to each family that welcomed a new arrival, and she was there to hold the hands of those that lost a loved one. My brave, beautiful wife had no fear when it came to loving her people."

Elise frowned. "She sounds perfect."

Naima chuckled. "Not at all. She was stubborn, too trusting of people, a tad bit vain, and had a voracious appetite for pastries."

"You mentioned that she and her brother were twins," Grammy said.

Naima nodded. "Yes."

Grammy quirked a brow at Elise. "That certainly can't be a coincidence."

Elise shook her head. "Grammy, we are not bringing Marcus into this."

"Why not? Just as Aliya is your past life, Adnan could be his."

"We haven't even determined if the first is true."

Grammy looked at Elise as if she'd said something silly. "What did I tell you when you returned from your first trip to Nosy Be and told me about your experience?"

"But Marcus didn't have the same experience. He thought it was cool, but he didn't bawl like a baby when we left or feel the need to return after."

"That could just mean that nothing has triggered his past life to come forward," Grammy said.

Elise's head began to hurt just thinking about the ramifications of what it meant that both she and her brother could be the reincarnation of mythical royal siblings. "Can we just let Naima finish her story please?"

Grammy grinned in amusement. "Yes, please, Naima, finish. This is all so exciting."

Naima hid a smirk as she gazed briefly at Elise. "As I mentioned, we had another friend, a fellow jinn tribe member of mine, Malik." Her smirk turned to a frown as she continued. "He was in love with Aliya and despite knowing how she and I felt about each other, he held out hope that she felt the same way about him. He also aspired for the vizier seat when my brother, who would have normally been next in line to have the position, decided he was more soldier than diplomat. Malik had been captain of Adnan's royal guard and Adnan's best friend so he assumed he would be asked to take the role." Naima looked guiltily down at her lap. "But he asked me instead." She looked back up at Grammy. "When my brother chose not to follow in our father's footsteps, who was the vizier for Aliya and Adnan's father, my father trained me for the role since I was so close to the twins. Malik didn't take the announcement of Aliya's and my betrothal or of me becoming the next royal vizier well."

Naima told them of Malik's attempt to start an uprising of the younger jinn and his punishment as of result of his actions. Then of his coming back, with the help of a powerful black jinn, to seek revenge. All of which led them to where they were now.

Although his actions were extreme, Elise honestly couldn't blame him. He'd unintentionally had his heart broken and his pride stomped on by the woman he loved and his best friend. She could also see it from the royal twins' point of view. If what Naima was saying was true, Aliya never gave Malik any reason to believe she cared for him as anything more than a friend. Also, if the role of vizier was one held by Naima's family since the kingdom came to be, then Malik had once again assumed his relationship with Adnan was more than that of brotherly affection and had his pride hurt in return. Ultimately, Malik caused his own downfall. Elise refilled her mug and warmed her hands which had grown chilled from the thought of how betrayed the twins must have felt by one of their closest friends.

"I can't imagine having to watch my brother die at a friend's hand and then watch the love of my life be cursed to live her life trapped in a lamp at the bidding of others' whims and wishes. The past…" Elise found the words difficult to say, "six hundred years must have been even more difficult for you."

Naima turned toward her with a sad expression. "It wasn't ideal, but at least I've been aware of who I am these past centuries. It must be more difficult for Aliya to lose a bit of herself with every lifetime lived since this all began."

Elise didn't know how to respond to that. Thinking about it made her realize that she may very well have to sacrifice who she was to free Naima and Aliya from their curse.

Naima didn't need to see Elise's face to know her comment frightened her. She could feel it as if Elise's feelings were her own. She also didn't like what this could mean for her if they managed to break the curse. Would Aliya come through and be able to maintain the memories of her life without affecting the life that Elise had spent the past thirty-five years living?

"Well, now that everything has been revealed, what are we going to do about it?" Grammy asked.

Naima looked at the wizened woman with a smile. "We?"

"Yes, we. You didn't really think you could tell me all of this and then have me sitting on the sidelines watching, did you?"

"That's exactly what you should do," Elise said then turned to Naima. "I'm assuming Malik, or at least the black jinn that had possessed him, could still be around somewhere?"

Naima covered her face with her hand. "I had not thought of that. It is a possibility."

Elise frowned. "Which means he could have been watching you and anyone who carried Aliya's soul all these years and knows you may have connected. Could we be in danger?" She looked back at Colleen. "Grammy, that could put you in danger if you get involved."

Colleen gave them a cocky grin. "You don't have to worry about me. I have the strength and spirit of my past lives to protect me."

Elise rolled her eyes. "Grammy—"

"Don't you roll your eyes at me, little girl. You two are going to need guidance for what you have to do, and I can get you that."

Naima looked at Colleen curiously. "How would you do that?"

Colleen smiled. "Let me make a phone call and see if we can get started today. Elise, you won't mind if we skip our shopping trip?"

"Sure, it's not like I have to get a cocktail dress for the charity gala that YOU'RE organizing."

"Helloooo, you have a magical being at your disposal. I'm sure she could snap something up real nice for you," Colleen said with a wink at Naima before she left the kitchen and headed to Elise's bedroom.

Elise looked exasperated. "I apologize. My grandmother is a bit eccentric."

Naima smiled in understanding. "I think she's charming. I like her. She reminds me of my grandfather. Speaking of him, I believe he's the one who gave you both the toy lamp and my lamp. I don't know how he managed to get ahold of it, but your description of the man in the marketplace sounds too much like him not to be a coincidence."

Elise didn't look the least bit surprised by that revelation. "Of course, why wouldn't there be another jinn to add to the mix? I feel like I've entered some weird dream I can't awake from."

"I'm so sorry you've had to deal with all of this. You could always just make your wishes and get on with your life."

Elise shook her head. "I couldn't live with myself knowing I relegated you to spending the rest of your days in that lamp at the beck and call of others."

"You wouldn't have to if your last wish was to forget that you ever had the lamp," Naima hesitantly suggested.

"You could do that?"

"Yes."

Elise looked to be considering it, then sighed. "No, it just wouldn't be right."

Naima gazed down at her now cooled tea to hide her look of relief.

"Naima, tell me about you and Aliya."

"Are you sure you want to hear it?"

"No, but I feel like I need to in order to understand how important breaking this curse is not just for you but for her as well."

Naima was touched by Elise's concern. She smiled thinking back to when she'd realized she had fallen in love with Aliya. They had always been friends, but it wasn't until Naima witnessed Aliya completely trounce Adnan during a training exercise when they were only twelve years old that she saw the woman Aliya would become and fell completely in love with her.

Colleen came back into the kitchen. "Okay, we're all set. Did I miss anything?"

"Naima was about to tell me about Aliya," Elise said.

"Oh goodie." Colleen hurried to her stool.

Naima smiled. "Aliya was only twelve years old when I realized we would be more than friends, but because she was still a child, I didn't admit my feelings to her for another four years and found out she felt the same about me. From that point on we began to hear each other's thoughts and sense what the other was feeling. My grandfather said we were soul mates."

Naima looked over at Elise hoping to see something of Aliya, but her gaze was only met with curiosity. She pushed the overwhelming feelings of disappointment and frustration deep within her.

"Aliya was a gentle woman, but she could become a tigress when defending herself or the ones she loved. She bested any opponent sent her way during training, including me and her brother," Naima said proudly. "She had even begged her father to let her journey off the island to visit the neighboring countries and trade routes with Anand as each generation of Akiban ruler did before they were to take the throne, but it was too dangerous to have both future rulers take such a dangerous trip at once. If anything happened to Adnan during his journey, Aliya would have to take his place on the throne when the time came."

"She'd never been off the island?" Elise asked.

"Yes, but it wasn't until our honeymoon, and it wasn't the vast travel Adnan had been afforded."

"Wow, so the curse is the only thing that got her off the island and even then, she had to live her life through others' eyes. That's so sad." Elise frowned.

"Curses aren't usually placed to make anyone but the person cursing you happy," Colleen said.

They all sat quietly for a moment. Naima could feel Elise and Colleen both thinking about and sympathizing with Aliya's plight. It meant everything to Naima for them to understand and want to help.

"Aliya was a warrior princess with a heart of gold and my whole world," Naima finished, putting everything left unsaid in her eyes as she looked at Elise. Hoping that, somehow, the message would reach down to her very soul to where Aliya lay hidden, because if she couldn't find a way to reach her, all would be lost.

Elise looked into Naima's dark eyes and felt as if her soul was being pulled toward hers. As if she were having an out-of-body experience, she saw rather than felt, her hand reaching up to stroke Naima's cheek and a strange word in a language she'd never spoken came to mind. She said it out loud before she could stop herself.

Naima's eyes widened. "Aliya?" she asked hopefully.

Elise forced herself back into her body and snatched her hand from Naima's cheek as if she'd been burned. "What the hell was that!"

"I believe that was a knock on the celestial plane door," Grammy said.

Elise turned to Grammy, holding her hand against her chest trying not to panic. "What did I just say?"

"You said *my love* in Arabic. Aliya used to call me that," Naima said.

Elise turned back to Naima whose eyes glistened with unshed tears. She wanted to tell the beautiful jinn that this wouldn't work, that she couldn't do this, but the ache and loneliness in Naima's eyes kept her from speaking out.

"Okay, ladies, we need to go." Grammy stood and began cleaning everything up from their tea service.

"Go where?" Elise asked.

Grammy didn't answer right away. "To see my therapist."

"What? Absolutely not!" Elise said.

Grammy turned to her with her hands on her hips and a determined expression. "We...YOU...can't handle this without a professional. Judging by what just happened, Aliya is trying to make her presence known, and as long as Naima is here it will be harder for you to hold her back. It's best to find a way for you to coexist until we can find a way to break the curse."

Elise knew from the look on Grammy's face she wouldn't take "no" for an answer. She'd go, but she wouldn't be happy about it. "Fine," she said in exasperation.

"Who is this therapist?" Naima asked.

"Maureen is a doctor who specializes in past life regression. She uses hypnotherapy to help patients recover past life memories or incarnations."

"Hypnotherapy?" Naima looked concerned. "She won't hurt you?"

"No. Grammy has been going to her for years."

Naima looked over at Grammy who gave her a nod of reassurance. "She'll be gentle with Elise. That's who I called when I stepped away. I didn't tell her everything. Only that Elise has been showing signs of past life regression. I figured the whole truth might be too much even for her."

Naima nodded but still looked unsure. Elise wasn't feeling any surer about all of this herself, but she felt it was important to put on a brave face so as not to worry Naima. They headed out and were walking toward the subway when a thought occurred to her.

"You said it's been thirty years since you were last out of the lamp?" she asked Naima.

"Yes."

"Have you ridden an underground train before?"

"Yes."

Elise grinned. "Okay, good. Then this won't be a shock to your system."

Other than a few curious glances and open-mouthed stares in the statuesque and beautiful Naima's direction, which Elise couldn't blame them for, it was an uneventful ride uptown. Naima spent the entire time questioning Grammy about the hypnotherapist's procedures, and Grammy patiently answered them all. Elise, on the other hand, was trying to tamp down her anxiety over the idea of bringing Aliya forward. Maybe she'd seen too many horror movies about people who had the soul of a past life or a spirit of some long dead person taking them over as they completely lost the battle for their own soul in the end. She loved her life. She had a wonderful career, she lived in a great rent-controlled apartment, had a loving, close relationship with her family, a great group of friends, and was perfectly happy with being single right now. She couldn't help but wonder what kind of life a mysterious princess from another time would want in this modern world. Would it all be too overwhelming for her? Would she want to go back to the island she once called home with the woman she once called wife? It was all leaving Elise just as lost and confused as Aliya must be now.

Too quickly, they reached their stop and Elise hesitated to get off the train but another passenger rudely jostling her aside as she stood blocking the doorway moved her into motion.

"Are you okay?" Naima asked in concern.

She gave her a tentative smile. "I'm fine," she answered, but the knowing look on Naima's face told her she knew otherwise.

Naima took her hand. "We don't have to do this. You could make your wishes and be rid of all of this in a matter of minutes."

Elise sighed in resignation. "No, I couldn't live with myself if I sent you back into that lamp. I can only hope what you said about Aliya having a kind and generous soul will show when it comes time for us to coexist as Grammy says. I don't want to lose what makes me, me."

Naima gave her an understanding smile. "I can't promise what Aliya will do considering it's been many centuries since she was aware of who she was, but I can promise that if I think you will be harmed in any way, I will put a stop to it."

Elise felt somewhat better. "Thank you."

CHAPTER THREE

The scent of sage enveloped Naima as soon as they walked into the office of the doctor that would supposedly be able to help both Elise and Aliya. She was excited about finally connecting to her lost love while also nervous about how all of this would affect Elise. Naima was beginning to feel a connection with her, and she didn't know if it was because of her bond to Aliya's soul or something different. It could also be that she had been alone for so many years or with summoners who she felt nothing but an obligation to that she was confusing the physical attraction she had for Elise for something more.

They were greeted by a petite woman with bright blue owlish eyes, a salt-and-pepper short pixie-style haircut, dressed in a loose ivory tunic, wide-leg navy pants, and bare feet. She looked to be much older, not quite Colleen's age, but her eyes looked as if she'd seen so much more than was possible in her lifetime. Naima could feel a strong flow of energy from her, but it wasn't anything to fear. It felt comforting, like what she'd felt from spirit guides she'd encountered in the past.

"Maureen, thank you so much for seeing us on such short notice on your day off," Colleen said as she walked forward, took Maureen's hands, and briefly pressed her forehead to the other woman's forehead in greeting.

"How could I say no to such an intriguing case." Maureen turned and smiled affectionately at Elise. "It's so good to see you again. When was the last time? About ten years ago?"

Elise returned the smile and greeted Maureen with a handshake. "You too, Dr. Stanford. Yes."

Maureen chuckled. "We're all adults here now. There's no need to be so formal." She looked curiously at Naima. "Now, who is this gorgeous swirling ball of pink and purple aura?"

"This is Naima, a friend of Elise's," Colleen answered before Naima could.

Maureen cocked her head and narrowed her eyes at Naima. "Interesting," she said.

Naima knew from the way Maureen looked as if she were looking through her, that she had to have some connection to a spirit guide, which could be a good thing unless that guide was an archangel. Jinn and archangels were sworn enemies. She nodded then turned and headed toward a door.

"Elise, please follow me. Colleen and Naima, you're welcome to grab refreshments while you wait."

Elise stopped. "They aren't coming in with me?" She looked as if she might bolt from the room.

Maureen turned back toward her with a soft smile. "If you'd like them to, of course. Usually, my clients are hesitant about having family or friends attend their sessions because they're worried what might be revealed while they're under hypnosis."

Elise looked relieved. "I would prefer to have them there. Whatever I share will be important for all of us."

Maureen nodded. "I see."

They followed her into a dimly lit room with plush, comfortable chairs and sofa, candles burning with the scent of sage that Naima smelled upon their arrival, and the soft sound of flute-like music playing. Maureen directed Naima and Colleen to sit in a pair of chairs on one side of the sofa and Elise to sit on the sofa as she sat in a chair across from her. Naima could feel Elise's anxiety as if it were her own and wished she could comfort her somehow. She was no stranger to hypnosis as the Oxford professor that she told Elise about had a keen interest in the practice with various books on the subject in her library. She had even taken Naima to a lecture by the famous American hypnotist Milton H. Erickson. It had been equally fascinating and frightening to watch him manipulate people into believing they were climbing mountains or visiting places they'd never been before. It was the kind of manipulation she'd seen some of the higher jinn perform on humans who threatened to harm Akiba. They would enter their minds and make them see the most frightening things to make them never want to return to the island.

"Will this be safe for her?" Naima asked Maureen.

Maureen nodded. "Yes. If I notice that she's in distress, I'll bring her out of it. There's no need to worry. What I do is far different than what you've experienced in the past," she said knowingly.

"How…"

Colleen reached over and placed her hand over Naima's. "Elise is perfectly safe with Maureen," she said with a reassuring smile.

Naima looked back at Maureen suspiciously. "How did she know about my past?"

"Maureen has a spirit guide who speaks to her. Her guide sees things that she can't. They must have seen something in your past."

"They? She has more than one?"

"We say they because her guide isn't a he or she. Not really a person. Just They."

Naima met Maureen's open gaze and nodded.

"If you two are finished, I'd like to find out what's troubling Miss Elise," Maureen said.

"Sorry. Continue," Colleen said.

"Thank you." Maureen turned back to Elise who still looked like a bundle of nerves.

Naima tried to send a sense of calm her way but not enough for her to know it was coming from someplace other than her own mind telling her to take a slow, deep breath and that Grammy or Naima wouldn't let anything happen to her. It must have worked because she closed her eyes, took a calming breath, and gave Maureen a tentative smile.

"So, Elise, what have you come here for today?" Maureen asked.

Elise gazed hesitantly at Naima then back at Maureen. "As my grandmother said, I've been feeling some strange things lately that she thinks may have something to do with a past life."

"Do you agree with her?"

"I don't know but it wouldn't hurt to find out."

"Well, I guess that's as good a reason as any," Maureen said, humor in her tone. "Tell me what kind of experiences you've been having."

"Uh…I guess moments where I've felt like I've been some place before and I haven't. Or like meeting someone for the first time and feeling like I've known or met them before."

Maureen nodded. "Déjà vu could be a sign of a past life. I'm sure your grandmother made you aware of what these sessions entail, but I just want to make sure I cover everything."

Maureen went on to explain what hypnotherapy was, how it worked with past life regression, and the benefits of it. She also explained how the session could bring on a sudden release of deep emotions by possibly uncovering some very traumatic experiences or events from the past life. She explained it wouldn't be harmful, but Naima worried about the traumatic experiences that Aliya had that final day. As much as she disliked the idea of putting Elise through the gamut of emotions that would bring and wanted to keep her safe, she hoped this would work because she really would like to avoid having to seek out Malik and Jahir, which would only make matters worse.

Elise tried to hold on to the sense of calm that came over her moments ago. She knew from what Grammy told her of her sessions with Maureen that the process didn't work if you weren't relaxed. If she were honest with herself, she didn't want it to work. She didn't want to know the truth. But she also didn't want to send Naima back into that lamp. She could always do what the professor did. Wish for Naima to be her companion for the rest of her life. That would at least give her some reprieve from her curse, but what would that mean for her? Was she willing to spend her life with a woman she barely knew? A beautiful, sexy, magical woman she barely knew? Elise was the first to admit she had commitment issues. As soon as any of her past relationships reached the point where her partners began including her and the word "us" or "our" when planning their future, she always backed away claiming she wasn't ready. The oddest thing was, she wanted to meet a wonderful woman, get married, have a family and a home, but something always held her back. Like she was waiting for something, or someone, she knew was out there, but she hadn't found yet.

"Okay, Elise," Maureen said, drawing her from her thoughts. "I want you to get comfortable. Sit back, lie down, whichever you prefer, either is fine."

Elise sat back into the plush sofa, stretched her legs out in front of her, and took another deep breath. Maureen stood, picked up a blanket that lay on the arm of the sofa, and placed it over Elise's lap.

"Just in case you get a little chilly. It happens sometimes." She sat back down. "I like to record the sessions because sometimes I don't catch everything in the notes that I take. Also, in case you would like to have a copy to listen to later. Are you comfortable with that?"

"Yes."

Maureen nodded, placed a small recorder on the table between them, and pressed the button. "Are you comfortable?"

Elise nodded and Maureen gave her a pleasant smile.

"Good. Now I'd like you to lay your head back and look up at the ceiling toward the gold dot above you and stare at it. Keep staring at that spot while I'm talking. Take a long, deep breath…"

Elise focused on a gold spot that was about as big as her head painted on the white ceiling, then took a deep breath as Maureen instructed.

"Exhale slowly…that's good. Now breathe normally. As you do, become aware of the rhythm of your breathing…"

Elise once again did as she was instructed already feeling the relaxation she felt when Grammy managed to talk her into meditating with her.

"Your eyes are probably getting tired, fatigued by now. Just think of how good it would feel to close them. Your eyelids are getting heavier and heavier, just allow them to close on their own and relax."

Maureen's voice had taken on a quiet, soothing tone, and Elise felt her eyes growing heavy. Her nerves began getting the better of her and she fought it for a moment but eventually gave in to the drowsiness and her eyelids fluttered closed.

"Good. Allow the feeling of relaxation to go through your entire body to the tips of your toes and just rest there for a moment."

Elise felt her body melt into the cushions, feeling more relaxed than she'd ever felt before.

"You should begin to feel a sense of comfort, calmness, and peace. Become aware of the sofa supporting you…the temperature of the room…and how they're just right for your purpose here today."

Elise tensed for a moment at the reminder of why she had come to Maureen today. "No, this is important," she told herself and took another breath to stave off the panic that was waiting on the periphery.

"This process only requires you to follow some simple instructions that your mind and body already know how to do…just close out any other sounds you hear, whether it's movement or voices outside, and focus on the sound of my voice…know that it can help you to go even deeper."

Elise blocked the sound of traffic outside the window and tuned only on Maureen's soothing voice, feeling lighter in her body as if she floated on a raft in a pool.

"Now, Elise, imagine a ray of pure light coming from above, from the golden spot on the ceiling, and entering your body through your head. Notice how it relaxes you even more as it travels along your body…making you loose and limp…relaxing all the areas of your head, spine, limbs, to the tips of your toes. That's it, you're doing wonderfully."

Elise no longer felt the raft beneath her. She was floating directly on the water. Letting it leisurely carry her down an endless stream.

"In a moment I'll count from ten to one. With each descending number you'll relax deeper and deeper. By the time I reach one, you'll reach a level of relaxation that's just right for you at this time. Ten… going deeper now…nine…even deeper…eight…you're so relaxed… seven…getting more relaxed with each number…six…drifting deeper…five…deeper still…four…every fiber of your being is so relaxed…three, two, and one…just let it all go…"

Elise no longer floated. She was now beneath the water, lying on a soft bed of earth. There was no sound and everything above her was awash in watery sunlight. She didn't feel a sense of panic that she would drown, only curiosity.

Maureen's voice still reached her as clearly as if she lay beside her in the water. "As you continue to relax, you'll be traveling back to a previous lifetime to a greater understanding of an important event that affects you right now. Stored deep in your unconscious mind are memories of another time and place…you can retrieve those memories. If you choose to at this time, you will be able to access the record of your soul's journey…look deep into your subconscious mind, you can see, hear, feel, and sense in the way that's best for you. You will feel completely at peace knowing that your mind is no longer limited by time and space…You will be able to remember events, people, and places in vivid details."

Elise could hear other voices drifting down toward her through the surface of the water. They sounded so far away, but she felt pulled toward them.

"I will begin counting from twenty down to zero…with each count, you will be drifting back through time and space of your current life, to a teenager, to a young child, to a baby, and then back through the womb into your spirit surrounded by a beautiful white light…You will allow your mind to regress into a lifetime that will have the most valuable information for life today…"

Maureen slowly counted down until she reached twelve. "You're going back through the years of your life…eleven…ten…nine…eight…"

Elise saw the day she opened her interior design business… her college graduation…holding her grandmother as they wept at her grandfather's funeral…the first time she stepped foot on to Nosy Be…her and Marcus's first day of kindergarten…and, somehow, the sense of being in her mother's womb. Through all of this she heard Maureen counting down and felt herself floating through a tunnel of water with all these images flashing on the walls around her like an old movie reel. Then she was surrounded by a brilliant white light and felt as if she were leaving her physical body. As if she were becoming the light and air around her. She could faintly hear Maureen's voice out on the periphery telling her to relax and enjoy the experience. To feel the peace, love, and joy surrounding her. Then she heard Maureen count from three to one and felt herself slowly being lowered toward earth again. The closer Elise got, the light faded, and she could hear Maureen's voice more clearly.

"Take a deep breath in, look down at your feet, trust what appears before you, and tell me what you see?" Maureen said in her soft, calming voice.

Elise took a deep breath, let it out slowly, and looked down. "My feet are bare and partially buried in damp sand." Was that her voice? It didn't sound like it.

"What are you feeling?"

"Like I'm myself but not."

"Are you looking out as yourself or are you an observer of what's happening?"

Elise had to think about that. "I'm looking out as myself...I think."

"What are you wearing? Are you male or female?"

Elise's line of vision went from her sand-covered toes, up her bare calves to layers of silky colorful mandala print material gathered around her thighs and bunched in her hand. "I'm a woman wearing a sari, but it's gathered up around my thighs to keep from getting sand and water on it." She looked in confusion at her hand. Why was she wearing so many huge, gaudy, rings? There was also a henna tattoo that covered both of her hands and went up her arms to her elbows. Elise was starting to feel anxious, but Maureen's voice pulled her away from the feeling.

"Just relax, there's nothing to be anxious about. Breath in...and out...in...out. There you go. Would you like to continue?" Maureen said.

Elise still felt disconnected from her own self but didn't feel as anxious. "Yes."

"Can you look at your surroundings? Do you know where you are?"

Elise looked up to find she was standing on the shoreline of a bright, clear blue body of water that was refreshingly cool as it came ashore and brushed along her feet. She could hear voices. "I'm on a beach and I'm not alone."

Hands wrapped around Elise's waist and pulled her back against the soft curves of a womanly body.

"Does the sea call out to you, wife?" a familiar, deep, feminine voice whispered in her ear.

"I love when you call me that," Elise said. She didn't know if it had been aloud or in her head.

"Wife...my wife...forever and always," the woman said, followed with a soft kiss on the nape of Elise's neck.

Elise shivered with desire. She wanted to turn around, to pull the woman into her arms and kiss her without a care of who saw, but she was afraid if she did, the spell would be broken. It took her a moment to realize Maureen was softly, but firmly calling her name. "Yes," she answered.

"Stay with me. Tell me what's happening? Who are you talking to?"

"My wife."

"So, you have a family?"

Elise took a moment to think about that and instinctively knew the answer. "Yes. I have my wife, my parents, my grandparents, and my brother." She felt herself smile happily.

"Do you have a job? What do you do?"

"I care for my people," Elise said, but once again didn't recognize her own voice.

"Now, I want you to go to a specific moment of this lifetime that will help you find the answers you're looking for."

Elise took several breaths and felt a sense of loss as her surroundings faded. The last thing to disappear was the woman holding her. She was surrounded by that brilliant light once again but only for a moment before it dissipated and left her standing in the middle of a grand room with marble floors, high vaulted ceilings, and extravagant decor.

"Do you know where you are?" Maureen asked.

"The palace," Elise said without hesitation.

"What's happening?"

As Elise gazed around the room ghostly images began to appear. A man on the throne, a sense of dark evil emanating from him, two people suddenly appearing before her, but she couldn't see their faces clearly, then the man coming off the throne and toward them so fast that he was just a blur of black before he grabbed a man beside her... she sensed that he was her brother. He was being choked by the dark cloaked figure. Elise wanted to scream, to run to him, but she couldn't move. An invisible force held her in place as she felt the life drain from him. Elise grew more anxious by the second and felt as if her heart was about to explode from her chest.

"ADNAN!" she screamed, but it wasn't her voice.

Somehow, through the pain and grief she felt, Maureen's voice firmly calling her name came through. She focused on that, and the intense emotions began to ease.

"Take a deep breath, stay calm, and let the experience fade. You can come out of it anytime you like. Nothing is holding you there."

Elise closed her eyes to the scene, fighting the pull of something stronger trying to keep her there. She sought the calm, peaceful light and felt herself being carried upward, away from the anger and grief that threatened to overwhelm her. When she reached the top, she felt more like herself. Like she was in her own body. She could feel the sofa cushion against her back, smell the sage incense burning, feel the blanket Maureen had placed on her lap gripped tightly in her hands.

"Are you with us, Elise?" Maureen asked.

"Yes," Elise said hoarsely before slowly blinking her eyes open and loosening the death grip she had on the blanket.

She was met with Maureen's calm, smiling face. "Good. Just take a moment to settle into yourself and your surroundings. You're probably feeling some residual anxiety and heaviness."

"I feel like I've been put through a couple of wash cycles before being hung out to dry."

Maureen gave her a comforting smile. "That's understandable. Just take a moment."

"What happened while I was regressed? I feel like something major happened, but I can't remember what. When I try to recall it all I see is a fog and I feel anxious," Elise said.

"That's normal. Our subconscious will sometimes block memories to protect us. It's like your mind's very own bodyguard. I do have some concerns though." Although Maureen managed to keep a neutral smile on her face, Elise didn't miss the concern in her eyes.

"What is it?"

"With past life regression, the memories and emotions of that past life usually come to the present life as if it's their own memories and emotions. That wasn't the case with you. When you spoke about the memory you were experiencing, I didn't get a sense of your connection to the memory, and your voice changed as I questioned you about it."

Elise wasn't liking where this was going. "Are you saying the memory isn't from a past life?"

Maureen leaned forward, narrowing her gaze at Elise's then nodded. "It's a past life but not one that you've experienced. The spirit connected to that life is a wholly different spirit than yours. You're not intertwined as one soul experiencing different lifetimes, you're two souls with different lifetimes."

Elise looked from Maureen to Grammy who chewed her lip, then Naima who looked just as uncertain and confused as she felt. She looked back at Maureen. "So, I'm possessed."

Maureen smiled in amusement. "No, I wouldn't say you're possessed. Your head's not going to start spinning and you won't be vomiting pea soup, but there is another soul inhabiting your space, and the sooner we're able to connect with that soul and free it, the better for both of you."

That didn't sound too comforting. "Am I in danger of this spirit trying to take over?"

"It's obvious, from what Colleen has told me over the years that this spirit has been with you for most of your life and I'm assuming you may have attracted it during your first trip to Madagascar when you were younger. It's also why you've always felt a pull to go back. I don't believe whoever this spirit is wants to harm you, but they may have unfinished business that they feel needs to be taken care of before they can rest. I want you to keep a notebook by your bed to write down everything you dream about, no matter how silly or inconsequential you may think it is. Our thoughts and memories can make their appearances in the form of dreams. Then, when you're ready to try this again, call me and we'll go from there."

Elise wasn't sure she wanted to do this again, but she nodded anyway. "Okay."

Maureen turned toward Grammy and Naima. "I know there's more to all of this, but I understand if you're not ready to tell me everything. I just ask that neither of you push Elise about any of this.

Let her go through the process at her own pace. Colleen, you know the deal."

Grammy nodded. "Don't worry, I'll make sure she's not pushing herself or being pushed."

Despite her own concerns, Elise grinned at the pointed look Grammy gave Naima who looked offended at having been called out for something she hadn't even done yet.

Maureen turned back to Elise. "I want you to take it easy today. Find something relaxing to focus on the rest of the day so that you're not thinking about the session and feel free to call me any time if you're having a difficult time or just need to work through something." She handed Elise a business card. "That's my office and cell number."

"Thank you, Maureen. I appreciate you seeing us on such short notice."

"It was my pleasure. Colleen is my favorite client; I couldn't say no."

They said their good-byes and left the office.

"I have an idea," Grammy said as they headed toward the subway. "Why don't we head downtown, grab some lunch, and maybe do a little shopping."

Elise frowned. "Grammy, it's a Saturday afternoon, it's going to be packed down there."

"I know, but it's just what you need to keep your mind busy and focused on other things. Besides, we still need to find you a dress and I know the perfect little boutique."

Grammy hurried them along chattering away. Elise knew it was her way of trying to keep things light when she was worried. Her laid-back, easygoing grandmother worrying made her worry more.

Naima could feel the anxiety rolling off both Colleen and Elise. It seemed the cheerier Colleen appeared, the more they both worried, but she was more concerned about Elise. Once Elise was deep within the hypnosis Maureen put her under, Naima could no longer read her mind or feel her emotions. It took everything she had not to shout for Maureen to stop and bring Elise back, until she began describing her and Aliya's wedding day. They had chosen to marry on the beach, rather than the palace, on the very spot that their forefathers had met and gathered, surrounded by all the descendants of the original tribespeople who had first set foot on Akiba's shores. The moment Elise had described was during the celebration after the ceremony when Aliya had slipped away from the festivities. Naima remembered it as if it were yesterday.

As Naima chatted with Adnan, she spotted Aliya slip away from a group of villagers that had been wishing her well. She watched her lift each foot to remove her sandals, gather her wedding sari in her hand, and walk to the shoreline. She was so breathtaking as she watched the waves crashing in the distance and rolling in over her feet. She still couldn't believe Aliya was finally her wife.

Adnan waved a hand in front of her face, startling her. "Go to her. You're too distracted by love to hear a word I said."

Naima felt her face heat with embarrassment. "My apologies, Your Highness."

Adnan waved dismissively. "No apologies needed. I'm simply happy that you two are finally settled down, and once again, we're family now, there's no need for formal titles when it's just us. Now, go. I'm sure Mother has a prospective wife or two for me to woo," he said, grinning.

Naima gave him a bow in departure and hurried toward Aliya. She walked quietly up behind her and wrapped her arms around Aliya's waist. "Does the sea call out to you, wife?"

"I love when you call me that."

"Wife…my wife…forever and always." Naima placed a soft kiss on the nape of Aliya's neck. She felt her shiver in her arms and knew it had nothing to do with the ocean breeze.

"You never answered my question, does the sea call to you?" Naima gazed out at the ocean over Aliya's shoulder.

"Yes, it does. Do you think Adnan can do without you for a bit so that we can do a little traveling?" Aliya asked wistfully.

Naima grinned. "Funny you should ask that. He has gifted us with the fleet's most luxurious vessel so that we may take a sabbatical to enjoy our first month of marriage in private."

Aliya turned in her arms looking at her in disbelief. "Do not fool with me, Naima."

Naima reached up to smooth a stray lock of hair from Aliya's face. "I would never do that when it comes to your dream of sailing off across the seas. My father will step back into place as the king's vizier while we are away."

"We're truly going to sail across the oceans. Just the two of us." Aliya said with childlike wonder.

Naima chuckled. "Maybe not all of them, my love, and not completely alone. Of course, we'll have a captain, crew, and a few royal guards."

Aliya frowned petulantly. "Can't you just use your magic to sail the boat and protect us? You are a blue jinn, after all."

"Yes, I could, but your parents refused to give their blessings to let you go unless we had an experienced crew and guards. They trust me with your heart and life, it's the outside world they don't trust."

Aliya seemed to take a moment to think about that then nodded. "Although I'm a bit annoyed that they still see me as their pampered little princess instead of the warrior-trained, politically savvy woman I've become, I can see their point."

Naima smiled. "I'm glad you do because we depart in two days."

"Two days! Surely you don't expect me to be ready in two days! I have a month's worth of outfits and jewelry to choose and pack."

"It won't matter what outfits you choose, you won't be clothed for long, wife." Naima swept Aliya up into her arms for a passionate kiss that quieted any further complaining.

Up until that moment, Naima wondered if she had been wrong about Elise's connection to Aliya. Then she heard Aliya's voice speaking clearly through Elise and now that she had seen for herself that they were not only connected but that Aliya's soul was in no way meshed with Elise's, she worried for both Aliya's and Elise's well-being.

"Is everything okay?" Naima whispered as they boarded the train and Elise sat between her and Colleen.

"I don't know," Elise said. "I feel strangely disconnected right now. As if I'm here but I'm not."

"Is there anything I can do, any questions I can answer for you? I know we aren't supposed to push you. I just want to make sure that you're all right."

"Of course, she's not," Colleen said, looking around Elise at Naima in annoyance. "The first session is always the toughest. Give her mind time to right itself before you go fishing for answers."

Naima felt rightfully chastened. "My apologies. I didn't mean to cause harm."

Elise patted Colleen's knee and gave Naima an understanding smile. "You haven't. This affects you just as much as me, so it's understandable that you're worried and want to do whatever you can to help. I think I just need some time to reconnect to myself."

"Yes, of course." Naima wanted so much to pull Elise into her arms and stroke her hair to ease her worries like she used to do to Aliya so long ago. Instead, she folded her hands in her lap and focused her attention on the people and conversations going on around her to learn as much as she could about this time and people.

• 83 •

CHAPTER FOUR

Elise felt more like herself by the time they arrived downtown and was looking forward to an afternoon in her favorite part of Manhattan. She spent most Saturdays at the office working, but she sometimes liked to come down to the Village, Chelsea, Soho, or Chinatown to help get her creative juices flowing. She always found the best fabrics, art pieces, or décor items for either current clients or to store in her warehouse for future clients, as she wandered for hours in and out of small shops and galleries.

"Why don't we have lunch at Seamore's. We'll make it just in time for the start of brunch and order a pitcher of mimosas," Grammy said.

"Sounds good to me. Do you drink alcohol?" Elise asked Naima.

"Yes, I've enjoyed libations over the years." Naima smiled, causing Elise's heart to skip a beat.

Her beauty was otherworldly, which shouldn't be a surprise considering she probably did come from another world. At least Elise thought she must have come from another world. Weren't genies... jinn...from another plane of existence or something? She was going to have to make a point of asking Naima more about that. They arrived at the restaurant and managed to get a table outside. Grammy ordered a pitcher of mimosas before they were even seated. Naima absentmindedly took the menu from the waitress as she seemed absorbed in people watching with wide-eyed amazement.

"Naima, when was the last time you were out of that lamp?" Grammy asked, grinning in amusement.

Naima managed to tear her gaze from a woman walking by dressed in a floral sundress and combat boots, with her hair styled in a long pink mohawk, heavy dark kohl on her eyes, tattoos covering every inch of her body from her neck on down, and piercings in her brow, nose, lip and along her earlobes.

"Thirty years ago," Naima said distractedly.

"This must all be so strange to you," Elise said.

"It will take some getting used to. Modesty doesn't seem to be a concern these days." Her gaze followed another woman in a tank top with no bra and shorts so short that if she would've bent over her entire ass would've been on display.

Elise tried tamping down the sudden rise of jealousy over Naima's appreciative glance. "So, does everyone know what they want to order?" she said a little too loudly.

Grammy gave her a knowing grin. "I think I'll have the lobster Benedict. Will you be getting your usual?"

Elise gazed down at the menu. "Probably."

"What is your usual?" Naima asked.

"The green skillet," she said, pointing to the item on the menu.

Naima nodded. "I'll have the same."

Their pitcher of mimosas was brought out, they placed their orders, and Grammy filled their glasses.

"Naima, if you don't mind me asking, where do jinn come from? I know you're from Akiba, but where were your people before arriving on Akiba?" Elise asked.

Naima sat quietly contemplating for a moment. "I'll try and explain this as simply as possible. There are three realms in which the world exists, the terrestrial, where we are now, the celestial, where angels reside, and in between those realms is the imaginal, not to be confused with the term imaginary, where psychic and spiritual beings such as the jinn exist."

"So, you're spirits? Like ghosts?" Elise asked.

Naima gave her a patient smile. "No, spirits or ghosts are noncorporeal beings with no true thought or physicality of their own. Jinn are corporeal, rational, and more humanistic in our nature. Like the human world, the imaginal world has nations of jinn who form tribes or societies. We have free will, follow different faiths, and are capable of good and evil. My grandfather and his tribe chose to create Akiba to be able to live as free and peaceful beings rather than stay within the imaginal realm and be amid a battle that has gone on since the beginning of time between the angels and jinn for God's favor."

"Wait, there's an actual battle going on above us?" Grammy said, looking up and making the sign of the cross before taking another sip of her mimosa.

Naima chuckled. "Not like you're thinking. Yes, a millennia ago there were actual battles going on, but now it's more spiritual. As the celestial plane is closer to God and the Heavens, angels have deemed themselves God's personal army. They've forgotten that the jinn had once been at God's side as well, but when God seemed to put the humans that he created above the jinn, they grew jealous and lost favor in God's eyes."

"Wow, that's a lot to unravel," Elise said. Her head spun with so many questions, but their food arrived, and she chose to save them for another time. "We will definitely have to finish this conversation later."

"I'm happy to answer any questions you have. The human Akibans were given the history of the jinn when they chose to stay on the island. My grandfather thought it was important because of the fear and confusion many had of jinn due to their religious teachings. After that, it became part of an Akiban child's education, whether they were human or jinn."

"During my travels in the Middle East, I learned that within the Islamic religion, jinn are put on the same level as demons. If someone begins acting out of character or mentally unstable, they say they've been possessed by a jinn," Grammy said.

Naima frowned. "Yes, exactly. It's believed jinn are evil spirits that are only out to possess and trick humans. Unfortunately, there are jinn who gleefully live up to that reputation, which doesn't help the ones who only wish to assist and guide humans, not harm them. My grandfather and his tribe accepted the humans that were shipwrecked on Akiba to guide and keep them safe after the cruel life they had led as slaves."

"That's terrible." Elise felt Naima's sadness over the bad reputation the jinn had obtained due to some bad apples in the bunch.

She reached across the table, took Naima's hand, and tried to give her an encouraging smile. "Well, I for one, am glad you're not all like that."

Naima's face softened beautifully with her smile. "Thank you."

Their gazes held for a moment before a clatter broke the spell and Elise eased her hand from Naima's guiltily.

"Oops, sorry, I dropped my knife," Grammy said. "So, Naima, can you tell us any fun stories about wishes you've granted in the past?"

Elise only half listened as Naima talked about previous holders of the lamp. She was lost in how right it felt holding Naima's hand and looking into her eyes. Like she could spend the rest of her life just doing that and be content. She wanted to believe it was residual of Aliya's feelings, but she knew otherwise. She felt herself being drawn to Naima by her own attraction.

"NO!" a familiar voice shouted in her head, making her almost drop the glass of water she was picking up.

"Are you feeling okay, honey?" Grammy asked in concern.

Elise smiled to reassure her and placed her hand, which was trembling now, in her lap. "I'm fine. I guess the condensation made the glass more slippery than I expected."

Grammy looked as if she didn't believe her but let it go. Naima looked at her worriedly, but she gave her the same smile she'd given Grammy. "I'm sorry, you were saying something about someone asking for a harem?"

Naima held her gaze for a moment, then continued with her story. They chatted the rest of their lunch about wishes and Grammy telling Naima what she missed during the years she was in her lamp before it found its way to Elise. Afterward, they strolled around the neighborhood heading to the boutique Grammy insisted they needed to go to to find Elise the perfect dress. She tried on a few but didn't like them well enough to come out of the dressing room for Naima and Grammy to see.

"What are you doing in there, child?" Grammy said through the door.

Elise frowned at her reflection in the mirror. "I don't like any of these. Maybe I'll just wear something I already have."

"Here, try this one." The hem of a dress came over the top of the door. Elise grabbed it and looked it over.

"You better come out and let me see since I chose it," Grammy commanded as she walked away.

Elise put the dress on and loved it. As usual, Grammy was right. It was a black double layer silk slip dress with a double V-neck in front and back, gathered triple layered tulle at the hem, and raw cut edging and trim. It was flowy and feminine, just the way she liked. She didn't know how she missed this one while she was looking around. Elise exited the dressing room performing a runway style walk, then struck a pose in front of Grammy and Naima sitting in their chairs.

Grammy clapped happily. "I knew it was perfect."

"You look beautiful," Naima said, her eyes turning a swirly pool of darkness as she looked her up and down.

Elise felt as if she were being physically stroked. She tore her gaze from Naima's to meet the look of amusement in Grammy's eyes.

"I guess we've found the dress." Grammy stood and began gently pulling and adjusting the dress, pinching about two inches of fabric in the back to narrow the waistline. "If this weren't silk, I'd be able to take it in a bit in the waist and tighten the straps, but it should be fine as is."

"Like this?" Naima subtly lifted a finger and Elise felt the dress softly shift on her body until the straps were tighter and the waistline fitted.

Grammy walked around to look Elise over, smiling in approval. "Well, that was weird but fun, and you look fabulous."

Elise realized this was the first time Grammy was seeing Naima's magic in action. She also noticed it no longer surprised her. You would think feeling your clothes moving on your body on their own would freak a person out, but it felt completely natural.

She turned to look at herself in a nearby mirror and had to admit, the dress looked even better after Naima's magical alterations. "It does look great on me."

"I've never seen that dress fit anyone so well before. It's like it was made for you," the salesperson said as she walked over and stood beside Elise looking in the mirror.

She heard Grammy snicker behind her and simply smiled at the woman. "I guess I'll take it then."

"I hope that was all right," Naima said as they left the boutique. She remembered too late that Elise had asked her to warn her before she performed magic. She had altered the dress without thinking, like she had done many times in the past for Aliya when she didn't want to wait for a seamstress to do it.

"It's fine," Elise said. The sweet smile she gave Naima made her heart skip.

"We should've found something for you to wear," Colleen said.

Naima looked at her in confusion. "Me? Why?"

"Because you're coming to the gala as well," she said, as if it should've been obvious.

"Grammy, I don't think that would be a good idea," Elise said.

"Why? Your invitation is for you and a plus-one, Naima could be your plus-one," Grammy said.

Elise looked nervously at Naima then back at Colleen. "Mom, Dad, and Marcus will be there. How do I explain Naima to them?"

Colleen waved dismissively. "You don't have to explain anything to them. If they decide to be nosy, tell them you met on one of those dating apps. Besides, she's been cooped up in a lamp for the past thirty years. She's due for a night out."

Despite how appealing that sounded, Naima didn't want to put Elise in an uncomfortable situation. "I'll be happy to stay at the apartment while you're out. I'm sure I can find something to occupy me. I saw you had an extensive book collection and I love reading."

Elise looked as if she were thinking it over then sighed. "No, it wouldn't be fair to keep you locked away. I'm sure we can produce a plausible story if anyone asks and, knowing my family, they will."

"Excellent! Shall we find you something to wear?" Colleen asked.

"No. I think I can come up with something on my own, but thank you," Naima said, remembering an outfit she saw in the fashion magazine she had taken her current attire from.

As they continued walking Naima suddenly felt a familiar presence nearby. She slowed her pace, looking at the passing people. There were so many it could be any one of them.

"What's wrong, Naima?" Elise asked, looking back at her. She must have felt Naima's anxiety.

Naima didn't answer right away. She let the feeling guide her as she turned in a circle and was drawn to a distinguished looking older gentleman walking toward a park across the street. Could he be another jinn posing as human and that's what was drawing her to him?

"It's nothing. I thought I recognized someone," she said, smiling.

Colleen gazed in the same direction then looked back at Naima doubtfully, but they continued walking. Naima couldn't shake the feeling that the connection was something more, but she chose to let it go.

That night as she lay in bed in Elise's guest room, she tried not to think about the fact that her wife, the love of her life, was just across the hall and there was nothing she could do but either wait to see if Maureen could find a way to separate Aliya's spirit from Elise or for Elise to make her three wishes, sending her back to the lamp and praying that she and Aliya would meet again in another lifetime. She gazed over at the lamp sitting on the dresser and couldn't stand the thought of being so close to freedom and finally reuniting with her love and losing it because Aliya's soul had been through too many lifetimes and was lost to her forever. Her curse wouldn't allow her to interfere and use her magic to force Elise to allow Aliya to come forward. She knew she wouldn't do that even if she weren't bound not to. Elise had a life and a family. Naima could never take that from her no matter what it would cost her. She would bide her time and do whatever she could to help Elise. She'd waited centuries, what was a few more years, if needed.

Elise stood within the ruins of the palace on Nosy Be before a grand throne that stood out amongst the rubble surrounding it. One moment, the throne was empty and the next, a dark mass began to appear forming into the shape of a man. As the details of the man appeared, he was dressed in the rich dark attire of an Arabian prince of long ago. His face looked familiar but something about him seemed off.

"Could it really be you?" the man asked as he stood and walked toward her.

Fear had Elise backing away. "Do I know you?"

He smiled affectionately. "It is you. I can feel it." The man stopped, looking around nervously, as if he were expecting someone to walk in any minute. "We don't have much time. You must tell Naima not to do anything foolish. I won't be able to help you if she rushes into attacking without a plan. One which I will have soon and will contact her."

The sound of thunder rumbled, and Elise looked up to find the sky quickly darkening.

The man grasped her hand. "Aliya, I must go. Please, tell Naima to wait for me to contact her, for both of your sakes." He looked up, then back at her with a tentative smile. "Go, quickly, before he senses you," he said before disappearing into the dark mass once again, then fading away.

Elise awoke feeling as if she'd just managed to escape something truly frightening. She untangled herself from her bed sheet and rushed out of her room to the guest room. She raised her hand to knock then changed her mind and turned away. It was just a dream. Probably brought on by discovering a jinn in a lamp she bought, learning that she was carrying the spirit of a cursed princess, and the aftermath of her regression session. She heard the click of the door opening behind her and stopped.

"Is there something wrong?" Naima asked.

Elise turned to her feeling embarrassed, which quickly turned to arousal when she saw how the pajamas she'd lent Naima fit her. Naima's body was pure muscle but not in a masculine way. She still had soft, womanly lines and curves, but there didn't seem to be an ounce of fat on her. The shorts that normally covered her to midthigh sat high on Naima's muscular thighs, and the camisole crop top showed off her firm six-pack abs and Michelle Obama arms. She forced her gaze up to meet Naima's who was watching her in concern.

"I had a dream. It's nothing. I didn't mean to wake you."

Naima gave her an understanding smile. "I wasn't asleep. It's been quite a day."

"That's the understatement of the year," Elise said.

"Would you like to talk about your dream? It may help to ease the anxiety you're feeling from it."

It was so weird having someone besides her grandmother being able to read her so well. "I guess. You were in it." She wanted to pull the words back as soon as they left her mouth but more so because of the look Naima was giving her. "It wasn't that kind of dream," she quickly said.

Naima gave her a playful frown. "One can only hope. Come, tell me about it anyway."

She stepped aside to allow her to enter the bedroom. Elise chose to sit on the bench at the end of the bed and Naima sat cross-legged in the middle of the bed.

"Tell me what about this dream that has you worried," Naima asked.

Elise closed her eyes to remember the details of the dream and they came back as if she had just woken up from it. She told Naima everything and when she was finished, she looked down at her hands feeling foolish for having bothered her.

"Like you said, it's been quite a day. It's probably my subconscious trying to absorb it all."

When Naima didn't respond Elise gazed up to find her frowning and looking at her in concern. "Can you describe the man?"

"Uh, yeah. He was tall, maybe Marcus's height, about six two, had your complexion, piercing silver eyes, like they almost glowed, a hawkish nose, and a goatee. His head was covered so I couldn't see what his hair looked like." Elise was surprised she remembered so much detail.

"It was Malik," Naima said in quiet awe.

Elise's heart skipped a beat. "The one that cursed us. I mean you and Aliya. Why would I be dreaming about him?"

"You weren't dreaming. He was reaching out to contact you. That must have been him I felt earlier." Naima stood and began pacing the room.

Elise could feel the nervous energy coming from her. It made the hair on her arms and the back of her neck stand up like she was near something electrical. "Naima, what's going on?"

Naima knelt in front of her. "Tell me what he said again. Word for word," she gently insisted.

Elise did as she asked, and Naima smiled then quickly frowned again. "It could be a trick. Jahir might have found out we were finally together and he's trying to keep us from breaking the curse."

"I don't know. He…Malik…seemed sincere in his concern about wanting to keep us safe."

"There was a moment, on that day when Malik did come through, after he'd killed Adnan. Maybe, over the centuries, he'd learned how to control Jahir's hold on him. But that would mean he's become just as powerful as Jahir."

Elise felt as if her heart was being squeezed in her chest at hearing Naima say Malik killed Adnan. For a moment she found it difficult to breathe and had the intense urge to scream and cry. Naima must have felt her distress. She quickly sat beside her and pulled her into her arms.

"I'm so sorry, my love, I didn't mean to sound so insensitive about your brother's death," she said as she lovingly stroked her hair.

Elise almost corrected her to remind her that she wasn't her love or that it wasn't her brother that died, but the sudden grief that was threatening to overwhelm her began to ease as Naima held her. Moments later, after it had passed, she didn't move from the warmth and comfort of Naima's embrace.

"Are you feeling better?" Naima asked.

Elise wondered if she told her that she wasn't, would Naima continue holding her? *She is not yours!* a voice said angrily in her head. "Yes, sorry." Elise gently pushed herself out of Naima's embrace, stood, and walked over to look out the bedroom window.

"So, if this dream, or psychic phone call, from Malik is real, what are we going to do?" she asked, focusing on a stray cat sitting across the street staring right up at the window instead of the sense of loss she felt at not being in Naima's arms.

"We're going to do as he asks and wait for him to reach out to me. I couldn't focus on exactly where the feeling I got earlier came from so there's nothing I can do right now."

"Why did he reach out to me instead of you?"

"Because he probably didn't think I would listen. Malik and I were no longer close after Aliya and I declared our love for each other."

Elise sat back down beside Naima. "That's right, he was in love with her also."

Naima nodded. "Aliya blamed herself for his exile for a long time. She felt that if she had been more sensitive to how he was feeling she might have been able to make him see she wasn't intentionally hurting him."

"Even princesses can't control who or how someone loves. She could've sat Malik down and been as honest as the day is long and his heart still would've been broken. You can't force people to love or not to love you. That's just the way love is." Naima smiled and Elise felt good knowing she'd been the cause of it.

"You are so different from Aliya. She was so worldly when it came to affairs with Akiba but so naive when it came to affairs of the heart."

"Well, unlike her, I wasn't fortunate enough to find the love of my life while I was still a child."

Naima looked at her curiously. "Have you ever been in love?"

Elise shrugged. "I've cared deeply for people in the past, but I can't honestly say I was in love with anyone."

She could count on one had the number of women she'd been in a relationship with and could genuinely say she loved them, but what ended those relationships was the fact that she couldn't see herself spending the rest of her life with them. Grammy had said she just hadn't found the right person. The one who connected not only with her heart but her soul. Elise just believed she was an aromantic and she was fine with that. It didn't mean she didn't want to be in a relationship, it just meant she would have to find someone who was the same way. A long and lasting relationship could be built on love and respect just as much as one built on fairy-tale love and desire. Naima was looking at her strangely. Had she read her thoughts?

"Well, we should probably get some sleep. The gala is tomorrow, and we promised Grammy we would help her set up, so we've got a long day." Elise stood and started toward the door, but Naima grasped her hand as she walked past her.

The warmth of Naima's hand enveloping hers spread throughout Elise's body. She turned to find Naima standing so close she could see her irises disappear into the swirling galaxy of her eyes as she gazed at her.

"You are so beautiful," Naima said as she tucked a curl behind Elise's ear that had escaped the ponytail that she'd hastily put her hair in before bed.

She shivered as Naima's fingers brushed her ear. "Th-Thank you."

She was so mesmerized by the unearthly glow that began to lighten Naima's eyes it took her a moment to realize they were drawing closer to her as Naima lowered her head for a kiss. Elise licked her lips in anticipation and when their lips met, she grew dizzy with the desire that began with Naima's touch. Their kiss was slow, sensual, and made her ache for more.

"NO!" That damn voice in her head screamed so loud Elise swore someone was in the room with them. In a way, she guessed they were. She tore her lips from Naima's and backed away.

Naima looked just as shocked by what she'd done. "I'm so sorry. I don't know what I was thinking."

"It's okay," Elise said, despite the mix of guilt and anger she was feeling. Guilt over kissing someone else's wife, past or present, and anger that she couldn't keep kissing Naima because of that past wife's hold on both. "I'll see you in the morning." She turned and rushed from the room.

Naima watched Elise leave, wanting so much to call her back. To kiss her until they were breathless. She felt a sense of guilt because she knew it had nothing to do with Aliya and everything to do with her attraction to Elise. It hadn't even been a full day since Elise had unknowingly released her from the lamp, yet she felt a growing desire for, and a need to protect her not long after. She touched her lips and could still feel the softness of Elise's on them. As brief as their kiss was, there was a passion there like she'd never felt before. She was a little relieved when Elise broke off the kiss because the pull that she felt toward her was too strong for Naima to deny. She walked over to the window and noticed a white cat sitting across the street staring up at the window. The apartment was six floors up, yet Naima knew the cat was looking right at her. Then she felt it.

"Grandfather?" she whispered.

The cat seemed to nod then turned and walked away. Naima watched until it disappeared around a corner of bushes, and she smiled. She knew then that Chirag had been the one to sell Elise the toy lamp when she first visited Nosy Be and the real one on her last visit. He had come back to help, but why now? Why this lifetime? If he knew about the curse all these centuries, why didn't he help sooner? Naima tamped down her anger at the thought that she'd spent six hundred years doing others' bidding as her grandfather just sat by and watched. She was tempted to go out and chase the cat down to find out why he'd waited so long, but something told her he would tell her in his own time.

CHAPTER FIVE

Despite having missed the past thirty years, Naima was adapting to this new world of advanced technology without a problem, but she didn't think she would ever get used to seeing so many people so obsessed with looking at their devices that there was barely any human interaction happening. Even while they were at the restaurant the other day, there were groups of people at tables who were barely paying attention to each other. As she and Elise waited for the car that Elise had called up with a few taps on her phone, two men almost ran into each other looking down at theirs. There were mumbled apologies and then they went on their way, eyes back down on their screens.

"How has humanity managed to thrive and procreate when they're always looking down and tapping away on their devices?" Naima asked.

"Dating apps," Elise said.

Naima looked at her in confusion.

Elise smiled in amusement. "There are ways to meet people through your electronic device."

Naima shook her head. "What happened to just good old-fashioned courting?"

"You can do that through the apps but more efficiently. Let me show you." She opened one of the little boxes on her phone. "These are called profiles. It has the person's picture, description, what they do, what they like and the type of person they're looking for. If you like them, you can send them a message, if they're interested, they message you back. To get to know each other, you can continue messaging, talk to each other on the phone or through video chat, and if you're still interested you can set up a date to meet."

Naima watched as Elise scrolled through a few profiles. "It seems so impersonal. How do you sense if you have a connection with a person if you spend most of your time communicating electronically?"

"I guess when you finally talk on the phone or video."

"And this has worked for you?"

Elise's phone chirped and a notification popped up on the screen. "Our ride is here," she said a little too cheerfully.

Naima smiled at her avoiding the question. She already had her answer from their conversation last night. She still found it surprising that a woman Elise's age had never been in love. Could it be due to Aliya's presence? Had any of the other humans who had shared Aliya's soul lived a similar life without sharing a deep love for another? She gazed out the car window wondering how many others were in Elise's situation. Sharing their body with another soul or spirit, possibly forever bound to whatever that previous soul's life may have been like. Not everyone would have someone like Maureen in their life to help them connect to, and possibly separate from, that life.

She gazed over at Elise who was tapping away on her phone completely unaware of the inner turmoil Naima was going through. What would happen if Maureen succeeded in separating Elise from Aliya? Would her wife be forever lost to her? Would she have to spend a millennium in that lamp at the whim of others? She had to figure out how to bring her Aliya back to reclaim their love and free them both without bringing harm to Elise. Her vision blurred with tears of frustration at so many unknown variables. She blinked them away and focused on the here and now where she knew her grandfather was attempting to intervene in some way and Malik was also trying to find a way to help. She just had to have patience and wait and see where it led.

Elise had been very aware not only of Naima looking at her but also what she was feeling. Her stomach had knotted into a ball of worry and frustration that was not her own. Yes, she was worried, especially after her dream and the jealous, angry reaction from Aliya whenever she and Naima seemed to be connecting, but her own worry didn't cause the anxiety she felt rolling off Naima in waves. She focused on answering emails rather than face what could be upsetting her so much. Focusing on her everyday life kept her grounded and from totally freaking out about the unbelievable things that had happened in the past twenty-four hours.

Twenty minutes later, they arrived at the venue located downtown near the boutique where they had been shopping just the day before. They made their way up to the rooftop space where the gala was being held, and Elise felt as if she'd walked into another world. The event was a fundraiser for an HIV/AIDS organization that Grammy had joined shortly after her brother died from complications due to AIDS thirty years ago. They had chosen an Arabian Nights Soiree theme, the irony of which didn't get past her as she heard the intake of breath from Naima standing beside her. One side of the large space had about twenty tables with seating for ten all under their own individual Moroccan tent with lush purple, gold, orange, and red linens and décor, stained glass Moroccan lanterns, colorful tea glass vases, and brass and silver plates and trays. The other side was set up like a lounge area with low tables, ottomans, and cushion seating. Large palm fronds and more lanterns and lamps were dispersed throughout the room. The doors to the outside area of the rooftop deck were open. It was set up like a hookah lounge with the similar low tables, cushions, lamps, and palm fronds. At the front of the room was a stage where a traditionally dressed Middle Eastern band was setting up.

"This is interesting," Naima said, humor tingeing her tone.

Elise glanced over at her to find her doing her best not to laugh. "What's so funny?"

She attempted a more neutral expression. "Nothing. It looks very festive."

"There you are!" Elise heard Grammy say and turned to find her walking toward them.

She gave them both a hug and kiss then gave Naima a knowing smirk. "I know it's too much and looks nothing like the real thing, but I swear we had this planned a year ago. If I would've known I was going to have a genuine jinn attending, I would've had you do your magic for more authenticity."

Naima chuckled. "It looks wonderful. If you would've seen the parties that I attended after the release of *Lawrence of Arabia* you would laugh. Live camels, men dressed in robes and turbans like some storybook sharif and darkening their skin with makeup, women dressed in bejeweled and sheer attire as if every woman at the time was a concubine." Naima shook her head. "It was offensive."

"Well, you won't have to worry about that here. We just wanted the atmosphere of a grand storybook Arabian night. The staff are all dressed in their regular attire, and we made sure guests knew this wasn't a costume party. The only authenticity we made sure to have were the band, belly dancers, acrobats, and henna artists," Grammy said proudly.

Naima smiled appreciatively. "I look forward to that."

"You're definitely giving your guests their money's worth," Elise said.

Grammy snorted. "At one hundred dollars a ticket, I had to make it worth their while. We sold two hundred tickets, collected another five thousand in donations online, and will get even more from the silent auction."

"Uncle Robert would be so proud of all the work you're doing."

Grammy smiled wistfully. "He would've loved all of this decadence."

Elise pulled Grammy into a half hug. She was young when her great-uncle passed so she never got to know him well, but she'd heard enough stories from Grammy to have a pretty good idea of what he was like.

Grammy returned the hug. "They gave us use of the bridal suite and groom lounge upstairs. You can put your things there to change into later and come back down to help me set up the auction tables. The rest of the committee are putting together the swag bags."

Two hours later, everything was done. The decorator was putting the final touches on the décor and Grammy did one final walkthrough before leaving it in the hands of the other four committee members who were already dressed. Once they were dressed, Grammy looked elegant in a black knee-length A-line cocktail dress with a sleeveless rhinestone embellished strap on one shoulder and a draped overlay over the other shoulder and bodice, and a pair of black satin, peep toe platform pumps with rhinestone embellishment along the back and heel of the shoe. She wore her salt-and-pepper hair in its short natural style and diamond hooped earrings.

"Okay now, Grammy, don't go hurtin' nobody," Elise teased her.

Grammy did a little spin. "You think I'll catch myself a younger rich friend tonight?"

"I think you may catch a few."

Grammy smoothed her hands over her svelte figure. "Good, I like having options."

They both laughed and Grammy walked over to Elise and fluffed her natural curls a little. "You're looking quite fabulous yourself. You're a knockout in that dress."

Elise gazed at herself in the mirror and was very happy with what she saw. The dress really did fit her perfectly, thanks to a flick of Naima's finger. Where Grammy was bold with her fashion choices, Elise was more sedate. She wore black strappy heeled sandals, an African woman cameo choker and matching earrings in an antique gold setting. The dress was flirty and made her feel rather sexy.

"What is taking Naima so long? She's a jinn, all she needs to do is snap her fingers and she's dressed." Grammy walked over to the bathroom where Naima had gone only ten minutes ago and knocked on the door. "Did we lose you in there?"

"No, I needed to make some changes."

The door opened and Elise thought her heart had stopped for a moment. Naima walked out with her long, thick hair pulled back into a pleated twist at the back of her head, drawing attention to her beautiful face. Her wide, full lips were a deep burgundy, and her eyes were outlined in black kohl making them seem even more iridescent than usual. Her chosen attire was a slim fitting burgundy velvet tuxedo with black shawl lapels, a black satin and lace camisole, and black velvet stiletto pumps giving her another three inches on her almost six-foot height.

"Wow," Grammy said, stepping aside to let Naima pass.

"You think it looks good? I changed at least three times to find something that felt more like me but fitting for today's fashion." Naima looked unsure as she studied her reflection in the full-length mirror.

With the initial shock over, Elise began feeling other things that she'd been trying to keep at bay since their kiss the previous night. They'd walked around that morning like it had never happened, and she was able to avoid Naima altogether when an urgent work matter came up that had her on a video conference call with her team for a few hours until they had to get ready to leave for the gala. Now she was wanting to taste Naima's full lips again, feel her strong hands gently grasping her face, and give in to the pull of their attraction. She looked up from Naima's firm, round buttocks lovingly encased in the velvet pants to find her watching her in the mirror with a look that told her she knew exactly what she was thinking and felt the same way.

"Well, I'm going to head downstairs before the steamy heat you two are giving off frizzes my hair," Grammy said, then left them alone.

"Do you like it?" Naima said.

"Yes. You look elegant and sexy as hell." Elise was surprised at her bold honesty.

"As do you." Naima turned toward her. Elise had to look up to compensate for the extra height Naima had from the heels. "That dress really is perfect for you."

"Thank you." Elise felt her face heat with a blush, but she didn't look away from the bright galaxy of Naima's eyes.

"Does looking up like that bother your neck?"

"No, but it's not often that I have to look up to another woman. I'm usually the taller one." Elise suddenly found that she wasn't looking up so high. "You lowered your heel, didn't you?"

"Just a smidgen. I like the way you look at me and wouldn't want you straining to do that."

Elise liked the way Naima looked at her as well, but she wouldn't admit that and risk being shouted at in her head. She looked at her watch. "We better head down. The event will be starting any minute."

"Let's go." Naima walked over to hold the door for her.

When they arrived downstairs, guests were already milling about the space while tuxedo-clad servers offered them hors d'oeuvres. With the lights turned down, leaving only the glow of the lamps and candles throughout, it looked magical.

"It's beautiful," Naima said.

Elise gazed over at her softly angled profile. "Yes, it is."

Naima turned to her as if she knew she was being looked at. Their gazes held for the longest moment before a server placed a tray between them.

"Falafel?"

"No, thank you," they said in unison, looking back at each other and smiling.

"Elise!"

She looked in the direction the voice had come from and frowned. "Marcus."

"Your brother?" Naima asked.

"Yes, which means my parents aren't far behind him. I was hoping we'd have more time to come up with a reasonable explanation of who you are." Elise pasted a smile on as her brother weaved through the growing crowd toward her.

His gaze went from her to Naima standing beside her and back to her with a sly grin. "Hey, sis," he said, pulling her into one of his bear hugs.

"Hey, broski." She squeezed him just as tightly.

Marcus was a big man at six feet two inches with broad shoulders, a wide barrel chest, and a large muscular build he maintained from the bodybuilding competitions he participated in when he was younger. He now worked as a pediatric physical therapist at a children's hospital where they had nicknamed him the Gentle Giant.

He held her at arm's length. "You look fantastic, but you always seem to glow after your trips to Nosy Be. One of these days I'm going to have to go back with you."

"You don't look too shabby yourself. Yes, you should. We haven't taken a vacation with just the two of us in a long time." She glanced around him and back. "Are Mom and Dad with you?"

"They're scoping out the silent auction items." Marcus turned toward Naima and offered his hand. "Since my sister is being rude, I guess I'll have to introduce myself. I'm Marcus."

Elise had been stalling hoping her parents would show up so she could delay introducing Naima until she could come up with how exactly she would do that. Leave it to Marcus to just jump right in with both feet.

Naima smiled and placed her hand in his. "I'm Naima."

"Naima, what a beautiful name." Elise didn't miss the way Marcus held her hand a little too long. "What brings you out tonight, Naima?"

Marcus's voice had taken on his Mack Daddy tone and Elise felt herself growing more jealous by the minute.

Naima continued smiling pleasantly as she slid her hand from Marcus's and took Elise's. "I'm Elise's date."

The warmth of her hand seemed to warm Elise's whole body. "Yes, Naima is my date." She liked the way that sounded and almost laughed out loud at the confusion then surprise on Marcus's face. She knew it was because Naima was not her usual type, which was cute, petite, mousy women, not the tall, glamorous, gorgeous ones that he usually went for. "Close your mouth, broski, before something flies in it."

Marcus chuckled. "Guess I'm finally rubbing off on you."

She punched him in the arm. "Let's go find Mom and Dad," she suggested, still holding Naima's hand as she began walking past a grinning Marcus.

Naima liked the way her hand felt in Elise's warm grasp. Liked not having to be the one in control. Ironically, not having control of her life for the past six hundred years had been frustrating beyond belief, but this was different. She had also spent so much of her relationship with Aliya in the protector role that, as much as she loved her, became tiresome. When she arrived at their rooms in the palace, she wanted to shed her protector and advisor persona with her vizier robes at the end of the day, but as strong and independent as Aliya was, she was still vulnerable and a bit naive. She was the princess, had been sheltered from much of the cruelty in the world, and was next in line for the throne should anything happen to Adnan before he had an heir. She would always need protecting and who better to do that than her wife?

With Elise, Naima still felt the need to protect her but more from emotional harm than physical because of how all this could affect her. She didn't feel the need to watch and be wary of anyone who approached Elise, or to feel the need to keep a protective arm around her waist in case they encountered a danger she would need to shield her from. As they walked through the crowded room, Naima was happy to stand quietly at Elise's side as she introduced her and chatted with people she knew. She was also happy that Elise had yet to release her hand. When they finally caught up with her parents, Marcus Sr. and Delaine, who were just as tall and beautiful as their children, introductions were made, and Elise took her hand once again. For the first time in her long life, Naima felt free to just enjoy being in the moment with someone she was beginning to care deeply for. Shortly after locating Elise's family, they went in search of their table. After a beautiful and emotional welcome speech from Colleen and the other fundraising committee members of the organization, dinner was served, and the moment Naima knew Elise feared had come.

"So, how'd you meet?" Marcus asked.

Naima could feel Elise's thoughts whirling through her mind like a tornado. *"Just breathe. I've got this,"* she wordlessly told her. "We met in Nosy Be and ended up on the same flight back from Madagascar," she said to Marcus.

Not quite the truth but also not quite a lie. Fortunately, Elise smiled and nodded convincingly.

"Really? Small world," Delaine said.

"Yes, it was as if we were meant to meet," Naima said.

"Don't lay it on too thick," Elise said in silent communication, surprising Naima.

"That's what my wife likes to say about us," Marcus Sr. said, smiling at his wife adoringly.

Delaine blushed and gave him a shy smile. "We had three different friends trying to set us up to no avail due to our schedules, until we finally met by chance at a party. What would you call it?"

"Luck?" Marcus Sr. said.

"Ha, maybe for you," Delaine said with a wink.

Marcus Sr. wrapped an arm around Delaine and pulled her close. "Definitely for me." He gave her a lingering kiss on the lips.

"Ugh! C'mon, guys, we're eating, and aren't you too old for all of that?" Marcus Jr. teased them.

Marcus Sr. chuckled. "Never too old for love, son. You'll find that out if you're ever lucky enough to meet a woman like your mother."

"I can't imagine that happening. They broke the mold when they made Mom," Marcus Jr. said.

Delaine blew her son a kiss. "Thank you, honey."

Marcus Jr. brought his attention back to Naima and Elise. "So, you met in Nosy Be, flew home on the same flight, then what happened?"

Naima was sitting between Elise and her brother and was about to answer when a small orange object flew past her, bounced off Marcus's chest, and landed in his plate. It was a carrot.

"Why are you so nosy? You don't see me asking about your love life?" Elise said, sounding mildly annoyed.

"That's because I don't have one, so I have to live vicariously through you." Marcus picked up the carrot and threw it back at Elise. It sailed past her and over the end of the table.

She snickered. "Still can't throw to save your life."

Marcus Jr. grinned. "Shut up."

"If you two can't behave we're leaving," Delaine scolded them, trying to keep a straight face.

"Sorry, Mom," the twins said in unison as if they were still children, grinning mischievously.

Naima smiled at the family's antics. She felt such a deep love flowing amongst them. There was love and teasing within Akiba's royal family, but it was more restrained due to the reputation they had to uphold as rulers of the kingdom. Elise's family interactions were so much more relaxed because they didn't have those restraints. Naima thoroughly enjoyed dinner with the Porters and their other table companions.

When conversation turned to her and what she did for a living, Elise quickly jumped in to answer. "Naima is a life coach."

Marcus Jr. looked at Elise in amusement. "I think she could've answered that one on her own."

Elise's face darkened with a blush.

"I'm between jobs at the moment. I'd only recently moved to New York when Elise and I met," Naima said, hoping to draw attention away from Elise.

"Where are you originally from? Your accent is so interesting," Delaine asked.

"I'm originally from Madagascar, but my father was a military consultant, so we traveled a lot," Naima told her.

"That must've been such an interesting life. Did you have siblings to keep you company?" Delaine asked.

"Yes, I have a brother who's in the military." Naima wasn't used to being the focus of so much attention unless it had to do with her granting someone's wishes. Most of what she was telling Elise's family was what she and the professor had come up with if anyone in her family questioned Naima. Unfortunately, with there being such a long gap between then and now and not having much time to get to know the time and place she was currently in, she would run out of reasonable answers to any further questions soon.

"Ladies and gentlemen, may I have your attention," Colleen's voice came over the speakers.

"Saved by Grammy," Elise whispered to Naima.

Naima smiled. "Thank goodness. I was starting to feel like a suspect being interrogated. Any more questions and I would've retreated to my lamp until you returned home."

The room grew quiet, and all eyes were on the stage where Colleen stood in front of the band who looked set to play.

"Now that you've filled your bellies, it's now time to fill your ears and eyes with tonight's entertainment with music from our wonderful band and performances from some talented dancers and acrobats. So, grab another drink at one of the three bars, visit the hookah lounge, sit back, relax, or feel free to dance, it doesn't matter as long as you're enjoying yourself. Also, don't forget to put your bids in for the silent auction. The sheets are filling up fast." She turned to the band. "The stage is yours, gentlemen."

The band began to play, one of the members stepped forward to sing, and Naima felt as if she were being transported to the past. Colleen had been serious when she said they had booked traditional entertainers. By the fourth song, one that talked about the joys of youth and love, Naima was filled with so much emotion she wasn't sure she could contain it. She felt Elise's hand grasp hers.

"Are you okay?" she asked.

Naima couldn't speak so she just nodded.

"Why don't we step out for some air?" Elise suggested.

Naima nodded again.

"We're just going to get some air," she told her family.

"Is everything all right?" Delaine asked, looking at Naima with concern.

"I think she's just feeling a little homesick," Elise said as she led Naima from the table.

❖

"Thank you," Naima whispered when they managed to squeeze through the crowded room and step out onto the large rooftop deck.

"You're welcome. I could feel you getting emotional. There was like a vibration coming off you and something told me that if I didn't get you out of there our little secret would be revealed."

Elise had sensed there was something wrong within moments of the band playing. In the beginning, it felt like she'd heard similar music before. She thought maybe it was during her visit to Nosy Be or at a Middle Eastern restaurant she may have gone to. Then the last song brought on a memory she knew wasn't her own. There were four children, two unbelievably beautiful girls dressed in saris and two just as handsome boys dressed in knee-length pants, pullover shirts, and embroidered vests each holding a strange looking guitar while a woman instructed them on how to play it.

"My apologies. I'm finding myself feeling emotions that I haven't felt in a very long time. My past summoning has never been emotional. Even when the professor passed on, it was sad, but it was also a part of life. I think I was more upset at having to return to the lamp than I was over her being gone. This time I'm feeling and seeing things on a more sensitive degree."

"Do you think it's because of me? Because you've finally been reunited with Aliya, which has never happened when you've been summoned before?"

Elise couldn't imagine what Naima was going through. How could she, a human who'd only been on this earth for forty years, never been in love, and whose only connection to the supernatural was finding out that her great-grandmother could talk to dead people and her grandmother was psychic, possibly understand what a six-hundred-thirty-five-year-old jinn, cursed to a lamp until she could be reunited with the love of her life in order to be set free, would be feeling? Naima looked to be seriously contemplating the question.

"I hadn't thought of that, but it could be the situation, not you directly. I believe I'm also feeling conflicted about how this will ultimately affect you and your life. In all this time I hadn't once considered the fate of the person who would be connected to Aliya. With each summons and return to the lamp, the less empathetic I've become." Naima's tone was laced with regret at her last statement.

It made Elise wonder about the previous people that had summoned Naima from the lamp. "Have you ever regretted granting a wish or refused to grant one?"

"There is one that I regret. I was summoned by a man who was barely keeping his family housed and fed with the meager income he was making from working in an African diamond mine, which was where he found my lamp. He had been fearful and skeptical of my presence in the beginning. His first wish, a small one which I believe was a test, was to replenish the soil in which his wife's garden struggled to grow so that it would flourish enough to put more food on their table. I granted his wish and within weeks his wife's garden grew so well they had enough to even help feed their neighbors. He was a humble and modest man so he took his time deciding what his remaining two wishes would be." Naima frowned.

"Unfortunately, his wife wasn't so humble. Realizing I was not a trickster trying to do them harm, and tired of living in poverty, she pleaded with her husband to wish for riches beyond compare so that they no longer had to struggle. For his second wish, to appease his wife, he asked for a diamond large enough to give them enough wealth to move to a nicer home, put his children in a good school, leave mining, and be able to open a little store where he could sell the furniture that he had been making to supplement his income as a miner. I granted his wish, he sold the diamond, moved his family to a nicer home, was able to put his children in a private school and open a warehouse and shop to make and sell his furniture. I hadn't thought his wish through before I granted it. I should have found another way to get him what he wanted other than a diamond. When some of the other miners heard he had obtained his new life from selling a diamond they accused him of stealing it from the mine. They knew he had found the lamp but hadn't known what the lamp was, and he hadn't told anyone but his wife about it, so they accused him of smuggling diamonds out of the mine in the rusted lamp he'd found. He was reported to the mining company, arrested, his home and shop were seized, and his family was put out on the street. I was able to come to him in jail since he still had one wish left. I could have made the charges go away and freed him if he wished it, but he didn't. He said it was only right since he had been too greedy. His last wish was for his wife and children to be taken care of and not have to pay for his greed." Naima grew quiet.

Elise placed her hand over Naima's on the rail they were leaning against. "If this is too difficult, you don't have to talk about it."

"No, it's fine. It's just that I've never told anyone about it before."

"Not even your professor?"

"No. You're the first to ask me about wishes I regretted. I don't think people really see jinn as having feelings."

Elise shook her head. "That's ridiculous. You have a heart like any other being, why wouldn't you have feelings and emotions like one?"

Naima smiled. "Not everyone is as open-minded as you. Especially humans who care only for what they can gain from my magic, not the guilt I possibly feel. The miner's wife was one of those people. When I came to her to tell her what her husband wished for, she didn't even ask about him. She just told me what would make her happy and waved her hand as if she were the one making it happen."

"What did she ask for?"

"A little plot of land away from the mines where she could grow her flowers and produce and sell them to make her own money. She also didn't want me to tell her husband where she would be starting this new life. She blamed him for their life of poverty before he brought his accursed lamp home and losing everything after. Once I provided her with everything that she thought would make her and their children happy, the last wish was granted, and I was sent back to the lamp to await the next summon."

"So, you don't know what happened to the miner?"

"No." Naima's sadness was heartbreaking.

"None of that was your fault. You granted his wish, there was nothing else you could've done."

"I should've known that there was no way a miner was going to be able to get away with selling a diamond and no one be suspicious of it. I should've warned him of what could happen."

"Are you a fortune teller as well as a jinn? Can you see what will happen to someone in the future?"

"There are some jinn who can, but no, I'm not one of them."

"Then there's nothing you could've done. He wanted to make his wife happy, give his family a good life, and in the end, his wish was granted. Not once did he ever wish for himself, even when you gave him the opportunity to do so. You did all you could've done."

Naima gave Elise a tentative smile. "I've carried this guilt for so long that I never thought about it that way. Thank you."

Elise gave her hand a gentle squeeze. "You're welcome. Any time you need a pep talk, I'm here."

Their gazes held for a moment and the universe in Naima's eyes no longer seemed strange to Elise. It was as natural and beautiful as looking at the night sky through a telescope.

"I guess we better get back inside before they send a search party out for us," she said.

They made their way back into the party just as the band leader was introducing the next performance. A spotlight shone at the top of the stairs where a woman stood dressed in a gold bead and sequin bra top, a long gold silk skirt with thigh-high slits up both sides, a gold and sapphire collar necklace, arm cuffs and wristlets, and a gold chiffon veil. A drum beat once, followed by the sound of clinking bells, which Elise guessed was probably from finger cymbals the belly dancer was wearing. With each drum beat and cymbal chime, she descended the staircase. When she reached the bottom, the drumbeat picked up and her hips and chimes matched the rhythm. She made her way to the center of the floor in front of the stage that had been cleared for her performance. She whipped off her veil and the crowd applauded happily at the beauty that was revealed. She continued her performance, accompanied by the band, her hips shimmying and gyrating as if they had a mind of their own. It was a breathtaking performance, and when it was over, she went around the edge of the crowd to pull several men and women onto the floor with her.

"She's heading our way," Naima said.

"I'm sure she doesn't even see us. There are two rows of people in front of us," Elise said.

As if the dancer heard her, she made a beeline through the crowd, grasped Naima's hand, and pulled her back toward the floor. Naima gazed back at Elise grinning in amusement. Elise followed until she was in the front row of the crowd. The dancer gave her impromptu class a quick instruction, then a male and female dressed similarly to the belly dancer, except the man had harem pants and a crop vest over his shirtless chest, came out of the crowd with scarves and hand cymbals which they helped the guests put on. Elise watched in amusement as Naima readjusted her hip scarf to lay loose and low on her right hip, clinked her cymbals together, then nodded in satisfaction. The dancer's assistants flanked her as the band started the drums and the guests, a few of which seemed to have picked up their lesson quickly, began to do the moves they were instructed to do. As the beat picked up, most of them lost their way and just did their own thing to the amusement of the audience.

Naima, on the other hand, kept up with the dancers. The lead dancer noticed and encouraged Naima to step forward with her.

"I see we have a ringer in the crowd," the belly dancer said.

"I took lessons when I was younger, but it's been a long time," Naima said.

"Well, let's see what you remember." The belly dancer turned and thanked the others that had joined them and were now being escorted back into the audience by her assistants leaving her and Naima alone center stage. "Are you familiar with raqs sharqi?" she asked Naima.

Naima seemed to think on it, then nodded. "I believe so."

The belly dancer quirked a brow at her and smiled before turning to the band to tell them what to play. Naima stepped out of her shoes and took off her jacket, leaving her in her pants and camisole top. Elise walked out to the floor and took them from her.

"Are you about to show up the entertainment?" she asked.

Naima gave her a wink. "Maybe," she said with a mischievous smile.

Elise chuckled and hurried back to her spot.

"Looks like the show is about to really get good," Marcus said, stepping up beside her.

"Looks like it," Elise said.

The music started, the dancer performed a move, and Naima followed. After a few more that way, Naima gave the dancer a wink and began moving with her instead of following her. They danced and twirled around the floor in perfect unison. The dance wasn't like the belly dancing Elise was used to seeing. Although there were the usual hip shimmies, most of the movements were isolated to the upper part of their body. Their bellies, waists, chests, and arms moved in such a fluid way it was as if they had no spine. Elise couldn't take her eyes off Naima as her hair loosened from its knot, flowed down to her lower back, and framed her beautiful face. She was grace, beauty, and desire wrapped up in one breathtaking package. The pure joy on Naima's face and the emotions Elise was feeling from her connection with her brought tears of joy to Elise's eyes. She felt overwhelmed with it.

She felt her brother's arm come around her shoulder. "What's wrong?" he asked.

Elise shrugged off his arm and quickly wiped away her tears. "I'm fine."

"Yeah, okay."

She wouldn't look at him because he knew her too well. He would know there was something more and she didn't want to involve him in any of what was going on. Especially if what Grammy said might be true about the possibility of Aliya's brother, Adnan, sharing Marcus's soul. The dance ended with a dizzying twirl by both dancers who gracefully lowered to one knee, their hair like a veil around their faces. The audience's applause was loud and boisterous. Marcus even let out a piercing whistle as he clapped. Naima and the dancer stood and gave their audience a bow before turning and bowing to each other. The dancer signaled for the band to play, and to Elise's surprise, they went into a popular dance tune that quickly got the crowd stepping to their own dance moves. Naima and the dancer exchanged a few words, embraced, and went their separate ways.

"You were amazing," Elise said as Naima joined her and Marcus as they stepped back to let the dancing crowd have the floor.

"Yeah, I think you outdanced the professional," Marcus said.

Naima's face practically glowed with something other than perspiration as she grinned happily. "Thank you. I haven't danced like that since I was a young girl." She held her thick mane of hair up off her neck with one hand and fanned herself with the other. "I think I'm going to go up to the suite and freshen up."

"Would you like me to come with you?" Elise asked, feeling so drawn to Naima's glow that she swore it was moving toward her.

Naima took her jacket and shoes from Elise. "No, I think I can manage. I won't be long." She leaned forward and pressed a soft kiss to Elise's lips then turned and stepped into the dancing crowd.

She stood so tall that Elise was able to follow her as she made her way to the stairs. She watched her move slowly and gracefully up them and disappear around a corner. It took her a moment to realize her brother was saying her name.

"Huh?" she said, turning toward him in confusion.

Marcus's brow was furrowed as he looked worriedly at her. "What's really going on with Naima?"

"What do you mean?"

He looked around then gently grabbed her arm and walked them to the outdoor deck. There were several tables filled with guests sharing a hookah, but Marcus led her to an empty one in the corner and lowered his massive frame onto a bed of cushions.

"Sit and start talking." He pointed to the cushions at her feet.

Elise considered just walking away. There was no way Marcus would be able to get his bulk up off the low seating before she was pretty much back inside, but she knew he would hound her until he got the truth out of her. They might not have been born identical twins, but they still shared that twin bond that had them knowing things about each other that normal siblings wouldn't. With a heavy sigh, she sat across from him.

"What do you want to know? We told you how we met. This is pretty much our first date so there's not much I can tell you about her." Elise hoped he'd leave it alone. She was just as bad lying to Marcus as she was to Grammy.

"I feel like there's more that you're not telling me. I've never seen you look at another woman the way you look at her. It's like you were mesmerized. And something feels off about her. I can't pinpoint what it is, but I feel like she's not what she seems to be."

Elise now knew she wouldn't be able to leave here tonight without telling Marcus everything. Their parents had thought her mother's family gift of intuitiveness may have skipped a generation until Marcus began showing signs of it when they were just seven years old. He had refused to get on the school bus one morning, begging their parents to drive them to school instead. He kept saying he had a bad feeling about the bus and that they shouldn't be on it. He was so hysterical their mother gave in and drove them to school. When they arrived, they found out their bus had been in an accident. There were some minor injuries, but for the most part, everyone was okay. After that, the family learned to listen to him when he felt something wasn't right or someone wasn't being honest.

"Okay, I'm going to tell you something and I need you to just be quiet and listen until I'm finished, no matter how unbelievable it sounds. Can you do that?"

"She's really a man, isn't she?"

"Marcus, I'm serious."

Elise figured he could tell by the look on her face that she really was serious.

"Okay. Go ahead."

Elise told him everything, and the wonderful brother that he was, Marcus didn't say a word, make a face, or even crack a smile the entire time. When she finished, he was quiet and looked at her as if he was waiting for the punchline of some bad joke or for her to say she was pulling his leg. A full minute passed without a word from him.

"Well?" Elise said.

"I'm just trying to figure out if you've finally lost your mind or if that beautiful woman is the best damn con artist in the world to have fooled both you and Grammy."

"I appreciate being called beautiful but not a con artist."

Elise hadn't even seen Naima approach their table. She walked around Marcus who didn't look the least bit embarrassed at having complimented and insulted her in one sentence and sat beside Elise.

Marcus looked at Naima skeptically. "Okay, so I'm really supposed to believe my sister found a real-life genie in a bottle?"

"Jinni," Elise corrected him.

"Does it really matter?" he said, sounding annoyed.

"Yes, it does," Naima said. "A genie is a fictional character. A jinni is a real being."

Marcus grinned in amusement. "Apologies, oh great and powerful jinni," he said with a mocking seated bow.

"Marcus!" Elise said, wanting to throw something at him.

"Fine. Prove it."

"What?" Elise said.

"I want her to prove it. Wish for something. I want to see some magic."

"You're such an ass. I told you what happens if I make my wishes." Elise realized how crazy all this was sounding. Grammy had believed it without question, which made her feel as if maybe she wasn't crazy, but she should have realized Marcus wouldn't be so easily convinced. She was the dreamer; he was the analytical one.

"It's fine," Naima said. "It's one wish. As long as you don't make the third one, we're fine."

"Are you sure?" Elise asked.

Naima smiled sweetly and nodded. "Make a wish."

Elise looked around them and noticed most of the people who had been out on the deck with them had gone back into the party. The few people still out there weren't paying them any mind.

She looked at her brother in annoyance then closed her eyes trying to think of a wish that wouldn't draw attention to them. Then she opened her eyes and grinned at Marcus. "I wish to have my Totally Hair Barbie Doll that Marcus ripped the head off of in one piece like brand-new."

Elise realized too late that she probably should have wished for something less personal and detailed, but Marcus was pissing her off. Even now he was looking smugly at her as if she just proved him right that all of this was a farce. That was until a box appeared on the table between them and Marcus's eyes widened in shock. It was now her turn to be smug as he picked up a boxed Totally Hair Black Barbie Doll in the exact outfit and braided hairstyle she'd done just before Marcus tried snatching it out of her hand and accidentally pulled its head off when they were six years old. He took it out of the box, looked down at the doll's feet, then up at her, then Naima in wonder. Elise took the doll from him and noticed what finally made him believe her story. Elise had oh-so-carefully painted the Barbie's toes in hot pink to match her dress. This doll's toes were painted hot pink.

❖

Naima hated doing such silly parlor tricks, but it was obvious Marcus wouldn't believe Elise without proof. She was proud of Elise for picking something out of the ordinary. Fortunately, because Naima was able to see the image of the doll in Elise's mind, she was able to grant her wish just as she requested. She felt some of the smugness she saw in Elise's expression, but then grew worried at the mix of shock and fear as Marcus looked from the doll to her. Then he started laughing. So hard he was holding his stomach and had tears in his eyes. She looked over at Elise who shrugged and looked at her brother in concern.

"Marcus?" Elise said.

Marcus held up a hand as he got his laughter under control. "I'm fine. I just find it hilarious that of all the wishes you could have made you chose a doll from your childhood."

Elise picked up a pillow and wacked his arm across the table. "Shut up. It was the only thing I could think of that you couldn't explain away."

"Are you serious? If a million dollars had popped up on the table, I couldn't have explained that away either."

Elise looked disappointed at her brother. "Is that what you would've done if you were the one in my place? You would've just made your wishes, relegating Naima back to the lamp and Aliya's soul to another for who knows how many more years of transferring from one life to the next never being free?"

Marcus looked guiltily at Elise. "I hadn't thought of that."

"Exactly. It's all I think about," Elise said sadly.

Naima reached over and took her hand. "I'm sorry you've been given such a burden. As I've said before, I can rid you of it if you choose."

"The answer is still no. I won't do that to you or Aliya."

Naima found she didn't feel the relief she had felt when Elise first turned down her offers to just grant her wishes and let her live her life. She realized she only wanted Elise to be happy, even at the sacrifice of Aliya's soul and her freedom.

"So, do you have a plan other than waiting for the guy who caused all of this to reach out to you?" Marcus asked.

Naima was glad he was past his initial shock and seemed to be taking everything in stride.

"I have one," Elise said.

"You do?" Naima asked.

Elise looked down at their clasped hands. "I'm going to go back to Maureen and have her put me under again."

"No," Naima said. "That was too difficult for you. I'll think of something. We'll keep that as a last resort."

The thought of putting Elise through that again and what it could possibly do to her mind frightened her more than she would've imagined.

"Naima, it's the only way to reach Aliya. To bring her forward to free both of you," Elise said.

"No. We have time. I'll figure it out." Naima raised her hand and brushed it along Elise's cheek. "I don't want you taking that risk."

"If you insist." Elise smiled and Naima felt her heart lift with joy.

"Uh, lovebirds, you do know I'm still here, right?" Marcus said.

Elise snorted and looked at him. "Of course. You're kind of hard to miss, broski."

Marcus stuck his tongue out at her. "Well, as unbelievable as all of this is, let me know if there's anything I can do to help."

"There's my grandkids who I've barely seen tonight," Colleen said, walking toward them. "You're missing a great acrobatic show."

"Hey, Grammy, we were just catching up," Marcus said.

She looked at each of them, then down at the Barbie lying on the table and smiled knowingly. "The more the merrier, but for tonight, let's just enjoy it as if we didn't have an existential dilemma to solve. Tomorrow is another day."

It was apparent to Naima that with this family Colleen had the final say as Marcus and Elise, pulling Naima up with her, followed their family matriarch back into the party with no argument.

CHAPTER SIX

A fter a couple of hours of dancing that included an impromptu dance competition between Elise and Marcus that Naima thoroughly enjoyed, she and Elise left the gala by nine because Elise had to be at work early.

"Whew! My feet are killing me." Elise took her shoes off as soon as they walked into the apartment.

"That's not surprising the way you were stomping around with Marcus," Naima teased her.

Elise looked at her in mock offense. "Stomping? It may not have been the shimmying and shaking you were doing," she did an exaggerated belly dance move, "but I'll have you know those were prime nineties moves we were doing."

"I'll have to take your word for it since I missed that decade." Naima grinned in amusement.

Elise dropped her garment bag and shoes in one of the chairs in the living room and flopped tiredly onto the sofa. She crossed a leg over her knee and began massaging her foot. "It's been a while since I danced in heels." She winced painfully.

Naima took off her jacket, laid it on top of the garment bag, and sat beside her. "Here, let me." She held her hands out toward Elise's feet. "I used to do this for Aliya after her monthly visits spent walking the town and village."

Elise hesitated, looking unsure, before shifting and placing her foot in Naima's hands. Naima laid Elise's foot in her lap and materialized a bottle of oil. She poured a small amount into her hand, then rubbed them together until they had warmed the oil in her palms.

Starting at her heel, she gently but firmly kneaded Elise's foot with her fingers taking great care to remember where the pressure points were so as not to trigger any unnecessary areas. Elise was tense at first, watching Naima warily, but it didn't take long for Naima to coax her to relax and lie back against the arm of the sofa. Naima used to love sharing private moments like this with Aliya. They had been so rare those last several years as her vizier duties kept her away often.

A pleasurable moan came from Elise when Naima began massaging the balls of her feet, then quickly cleared her throat. Naima could feel her embarrassment, but she ignored it, taking Elise's other foot and continuing her task.

"When you weren't altering clothes and massaging Aliya's feet, what were you doing?" Elise asked.

"My duties as Adnan's vizier."

"Tell me what a typical day in the life of a vizier involved."

Naima knew Elise was trying to distract herself from the pleasure she was feeling from the massage. With an inward smile, she answered her inquiry.

"Well, I was usually up at dawn to get some training time in, then I joined the royal guard for breakfast to go over the day's duties. After that I would meet with Adnan to go over his schedule, then I would begin my duties of overseeing the day-to-day functions of the kingdom, special projects, and events. I also sat in the high court, supervised the court officials, ensured that the royal family stayed well and healthy, and that there were no discrepancies with the kingdom's treasuries. If Adnan traveled, I would manage the kingdom in his place. I would travel at times as well to ensure that there were no issues with our trade partners and routes."

"Wow, when did you have time to just relax? Did viziers get the weekends off?"

Naima chuckled. "No, we did not get weekends off. A vizier is always on call when their king or queen needs them."

"So, you've spent your entire adult life in service of someone. Before and after being cursed to the lamp. That's sad."

Naima didn't like the pitying tone in Elise's voice. "Being vizier was an honorable position that carried great responsibility. It's an insult to compare it to being a slave to human greed."

"OUCH!" Elise tried pulling her foot from Naima's grasp.

Naima looked at her pained expression and realized she was pressing too hard in her anger. She released Elise's foot. "My apologies, I didn't mean to hurt you."

"No, I'm the one that should apologize. I didn't mean to offend you." Elise sat up and curled her legs up under her.

"I know, but in some ways, you're correct. I was in service of not only the royal family but of Akiba as a whole. The land, the people, were just as much my responsibility as they were Adnan's, and I took my role very seriously. Probably more seriously than I did my marriage," she said regretfully.

Naima stood and walked into the kitchen to wash the peppermint oil off her hands. It reminded her too much of Aliya, which she didn't want to think about as she was also reminded of how strained things were between them toward the end. The day that their worlds were turned upside down was the first day in weeks that they were to spend together. She would barely make it back to their rooms in time for dinner most nights, and even then, she was too tired to do anything but take a few bites before she was falling asleep while Aliya would try to tell her about her day. Aliya had seemed understanding, calling in their maid to help her put Naima to bed, but she hadn't missed the sadness she'd see in Aliya's eyes if she happened to be awake when Naima left for the day, or feel Aliya blocking her feelings from her during those times.

Elise followed her into the kitchen. "Were you unhappy?"

Naima picked up the dishtowel to dry her hands and gave Elise a sad smile. "I was happy, but I don't think Aliya was. I had no doubt that she loved me just as much as I loved her, but there were times that I wondered how different things would have been for us if I hadn't accepted the vizier role. Aliya and I could've traveled more the way she wanted, and she wouldn't have spent stretches of time alone feeling as if everyone had something more important to do than her."

"I thought you said she had her own duties to attend to."

"She did, but they weren't duties she had every day. Most of her days were spent reading, painting, practicing music, and in weapons training. She also accompanied her mother as ambassadors of Akiba on trips to visit the royal families of our trade partners, but it wasn't the travel she had always dreamed of doing."

Naima realized that Aliya had been a prisoner in the palace just as much as she was to the lamp. She had only been able to come and go at the whim of her parents or brother. When Naima had asked for Aliya's hand in marriage, being vizier was the last thing on her mind so she and Aliya had made all these plans of what their life together would be like, especially once Adnan took a bride and had children of his own to take the responsibility of being a royal heir off Aliya's shoulders, but then Naima's brother had decided not to carry on the family's role to the royal family and her life changed. She hadn't even considered doing as her brother did and turning it down. Aliya seemed to be fine with it after she'd told her, but Naima didn't think either of them realized how much it would affect their life together. Naima's vision blurred for a moment, then she felt tears trailing down her cheeks.

Elise wiped one away. "It couldn't have been easy for you either."

Naima shrugged. "I had chosen that life, Aliya hadn't. There was no protocol for who a Fadel could or couldn't marry. Man, woman, wealthy, poor, or even another royal from another land, it didn't matter, as long as their intended understood that Akiba and its people would always come first. Because of that, Aliya had known since she was a little girl that she wouldn't marry anyone with political aspirations. She would marry an Akiban who loved their country as much as she did. When we confessed our feelings for each other, she asked me if I would want to follow in my family's footsteps and I'd told her that the only aspirations I had were to be a good soldier and her wife. There were times after I became vizier that I felt as if I'd betrayed her by taking the position."

"I think I'm confident in saying that if Aliya didn't want you to take the position, she would've told you. From what little I know of her, she doesn't seem like the type of woman to sit quietly when she doesn't want something."

Naima couldn't help but smile. "You're right, she isn't. Before we had gotten together, her parents were planning a tour of the other trade kingdoms with Aliya and Adnan to meet the heirs of their families and possibly make a match. It was how they'd met and thought it might be how the twins would find their future mates. Adnan hadn't been happy about the idea, but as heir to the throne he knew a good match was important. Aliya wasn't as understanding about it. She knew that as the second born, she would probably have to move to her future mate's kingdom. Akiba was the only home she'd ever known, and as much as she wanted to travel, she always knew she would return there. She very bravely and confidently told her parents that she would sooner not marry at all before she married a non-Akiban. She also told them that if they still insisted that she go on their betrothal fishing expedition that she would behave so badly that no one would want her."

Naima shook her head at the memory of Aliya announcing all of that during a dinner with the royals and jinn council. "Her parents knew not to call Aliya's bluff by ignoring her threats, so they decided to let the twins choose their own path in finding a mate. Shortly after that was when Aliya confessed her feelings for me."

"Well then, that proves that Aliya wouldn't have hesitated in speaking up if she didn't think the vizier position was right for you or your marriage. If I had to guess, I would say she wasn't happy in the role she had. Maybe there was more she wanted for her life other than being a pampered princess."

Naima hadn't thought of that. Aliya never wanted the throne, but maybe she would've liked a more active role in Akiba's day-to-day functions. She and Adnan had been discussing giving Aliya the responsibility of working with their trade minister to become their full-time ambassador since her mother wanted to step back from her duties after the king had done the same, but then Malik arrived and destroyed their lives.

"You're probably right, I just wish I had paid more attention to her to know what was going on." Naima felt more tears coming on.

Elise pulled her into her arms and Naima did something she hadn't done since the moment she'd entered the endless, lonely realm of the lamp. She wept from the loss of her family, friends, and home, from the heartbreak of being torn from Aliya, and from the loneliness of the past six hundred years. Naima was so caught up in her pain that she barely noticed when Elise walked them to the sofa until she sat down, pulling Naima with her. Elise held her the entire time, whispering comforting words and combing her fingers through her hair. It felt so wonderful to be held. To be vulnerable without worrying about someone taking advantage of it.

When Naima was finally cried out, she looked up at Elise and wanted so much to be held not just in comfort but in desire. As if she read her mind, Elise grasped Naima's face and brought it close enough to hers for their lips to meet. The kiss was achingly gentle and tasted of her salty tears. Needing more, Naima grasped Elise's waist and pulled her closer. Once their bodies connected it was like putting a match to kindling as their kiss grew more passionate and seemed to burn through her body. Elise's hands went from her face to her shoulders, giving her a little nudge to lay back. Naima obliged her and Elise's lips tore from hers to sear a heated trail across her cheek, down her neck, to the tops of her breasts peeking over the neckline of her camisole. She almost cried out when Elise's warm lips left her heated flesh until she felt the silk of the top sliding down and her breasts laid bare. She opened her eyes to find Elise looking down upon her with an awed expression.

"You are so unbelievably beautiful," Elise said.

Naima reached up to brush her fingers along Elise's cheek. "So are you."

Elise felt her face heat with a blush. She hid it by lowering her head and taking Naima's nipple into her mouth and was rewarded with a moan of pleasure. Her strong fingers tangled in Elise's hair as Naima thrust her chest toward Elise's mouth. That moan was like a siren's call to Elise as her whole body responded as if a pilot light had been lit and set her on fire. She moaned into Naima's breast and hungrily switched to the other. Naima was breathing heavily and speaking in what Elise assumed was Arabic as it sounded like what she'd said yesterday. Suddenly, her head began to ache. She tried to ignore it, but it seemed the more aroused she and Naima became, the more intense the ache.

"NO! SHE'S NOT YOURS!" a feminine voice shouted angrily amid the pounding in Elise's head before everything went dark.

Elise woke to the smell of bacon which confused her because she didn't recall buying any when she went grocery shopping on Friday. She got up, slipped on her robe, and walked out to the unbelievable sight of Naima dressed in a pair of gray Victoria's Secret PINK logo sweatpants and matching tank top, and a pink floral frilly apron straight off some 1950s housewife. There was a gorgeous jinni looking sexy as hell standing in her kitchen cooking, not whipping it up out of thin air, breakfast. She felt like her life had turned into some weird *Twilight Zone* episode.

"Uh, good morning," Elise said.

Naima gave her a bright smile. "Good morning. I wasn't sure what you liked so I made a little of everything." She pointed toward the kitchen island with the spatula. "Feel free to start eating. I'm almost finished."

Elise looked at a complete feast laid out before her. There were scrambled eggs, bacon, sausage, toast, pancakes, a bowl of berries, and three different pitchers of juice. Then Naima added the omelet she had been making. Elise wasn't sure what to do. She always started her weekdays with tea, toast, and yogurt. The weekend was when she went all-out for breakfast.

"Where did you get all of this? I know I didn't have it in my refrigerator."

"No, your refrigerator was a bit sparse, so I had to improvise." Naima wiggled her fingers, which Elise assumed meant that she magically whipped groceries out of thin air.

"This was very kind of you—"

"But it's too much, isn't it?" Naima frowned.

Elise didn't want to hurt her feelings, so she grabbed a plate out of the cabinet. "No, I'm just not used to it, that's all. It looks delicious."

She was happy to see Naima's frown turn back into a smile.

"Don't feel obligated to eat everything. I won't be offended," Naima said as if reading Elise's mind as she tried to decide what to eat. Naima then grabbed a plate and placed several pancakes with berries on it and just a drizzle of syrup.

Despite Naima saying it wouldn't offend her if she didn't try it all, Elise loaded her plate with a little of everything except the pancakes. She took one bite of the omelet which was filled with vegetables and cheese and moaned in delight. "This is fantastic. Do all jinn know how to cook?"

"I'm sure if they wanted to, they probably could. In my case I never needed to know how. The professor insisted on teaching me. She thought it would make me feel more human. I found the task very enjoyable. Unfortunately, I haven't had a chance to use it since then. Usually, summoners chose to make their wishes as quickly as possible out of fear that I might take everything they wished for back or out of greed to obtain as much as they could while they could."

Elise cut a slice from one of the pancakes to see if they were as light and fluffy as they looked and was delighted to find that they were. "Well, you can cook for me anytime. I may not be able to stay awake in my client meeting this morning after all this food, but I'm sure a nice strong cup of tea will help with that."

As they ate, Elise noticed Naima looking at her worriedly. "I take it you're feeling better after last night?"

Elise looked at her in confusion. "Last night? Did something happen other than us coming home and going right to bed? I know I had a few drinks but not enough to forget anything that happened."

Naima frowned down at her plate. "No, you just seemed really tired, and I was concerned."

Elise felt like there was something else but didn't push it.

"Is there anything I can do for you while you're at work?" Naima asked.

Elise realized she hadn't thought about what to do with Naima while she was at work. For some reason, she didn't like the thought of having her hidden alone at the apartment as if she were something to keep locked away. Since it had been decades since Naima was last freed from the bottle and she'd never been to New York before, she also worried about encouraging her to go explore out of fear that someone would find out she was a magical being and try to kidnap her. Elise knew it was irrational considering Naima was a trained soldier with powerful magic who could probably take care of herself with no issues, but it didn't assuage her worry any less.

"Why don't you come to work with me? My office is within walking distance of Central Park. You could explore the area, we could have lunch nearby, you could explore some more, and then we could head back home around four." That idea sat better with her than leaving Naima alone.

Naima smiled. "I'd like that."

"Great, I'll help you clean up, hop in the shower and dress, then we can head out in the next hour."

"Oh, I'm sure I can handle cleanup. You go do what you have to do."

"Naima, despite whatever your past summoners made you think, you are not here to service me. You're a guest in my house."

Naima's face softened as she smiled in appreciation. "Thank you for saying that, but under the circumstances, it's the least I can do for you wanting to help Aliya and me."

Elise felt guilty at the irritation that arose at being reminded of Aliya. "Okay. Then I'll be ready in thirty."

She left Naima to do whatever magic she would probably use to clean up, wondering if the leftover food would just disappear into the ether somewhere as if it had never even existed. This time last week her biggest worry was whether a client was going to like the color palette she had chosen, now she was wondering if there was some celestial plane between worlds where magical food just floated around until it was needed by another jinn somewhere. Yeah, her life had definitely taken a turn into the Twilight Zone.

When Elise came out of her bedroom dressed and ready to go, the kitchen was spotless.

"I put the leftovers in the refrigerator in case you might want them in the morning," Naima said, once again either reading her mind or the questioning look on her face.

"Thank you."

"You look very nice."

Elise looked down at her outfit. Her weekend attire was usually casual bohemian style, but for work, especially when meeting with clients, she was more professional bohemian. She wore a pair of paisley wide leg linen trousers with an ivory silk T-shirt, navy blazer, silver chandelier necklace, and a pair of navy wedge heeled pumps.

Her face heated with a blush. "Thank you." She was embarrassed to admit even to herself that she had taken a little extra care in choosing her outfit not for her client but for Naima.

Naima looked down at her clothes and frowned. "I should probably change as well."

Elise didn't mind how she looked. Especially how well the pants fit her shapely behind, but she wasn't telling her that. "That's totally up to you. If you'd like to raid my closet, I'm sure there's something in there that will fit you despite our height difference."

"No, if you'll give me just a moment." Naima walked toward the coffee table and picked up the fashion magazine she'd been practically studying since the day of her appearance.

She nodded and showed Elise a picture of a model dressed in a pair of white skinny jeans, a long-sleeve burgundy tunic with a multi-color mandala design, and open-toe flats. "What do you think?"

"I like it."

"Good. I'm going to change now," she said, giving Elise the warning that she'd asked for before she performed any magic.

Elise chuckled. "I think I'm used to it now so you're fine."

Naima smiled, then the sweatsuit she wore morphed into the exact outfit from the magazine with the addition of a multi-color beaded earrings and necklace set. She unraveled her hair from the braided bun it had been in, and it flowed around her face and down her back in soft waves.

"You could wear a potato sack and still be gorgeous." Elise thought that was said in her head but realized it was out loud when Naima gave her a shy smile. "Uh…okay…let's go."

She walked past Naima to grab her work bag and keys before they headed out the door.

Naima enjoyed the way Elise made her feel so soft, sexy, and feminine. She'd taken on such a masculine role for so long as a soldier and Aliya's protector that she felt she'd lost much of her femininity. Especially around Aliya who was as close to a storybook princess as one could get. She'd been trying not to, but she found herself not only comparing Aliya and Elise to each other but how different she was with both. Even when the train came to a jolting stop and Naima stumbled, Elise reached out to wrap an arm around her waist to steady her. If it had been Aliya, it would have been the other way around with Naima holding on to her as if she were a delicate flower that she was trying to keep from getting trampled. She found herself blushing whenever she caught Elise looking at her and wanting to do whatever she could to make Elise smile. For the first time in her long life, she wanted to be the delicate flower and knew in her heart that Elise was the only woman who would ever make her feel that way. The guilt Naima felt over such thoughts, as if they were a betrayal of her love for Aliya, grew less with each moment she was with Elise. She was now sure that her growing feelings had nothing to do with Aliya's being a part of Elise as it was getting to know Elise herself.

They didn't speak the entire train ride, at least not with words. The shy smiles and glances they shared, and the warm feelings she picked up from Elise, told Naima that she felt the same way. Even Elise's arm never leaving Naima's waist told her that their situation was growing more complicated by the day.

"This is our stop," Elise said as the train pulled into a station fifteen minutes later.

Naima nodded, and when Elise's arm slowly slid from her waist, Naima grasped her hand. Elise looked back with a smile and tightened her grip to lead her off the train. They walked hand in hand for a few blocks as Elise pointed out places that she thought Naima might like to visit while she was walking around until they arrived at an office building.

"Would you like to come up and see my office or go explore?" Elise asked.

"I'd like to see where you work."

Elise released her hand to open the door. Until that moment, Naima never realized one could miss such a simple touch. They were walking toward a security desk when Elise stopped and turned to Naima with a look of concern.

"I completely forgot you're going to need to show some identification in order to be let up."

"What kind of identification?"

"A driver's license or passport. You wouldn't happen to have one of those on you?"

Naima smiled. "No, but I could. May I see yours?"

Elise took her wallet out of her bag, flipped it open to reveal the window pocket that held her driver's license, then took it out and handed it to Naima. A moment later, Naima reached into her jeans pocket, pulled out a wallet, and showed Elise a similar license except with her picture, vitals, and name.

"I hope you don't mind that I used your address."

Elise took it and compared it with hers. "Wow, I think even an expert would find it difficult to prove this was fake." Grinning, she handed the ID back to Naima. "Shall we, Ms. Fadel?" Elise said with a slight bow.

It felt strange for her to be addressed as Ms. Fadel. Since she had no surname of her own and had been addressed as Jinni Naima her whole life, she had chosen to use Aliya's last name for her identification. She was Aliya's wife, so technically, if she and Aliya were married in this time, she probably would've taken the Fadel surname as her own, she reasoned with herself to stave off a twinge of guilt. She followed Elise to the desk, provided her identification when they asked, and received a visitor's badge in return.

"Just out of curiosity, can you drive?" Elise asked as they entered the elevator.

"I used to."

"Let me guess, the professor?"

Naima grinned. "Yes. As she got older her eyesight weakened so she set up driving instruction for me so that I would be able to get around without me having to use magic to transport us from one place to the next. She thought us just popping up at places would cause questions."

Elise chuckled. "Yeah, I could see that being a problem."

They got off on the sixth floor and walked a few doors down to a door with *Porter Design & Décor* etched into the frosted glass. They walked in to the sound of classical music playing throughout the open studio with a wall of floor to ceiling windows opposite the entrance, a comfortable seating area next to an open conference area to the left of the entrance, a kitchenette to the right, and a glass cubed office in the center of the space. There were four other people already there. Three sat at drafting tables in front of the bank of windows, and the fourth sat at a desk just outside the glass cube.

"G'morning, Chief!" all four shouted in unison, then sent curious glances Naima's way.

"G'morning, everyone," Elise said, walking toward the young man sitting outside the glass office. "Hey, Micah, anything new since we spoke yesterday?"

It took him a moment to respond as he was staring at Naima in wonder then quickly averted his gaze to a notepad in his hand. "Uh...yes. Ms. Carter says she'll be about twenty minutes late for her appointment, Lenny says the tile was delivered to the Chambers house but in the wrong color, but he got it corrected at no additional cost to us, and your two o'clock consultation was rescheduled for next week."

"Well, I guess that leaves us more time for lunch," Elise said to Naima then looked back at Micah who was staring at her again. "I guess I should introduce you to the crew since they seemed to be very interested in you."

Naima gazed around the room at the others in the office who were now standing nearby unabashedly looking their way expectantly.

"Everyone, this is my friend Naima visiting from out of town. Naima, this is my currently spellbound assistant, Micah, and the rest of this motley crew are my designers, Landon, Phyllis, and Katrina." All three rushed over to shake her hand.

"You're absolutely gorgeous," Landon said in awe.

"Thank you." Naima grinned.

Katrina crossed her arms, narrowing her gaze at Naima. "I've met all your friends, and other than me, none of them look like they've just walked off the cover of *Vogue*. Where've you been hiding her?"

Elise chuckled. "Like I said, she's from out of town."

"I just want to know if you have a brother that's as gorgeous as you?" Phyllis said.

"Yes, but he's married."

"Wow, you're ready to just give up on my brother like that?" Elise teased Phyllis.

Phyllis shrugged. "Gotta keep my options open in case he never comes around to seeing how good I'd be for him."

"Are you all done? Can we get back to business as usual?" Elise asked in mock irritation.

"Yeah, I guess," Landon said. His petulant look matched the other two designers' as they headed back to their workspaces.

Elise shook her head. "Worse than children sometimes." She turned back to Micah. "How about you? Can I get you to stop staring long enough to make a twelve o'clock lunch reservation for two at Gardenia Terrace?"

Micah's face darkened with a blush as he looked at Elise. "Yes, I can do that."

Elise gave him an understanding smile. "Thank you." She turned back to Naima. "I have a few minutes until I need to get ready for my meeting. Let's have a seat in my cage." She pointed toward the glass cube that really did look like a cage sitting in the middle of the room for everyone to see into.

"Why would anyone want to sit on display like this?" Naima asked after they sat down.

"It was already here when I got the studio. It was originally a conference room. There was no dedicated office in the space unless I wanted to convert the windowless storage closet into one. At the time it was just Micah, Katrina, and me so I didn't see any point in doing any major construction to build out an office and just chose to use the cube. Now it's a funky feature that I kinda like. It also has soundproof glass so when I need to yell at anyone no one can hear it," she said with a teasing grin that Naima thought was very sexy.

"That makes sense. Is it a good business?"

"Yes, especially since adding Landon two years ago. He started his career as a carpenter and designs incredible pieces of furniture. We're looking at spaces downtown to open a storefront. It'll be a subsidiary of the design business, but Landon will manage it."

Naima could see the joy on Elise's face as she spoke about her business. She could also feel the love her employees had for her. After spending the evening with Elise's family and now at her job, Naima knew there was no way she was going to let Elise chance losing all of that to help her and Aliya. It was too much to ask of her. She was going to have to find another way to end their curses without involving Elise any more than she already was.

"Well, I won't keep you from your work." Naima stood.

Elise walked around her desk. "Would you like me to go down with you? Are you sure you'll be okay on your own?"

"I'll be fine. Shall I meet you back here for lunch?"

"Yes, the visitor badge should get you back up if you finish your sightseeing early, or you can meet me in the lobby at noon. Here." Elise took her watch off and handed it to Naima. "I'm assuming since watches have been around for some time that you know how to use it?"

Naima smiled in amusement as she strapped the watch onto her wrist. "I think I can handle it."

Elise looked embarrassed. "I'm sorry, I didn't mean it that way. I'm not quite used to having a jinni for a roommate."

Naima took her hand. "No need to apologize. You've taken all this much better than I would've ever imagined."

Their gazes held for a moment and Naima saw herself reflected in Elise's beautiful eyes and felt the depth of feelings growing within her heart. Naima touched Elise's mind just enough to graze the surface of her thoughts. She wondered if she could be falling in love with Naima and if it was even possible for Naima to love her back. It took everything Naima had not to pull Elise into her arms and tell her "Yes, it was possible." Instead, with her heart and head churning with confusion, she released Elise's hand and hesitantly left the office.

Naima walked a few blocks until she came to the park Elise had pointed out on their walk from the subway station. From what Elise told her about Central Park, Naima knew she wouldn't have enough time to explore all 843 acres before she had to meet her for lunch. She wouldn't mind as long as she was able to spend some time within nature. Naima wasn't used to so much concrete, people, traffic noise, and so many buildings seemingly on top of one another leaving no room for anyone to breathe. A few hours in the park would be a nice reprieve from it all. Not long after she entered the park Naima came upon a decorative wooden gate and a sign for the Hallett Nature Sanctuary. A sanctuary was just what she needed. Some place where she could sit and think. She strolled through the gate and followed the winding paths until she came to an area where the noise of vehicle traffic and children playing were drowned out by the music of birds chirping in the trees overhead. She sat on a beautifully carved wooden bench and allowed herself to just relax for the first time since she had been summoned from the lamp.

What was she going to do about Elise? She had a feeling that Aliya was making her presence known more each day. It was the only explanation she had for why Elise was making passionate love to her one minute and grabbing her head and passing out the next. She had a good suspicion Aliya was not happy with what they were doing, and it worried Naima that she'd hurt Elise to stop it. What was more worrisome was that Elise didn't even remember any of it. She had to find a way to break this curse without hurting Elise.

During her years with the professor, she had searched for ways she could break Jahir's curses on her own, but she couldn't find anything within the human books that would help her. Bound to the lamp here on the earthly plane, she also couldn't visit the imaginal realm to seek assistance from a more powerful jinn. She did try to seek out other jinn on earth, but the ones she did find were either not powerful enough or were too busy being a nuisance to humans to bother with her. She wanted to scream in frustration but sighed heavily instead.

"I know the feeling," a male voice said.

Naima looked up to find a distinguishably dressed older man in a soft gray three-piece suit, pink-and-gray plaid bowtie and matching pocket square smiling pleasantly at her. He had a head full of gray hair pulled back into a ponytail, wire rimmed eyeglasses, and a neatly trimmed gray goatee. There was something familiar about him.

"Maybe this will help." His gray hair turned a midnight black, his ponytail which had only reached his collar, lengthened just past his shoulders, the wrinkles in his face faded away to a smooth copper brown complexion, and his eyes glowed with a silver light.

Naima stood with her hands raised in self-defense and glowing a deep purple with magic. "Malik or Jahir?"

He smiled that playful crooked smile that always charmed human and jinn alike. "Do you really think we would be standing here having a pleasant conversation if Jahir were here?"

Naima was hesitant to lower her hands, but she didn't feel the heavy darkness that had accompanied Jahir's malevolent presence. "How did you know where to find me?"

"I know the presence of every jinn within this city. A little trick I learned from Jahir. May we sit and talk?" Malik asked.

Naima nodded but watched him warily. She sat back on the bench, and he sat beside her.

"I would ask how you have been, but I believe I already know the answer to that. I truly regret what happened that day and the days that followed." He looked genuinely remorseful, but Naima didn't trust it.

She snorted in derision. "Do you? Then why did you let it happen? You could've fought Jahir, stopped him from wreaking so much death and destruction." Naima knew she wasn't being fair. Jahir had been able to fight off the entire jinn council, there was no way Malik's weakened magic could have stayed his hand, but she was too angry and hurt to care about the truth.

"You don't know this, but as her final act of defiance, Aliya cursed Jahir and me before he separated her soul from her body." Malik smiled. "I was quite proud of her despite what it meant for me."

"What do you mean she cursed you? Aliya was a human. She didn't have the ability to curse anyone?"

"Ah, but that's where you're wrong. I believe her love for you and Akiba gave her the power to do what no other human could. She cursed us to be trapped in human form until the day you two were freed from your curse."

Naima looked at Malik in disbelief. "It worked?"

Malik smiled sadly. "Unfortunately, yes."

"If you're bound to each other, where is he?" Naima narrowed her eyes as she tried to sense another presence nearby.

"Let's just say he's asleep for now. You see, over the centuries, being bound to him also meant being bound to his magic. I've been able to strengthen my own by siphoning off his, making me just as strong. He's too arrogant to notice what I'm doing, and about a century ago he began giving me more control of our human form as he grew bored with being a human. There are times when I've gone decades without even a whimper of his presence as his spirit lay dormant within. Those are the times when I can fully stretch and practice my magic."

Naima found it difficult to wrap her head around her gentle Aliya cursing anyone, but she couldn't sense a lie in what Malik was telling her. Then she realized something. "You were who I sensed the other day while I was out with Elise and her grandmother." She remembered seeing an older gentleman at a park across from them and now knew it was Malik.

"Yes, that was purely coincidence. I sensed you as well, but when I turned you were walking away. I knew it was you because I sensed Aliya's presence within your Elise."

"She's not my Elise," Naima said, despite liking how it sounded.

Malik quirked a brow. "Are you sure?"

"Get out of my head," Naima said irritably.

"It's all over your face when you look at her."

"You've been watching us?"

"Only since yesterday and only when you leave the apartment."

"When you reached out to Elise in her dream, she told me she felt a dark presence. Was Jahir with you? Is Elise in danger?"

Malik looked annoyed. "No, he wasn't completely there but I think using my telepathic powers triggered him awakening sooner than I expected."

"How long had he been dormant before that?"

"Ten years, but he didn't fully come through. It was as if he had sensed Aliya's presence and cowered back in fear. He's quiet once again."

Naima found it difficult to believe that a powerful black jinn like Jahir would be afraid of a human soul. Then again, if what Malik said was true about Aliya having cursed them, then she could see why he might fear encountering her again after all this time. Naima looked at Malik suspiciously. Could it truly be coincidence that he showed up within the same lifetime she had finally been found by Elise?

"Why are you really here, Malik? Why now?"

"I know you don't trust me, and I don't blame you, but I want to be free of this curse just as much as you want to be free of yours. The only way to do that is to help you and Aliya do what you need to do."

"And if Jahir decides to raise his ugly head, what will happen to you, or to us if it's while you're with Elise and me?"

Malik sighed. "That's the part I'm still trying to figure out. But I think we were all brought here, to this time and place at the same time for a reason. I don't know if it's fate or God's cruel joke, but I think we need to see it as an opportunity to right so many wrongs."

"Wrongs that you brought down upon our heads. Our home, our people, are gone, Malik, because of your need for revenge. Wiped from history as if we never existed. Elise tells me that there's no record of Akiba. That the ruins on the island that was once our home are rumored to be the remnants of the lost city of Atlantis," Naima said bitterly. "What you wrought upon us is unforgivable."

Surprisingly, Malik looked ashamed. "I'm not asking for forgiveness, Naima. I'm asking you to let me at least try to make things right for you and Aliya."

Naima felt in her heart that Malik was sincere, so she tamped down her anger to hear him out. "How do you propose to do that?"

Malik looked relieved. "I have a…friend…who's a spiritualist. She can try to bring Aliya forward so that you two can connect, renew your love, and then Aliya can make her wishes and free you both."

"What happens to Elise when this spiritualist brings Aliya forward? Will she take over Elise or will her soul finally be free to move on into the afterlife?" As much as Naima hated the thought of Aliya's soul being forever out of reach until Naima ascended, the thought of Elise losing herself to Aliya's possession the way Malik had lost himself to Jahir's was even more painful. It was the same fear she had thinking about Elise returning to Maureen for another session.

"There's no guarantee that Aliya won't want to stay within Elise in order to be with you." Malik watched her curiously. "Is that not what you want? To be reunited with Aliya, free of the curses that kept you apart for so long?"

"Of course, it's what I want. It's all I've thought about for six hundred years." Naima wondered if she was trying to convince Malik or herself.

Malik smiled in understanding. "But you're starting to develop feelings for Elise."

Naima couldn't bear to say the words out loud, so she nodded. "I don't wish to see Elise hurt or for her to lose who she is. I would never forgive myself if I were the cause of that."

Malik took Naima's hand. The friendship they shared before their love for Aliya separated them rose to the surface. "I'll speak with my friend and find out how we can do what needs to be done without hurting Elise."

"Thank you," Naima managed to say past the lump of emotion in her throat.

"Together we will end this, Naima, I promise you."

❖

"So, you and Ms. Tall, Dark, and Gorgeous are just friends, huh?" Katrina said as soon as she walked into Elise's office for their weekly one-on-one meeting.

"Yes. You know you would be the first one I called if I was dating anyone."

Elise and Katrina had been best friends since college when they went out on a blind date and realized they'd be better off as friends than lovers. While Elise was easygoing, quiet, and avoided drama, Katrina was a bold extrovert who thought a little drama made life more interesting. Their friendship was about Elise keeping Katrina grounded while Katrina helped Elise be more adventurous. They balanced each other out.

Katrina smirked. "You don't have to be dating someone to be knocking boots. The heat coming off you two right before she left almost fogged up the cube's windows."

"It's not like that. Naima is staying with me until she gets a personal matter taken care of. Besides, she's not interested in me that way." Elise didn't know why she added that last part. Maybe to remind herself of that fact.

"Really? Does she know that? I saw the way she looked at you."

"Okay, we aren't here to talk about my love life. What's going on with the Herman brownstone?"

Katrina looked as if she were about to say something else then shrugged and went into updating Elise on her current project. Elise wished she could talk to Katrina about what was going on, but that would require her revealing all. Under normal circumstances, Katrina's straightforward, no-nonsense advice would have been perfect, but considering how unbelievable her situation was, Elise knew her friend would think she had completely lost her mind. If Grammy and Marcus hadn't witnessed Naima in action, she probably would still be thinking that she'd lost her mind. But as comforting as it was to know that she had their support, it didn't make her decisions any easier.

She wanted so much to free Naima from that accursed lamp but that involved communing with Aliya which frightened her, especially after the experience she had when Naima was talking about her relationship with Aliya and Elise had spoken in a language she'd never learned and touched Naima so lovingly. The moment was so surreal because it was as if she were watching herself from afar. It had been more than just Aliya knocking on the celestial door as Grammy had put it. She had completely taken over Elise's body. She felt that if she hadn't been mentally aware of what was happening, Aliya would have shoved her aside and completely taken over. Fear of that was what was holding her back from returning to Maureen for another session. She was going to have to speak to Naima about whether or not she could trust Aliya to let go when the time came because no matter how sweet and loving she said the princess was, the angry shouts and jealousy in Elise's head from Aliya whenever she thought Elise and Naima were getting too close made her feel like it was going to be difficult to get Aliya to go wherever she needed to go once the curse was broken.

Elise met with her other team members for their individual catchups and finished with twenty minutes left before she was to meet Naima for lunch. She tried answering more emails but found herself too distracted with watching the time, so she gathered her wallet and phone and decided to wait for Naima in the lobby.

"Have a nice lunch," Micah said, giving her a wink.

Elise rolled her eyes. "Thanks. I should be back in time for our team meeting."

"Don't rush back on our account," Katrina said from the kitchenette as she grabbed her lunch from the refrigerator.

Elise was tempted to give her the finger but chose a wave in parting. She hadn't been in the lobby for five minutes before Naima walked through the revolving door. Her face lit with a bright smile when she saw Elise. It hit Elise that she'd missed Naima not being nearby and realized that this had been the longest they had been apart since she magically appeared in her kitchen two days ago. With all that had happened since then, it felt more like weeks.

"How was your sightseeing?" Elise asked.

There was a subtle shift in Naima's smile. "It was nice. I spent most of it sitting in Central Park. They have a lovely sanctuary, which I'm sure you already know about."

"Yes. I go there sometimes when I need a break from the office. I had Micah make us reservations for a Mediterranean restaurant just a couple of blocks from here that I thought you might like."

"That sounds wonderful."

The cheerfulness in Naima's smile and voice didn't reach her eyes which looked dark and stormy. Something was wrong and Elise had a sneaking suspicion she wouldn't like what had brought on those storm clouds.

Chapter Seven

O nce they were seated at the restaurant and had placed their order, Naima started small talk by asking Elise how her day was going. She was trying to delay telling her about Malik and how he suggested helping with their situation. His suggestion about his spiritualist friend and the revelation that Aliya had somehow cursed him and Jahir to their human form worried her. Malik had said Aliya's love for Naima and Akiba had given power to her words, but Naima wondered if the pain and anger of seeing her whole world taken away by Jahir was what might have given them strength. So many of her memories were of a loving, gentle princess that she forgot that her wife was also a warrior at heart when it came to defending her home. A long-forgotten memory came to mind.

Aliya was just sixteen years of age when she, Naima, and a handful of human royal guards were making their way to visit the mountain villages of the clans that had chosen not to live within vicinity of the palace because of their distrust of the jinn. Unbeknownst to them, a small group of recently freed slaves that had been brought to the island decided to attempt a coup by kidnapping Aliya. They lay in wait using the trees for cover as they took out the guards with poison arrows while dropping an iron net on Naima to weaken her. She had been so immersed in her conversation with Aliya that she had let her intuitive guard down, so she hadn't sensed the danger coming. They had made the trip so many times without incident that she depended on the royal guard to handle any trouble that might arise.

Half a dozen men surrounded Aliya while the other three kept Naima trapped in the iron net while poking her with the iron tips of their spears. If all Naima had to worry about was the iron net, she could get away, but the spear tips drew blood, causing the iron to get into her bloodstream. The men surrounding Aliya obviously hadn't heard of her skills with a sword as they only laughed when she removed hers from the scabbard at her hip and took a defensive stance.

"Look at this, they gave her a sword to play with. Do you even know what to do with that, Princess?" A man whom Naima assumed was the leader taunted her.

"Why don't you come find out?" Aliya said haughtily.

"Salim, show the princess what a real swordsman looks like," the leader said.

To Naima's horror, a man twice as tall and wide as Aliya stepped forward with one of the dead guard's swords and a deadly leer. She struggled against her iron bonds to no avail. Aliya was on her own, and Naima worried that even with her skills, she wouldn't be able to take on so many opponents on her own. Especially as large as the one that was presently stalking toward her. With a loud battle cry that Naima had never heard come from her, Aliya ducked out of the way of her opponent's sword swipe and brought her own up under his arm, almost detaching it from his shoulder. With a yowl of pain, he dropped the sword, fell to his knees, and grabbed his barely attached limb. Aliya now faced the leader, once again in her defensive stance. He looked from her small frame toward the wounded giant in disbelief.

"I believe you were going to show me what a real swordsman looks like," Aliya said.

The leader's shock turned to anger. "I had hoped we could do this without injuring you, Princess, but you are wearing on my patience." He nodded toward the other three men surrounding Aliya. "Don't kill her," was his only instruction.

They sneered as they moved in on Aliya who couldn't manage to watch all three at the same time. The most opponents she'd been trained to handle were two at a time. Naima watched helplessly, praying that the men would follow orders and not kill her, but they wouldn't have to kill her to severely wound her. As they approached, they always kept one of the men at Aliya's back. The two facing her raised their borrowed swords while the third unsheathed a blade from his hip. Naima almost called out for Aliya to watch her back, but she knew that could distract her and possibly get her killed. She didn't need to worry. As if Aliya had eyes in the back of her head, she whirled on the man behind her, and thrust her sword just as he swiped his blade through her headscarf and across her cheek. Naima saw a line of blood on Aliya's face and screamed, receiving an iron jab in response.

Aliya continued as if she hadn't even heard Naima, moving like a whirling dervish as she grabbed her own dagger from her hip, and turned back toward the other two, meeting and parrying their attacks like a true trained soldier. Naima watched in fascination as her normally playful kitten of a mate became a dangerous tigress before her eyes. The way she fought was nothing like the moves she had learned when she, Adnan, and Malik trained together. They were the moves that only the royal guard had been trained in.

Aliya took out her other two opponents within minutes and once again faced their leader, barely breathing heavy. "Shall we play?" she said to him.

Naima saw fear in his eyes and felt a triumphant sense of pride in Aliya. Then he narrowed his gaze on Naima and back at her.

"You touch me, and they kill your jinni friend."

A spear was jabbed deeply into Naima's side, and she screamed as white-hot pain seared through her from the iron.

"NAIMA!" Aliya screamed.

"I'm fine," Naima said through clenched teeth.

"Drop your weapons, Princess," the leader said.

There were several flashes of light as a dozen jinn royal guards appeared and surrounded them all.

"No, you drop your weapons," Malik said, holding a sword at the man's throat.

He quickly dropped his borrowed sword and with the threatening looks of the other guards directed their way, his men dropped the spears they'd held Naima in place with. The iron net was quickly removed, and Naima struggled to stand as her magic tried to fight off the effects of the iron-tipped spears.

"Let me help you." Aliya wrapped an around her waist to steady her.

Naima quirked a brow at Aliya. "I believe someone has been holding out during training."

She blushed, but she couldn't hide the fire of battle that still lit her eyes. "At my request, Malik has been training me on the side."

Naima glanced up at Malik who watched them in concern, and possibly envy. "Do your parents know this? You could be injured learning the tactics of the royal guard."

"No, and I don't plan on telling them. I want to learn to protect my people as best I can. That won't happen with the sedate training I receive."

"Sedate? We all take the same training."

"No, you, Adnan, and Malik all take the same training, then you attempt to appease me by teaching me the basics while you play along. I'm just as capable as Adnan of learning more advanced techniques. I've proven that today."

Naima looked at the first man whose arm was being healed by one of the jinn soldiers and the other two attempted kidnappers that Aliya had practically maimed also being healed and couldn't argue with her. She had more than proved her abilities. Naima was proud of her but also frightened for her. The look she'd seen on her face, and the thrill she felt from Aliya during her battle was such a contradiction to her loving and caring demeanor. By the time she was facing the leader there was a sense of joy at the violence she'd wrought coming off her. Fear for Aliya's life had pushed what she was feeling from her aside, but now that they were safe, they were forefront in Naima's mind, and she hoped to never have to experience those feelings from Aliya again.

The memory of that day had Naima worrying about how Aliya would react to being forced from Elise and having to give up the chance to live freely once again. Would she fight it, or would she be willing to let go and ascend as she needed to for Elise to continue living her life?

"You're barely listening to a word I'm saying. You seem distracted. Is something wrong?" Elise asked.

Naima was a blue jinni, a trained warrior who had fought in actual battles to free enslaved people, had even faced death once, yet the thought of telling Elise about her conversation with Malik frightened her more than any of that had. Elise reached across the table and placed her hand atop Naima's.

"Please, Naima, talk to me. The anxiety coming off you is as thick as the humidity outside," Elise said with concern.

Naima flipped her hand and grasped Elise's. "I spoke with Malik today." She thought it was best just to say it rather than prolong the inevitable.

"Telepathically?"

"No. He approached me while I was in the park. He'd aged himself so I didn't recognize him at first, then he removed his glamour, and it was the same Malik of that long ago day." Naima still found their reasonable conversation difficult to believe considering all that had happened.

"How did he know where to find you? Do jinn have a special radar to track down other jinn?" Elise gave her a small smile, but Naima could feel her worry.

"Something like that. We can pick up on each other's energy, but more powerful jinn like Jahir can sense power from other magical beings like you can sense a change in temperature. Malik has managed to feed off Jahir's powers to grow his own through the centuries. He located me at your apartment and has been following us."

Elise's grip on Naima's hand tightened as she tried to discreetly look around the restaurant.

"He's not here," Naima reassured her.

Elise's shoulders visibly relaxed. "What did he want? Has he found a way to help you and Aliya?"

Naima didn't miss the way Elise asked about helping her and Aliya and not herself. She was just as much entangled with their curse as they were, yet she only thought of them.

"Yes, but I'm not sure if it's something I want to do. It could put you at risk."

Elise gazed down at their clasped hands then back up at her. "Will it free you?"

"I believe so. But it could also put you in danger. He told me something about Aliya that has me concerned about bringing her forward."

Naima went on to tell Elise everything Malik had told her of Aliya's curse and how his spiritualist friend could help. When she finished, Elise was quiet for a few moments as her brow furrowed in thought. She sighed and was just about to speak when their server arrived with their food. Naima looked down at her salad and thought she should've ordered the soup because her stomach had been in knots since talking to Malik.

"So, this spiritualist can bring Aliya forward for you to speak with, have her make her three wishes, then you'll both be free after you've granted them?" Elise asked.

"Yes, as long there aren't any issues, that's what should happen."

Elise looked down at her sandwich as if she had also lost her appetite. "You mentioned some concern over Aliya. Do you think she won't cooperate?"

"My concern has to do with the curse she placed on Jahir and Malik. I believe her ability to do that had to do with the anger and pain of loss and not, as Malik thinks, her love for me and Akiba. Curses stem from black magic. Anger, violence, or pain can strengthen that magic, not love. Whether her soul was aware of the lifetimes lived or not, her anger has had time to grow. I fear that Aliya may not be the same loving woman I once knew." Naima didn't want to believe that could be a possibility, but with Elise's involvement, she had to be realistic.

"I've seen movies and read fiction stories about past lives, spirits, and even jinn possessing someone and eventually taking over their mind and body. Sometimes fiction can be based on fact. Could that happen to me? Could Aliya come forward and not want to leave? After all, she'll have you again and a way to live a life outside the world she had as a princess. There would be nothing holding her back." Elise's voice shook on the last statement.

"I would not let that happen. I won't sacrifice your life and freedom for mine or Aliya's. I'll spend the rest of the millennia in that bottle before I do that," Naima said vehemently, and she meant it.

❖

Elise could hear in the tone of her voice and the determined expression on her face that Naima was sincere about not allowing Aliya to take over, but she still had to say what needed to be said. "Aliya is your wife, the love of your life. Can you honestly let her soul continue to go through this lifetime after lifetime? What happens if you find your way to each other again? You'll end up with the same situation of having to put that person in danger as well. This needs to end at some point, it might as well be now." Elise sounded a lot braver than she felt.

Naima looked at her in concern. "What are you saying?"

Elise sighed in resignation. "I'll meet with the spiritualist. Maybe she'll be able to find a way to keep my soul and life unharmed while giving Aliya a chance to do what needs to be done to break the curse. Maybe Aliya wants this to end as much as you do."

"That's a lot of maybes. It's too risky. I think going back to Maureen would be a safer option."

"It may be safer, but if my first session was any indication, it may take many more sessions to make any progress. If you trust Malik and he trusts his friend, I think that may be the quicker route."

"I don't mind waiting. As long as you haven't made your last two wishes I have plenty of time. Unless you're in a hurry to get rid of me." Naima gave her a teasing smile.

"No hurry at all. If this doesn't work, I may have to make the same wish as your professor just to keep you around."

"I'd happily grant it."

Their gazes held and the storm clouds in Naima's eyes dissipated, clearing the way for the bright swirl of galaxy Elise had begun to love seeing.

"Is everything to your liking?" their server asked.

Elise tore her gaze from Naima's and looked down at her untouched food, then smiled up at the server. "Oh, yes, we were just so busy talking we forgot to eat."

The young woman nodded then walked away.

"If we do this," Naima said, "I think we should have Grammy and Marcus there. Maybe the more connections you have to your life the more likely they are to keep you grounded in the here and now."

"That sounds like a good idea. I'll call them both when I get back to the office."

Naima nodded. "I'll get a message to Malik."

Elise smiled to cover up the quiet fear building within her. As much as she believed Naima wanted to protect her, she was afraid that being faced with the chance to not only be free of that lamp but to be with Aliya once again would change that.

❖

"Have you lost your mind?" Marcus shouted over the phone.

"No, but I will if I don't do something about this. I can hear her in my head and feel her deep down in my soul. It's like a persistent ache that I can't seem to get rid of. Especially when I'm around Naima. Something strange happened last night. I remember coming home, Naima giving me a foot massage—"

"A foot massage, nice," Marcus interrupted her.

Elise rolled her eyes. "Then I think we talked about something from her past and everything is dark after that. Next thing I remember was waking up in my bed this morning."

"Alone?" Marcus asked.

"Yes, alone. Can you please take this seriously? First the voices, now I'm missing time. I need to do this for my own sanity and for Naima. I can't bear the thought of sending her back to that lamp."

Elise heard Marcus sigh heavily. "Look, sis, I can't imagine what you're going through, but I will support whatever you need to do to get through it. I just want you to be safe. Playing with the spirit of a long-gone cursed princess who somehow managed to curse two jinn in anger doesn't sound safe."

It didn't feel very safe to Elise either, but she wasn't going to admit that. It would only make her chicken out. She and Naima decided to go this coming weekend, so she had the rest of the week to let what they were going to do sink in, or to talk herself out of it.

"So, you'll be there?" she asked Marcus.

"Yes. At least with both Grammy and I there we'll be able to sense if the whole thing is a crock of shit."

Elise hadn't even thought about how their clairvoyance could possibly help protect her if something wasn't right. "Exactly. I'll text you guys the address as soon as Naima makes the arrangements."

"Okay, cool and, sis…"

"Yeah."

"If you find any more magic lamps, please send them my way. I could use a hot jinni in my life to grant me a few wishes."

Elise laughed. "Sure, I'll do that."

After their lunch, Naima decided to go back to the apartment. She walked back to the park, found a secluded spot to make sure no one witnessed her magic, and arrived at the apartment a moment later in a plume of purple smoke.

"I was wondering when you'd get back although I'm quite enjoying these Atlanta Housewives. They're very entertaining."

Naima stared wide-eyed at her grandfather lounging on Elise's sofa with a glass of wine watching a shouting match between three women on the television. He wore a blue jogging suit, white running shoes, had shortened his long white beard to a few inches past his chin, and his usually waist-length hair was pulled back into a ponytail, to just past his shoulders. He looked like a hip and kindly older gentleman just enjoying an afternoon at home.

"Grandfather," she said in greeting once the initial shock wore off.

He grinned mischievously. "Granddaughter."

"I see you've made yourself at home."

"Yes. Elise has wonderful taste in wine. Would you like a glass?"

A wine glass glided from Elise's cabinet toward her along with the bottle of wine that had been sitting on the coffee table. Naima grabbed both out of the air and set them back on the table.

"No, thank you. What I'd like is to know why you're here and why now? We were led to believe that you had chosen to ascend."

"Yes, about that," he said guiltily. "Akiba had grown beyond my wildest dreams. I felt I had done all that I could do and that it was time for me to leave it in the hands of the next generation of jinn and humans. I thought leading everyone to believe that I had chosen to ascend would deter them from seeking me out if an issue arose. I wanted you all to learn and grow without my interference."

"You lied to us," Naima said angrily.

He shrugged. "I didn't lie. I just didn't tell the whole truth."

Naima shook her head and picked up the wine bottle to pour herself a glass after all. She would need it talking to Chirag. He enjoyed riddles and games too much to get straight answers out of him sometimes. She took a long drink then sat in the chair across from him.

"Is my assumption that you've been the one steering Elise along with the lamp all these years, correct?"

He frowned, sat up, and placed his glass on the coffee table. "Yes. I'm so sorry I wasn't there for you, the royal family, and Akiba. If I hadn't left, then none of this would've happened."

"Do you really think you could've stopped Jahir? He was too hell-bent on revenge to see anything but his hatred of you. Malik unfortunately became a pawn in his game."

"He would've listened to me, but by the time I'd heard he'd found his way into Akiba it was too late. I returned to find nothing left but bodies and rubble. The only survivors were the mountain clans. Despite their distrust of jinn, they recognized me and knew I wouldn't harm them. I managed to get them off the island and settled someplace safe in the Madagascar highlands before I went back to bury our people." A tear rolled down his cheek. "So much loss and it was all my fault."

Naima placed her glass on the table and moved to sit beside him. She wrapped her arm around his shoulder. "Grandfather, you couldn't have known. The only ones at fault are Jahir and Malik."

"No, I knew something was coming and that Jahir would be the one to bring it. I'd seen it in a vision. It was the other reason I left. I thought that if I weren't on the island, he wouldn't come." He turned and placed a hand on Naima's cheek. "I didn't think he would seek his revenge through you and our people when he learned I wasn't there. I am so sorry, my child."

They held each other and cried for all they had lost. When their tears had dried, Naima felt a little lighter in her spirit as she'd never been able to share that loss with anyone who understood what Akiba was to her until now.

"When did you find out about the curse on Aliya and me? I assume that's why you've been keeping tabs on Elise all these years."

"I learned of the curse when I learned of Akiba's destruction, but it took me almost a century to locate the path of Aliya's spirit. Once I was able to do that it wasn't that difficult to locate you and the lamp following stories of humans finding a magic lamp. Believe it or not, that isn't a very common curse for jinn. It smacks too much of the silly stories of Shahrazad," he said distastefully.

Naima frowned. "Yes, well, the truth couldn't be further from the stories."

Chirag looked at her with sympathy. "I can't imagine what you've endured, but I'm here now to put an end to it."

"Speaking of that, if you've known all these years, why didn't you try to help sooner?"

"Because the reincarnated humans who carried Aliya's spirit weren't strong enough until Elise. That's why I was able to direct her to your lamp." He grinned happily.

"What's different about Elise than all the others over the centuries?"

Chirag's grin turned to a look of disappointment. "You cannot tell me that you don't feel the strength of her spirit as well as those surrounding her?"

Naima considered what he was saying. Other than last night, Elise had been handling Aliya's fights to come forward much better than she would've expected. Also, with such a loving and close family around her and their gift of clairvoyance, they'd no doubt kept Elise protected. As Malik said, love was a powerful magic all its own and Elise was surrounded by it.

"There is one other reason that Elise had to be the one to break the curse. She's your true soul mate," Chirag said quietly.

"No, you said Aliya was."

"I thought she was. I was wrong. I felt it the moment Elise stepped off that boat onto our homeland. I'd had a vision that the right soul would visit Akiba when the time had come to correct all the wrongs committed so I held on to the lamp and stayed close to Akiba to make sure I didn't miss the opportunity to connect you two. But when I finally met her in the market and saw how young she was I knew I had to wait until she was older and stronger."

"That's why I hadn't been summoned for so long," Naima concluded.

Chirag smiled proudly. "Yes, I kept you safe until the time was right. That time was when she returned a few weeks ago. I could see it when I placed the lamp in her hand and the opal glowed with your inner fire because your soul recognized its mate."

Deep down, Naima felt he was right. That the truth had been there the moment she'd laid eyes on Elise and recognized her soul but had mistaken it for Aliya's. The irony that the soul of the woman she'd believed was her soul mate for so long now occupied the body of her actual soul mate didn't get past her. She covered her face with her hands and groaned. Their situation just became even more complicated.

"I thought this would be happy news," Chirag said.

"It would be if what Malik told me earlier wasn't true."

Thunder rumbled throughout the apartment. "Jahir is here?"

Naima looked up into eyes that glowed red with fire and the hairs on her arm stood on end from the electricity charging the air.

"Grandfather, you're going to have to calm down. Elise doesn't need to come home to find her building a pile of rubble."

Chirag closed his eyes, took several deep breaths, quietly recited a chant, and the air felt normal once again. "Explain," he growled.

Naima knew her grandfather was a reformed black jinn and that his magic was some of the most powerful amongst the jinn. To make him angry would be like setting off a nuclear bomb. She tried to explain what happened with Malik as best she could without agitating him again, but just the mention of Jahir being in the same city had him growling under his breath which kept the rumbling thunder contained within the apartment.

"Do you honestly believe Malik is acting alone? That Jahir isn't using him to get to you to keep you from breaking the curse?" Chirag said.

"Yes, I believe him. Judging by what he told me, Jahir seems to be just as anxious to free himself as Malik is. Would you want to be unwillingly trapped in human form for eternity, unable to travel freely amongst the realms or change forms on a whim? I know how much you enjoy soaring through the skies in your hawk form. Think of how you'd feel not being able to do that. Then top it off with having to share that form with another jinn," Naima said.

Chirag seemed to consider what she said then frowned. "How do you know, once free of Malik's human form, that Jahir won't kill you and Elise for what Aliya did?"

Naima hadn't thought of that. In his anger, Jahir could wipe them all out with a snap of his fingers. Then she looked hopefully at Chirag. "You could be there to protect us."

Chirag laughed out loud. "My child, I'm the reason he did all of this from the start. Do you really think my presence will help the situation?"

"It will at least take the focus off us. Elise's protection is my main priority. I don't care what happens to me if she's safe."

Chirag looked at her curiously. "You're already falling in love with her."

Naima didn't see any reason to deny the truth to him. "Yes."

"This is good. I knew it was the right time for breaking the curse. I'll be there. In the meantime, let me give you my number in case you need to reach me. I'm staying at a lovely hotel nearby so I can be here in a flash." To Naima's surprise, he pulled a cell phone that looked like what Elise called her iPhone, from his pocket.

"I can't believe you actually have one of those distracting gadgets?"

Chirag held it up to his face, the screen lit up, and he smiled gleefully. "They're such a fascinating invention and you know how much I enjoy modern conveniences. If I didn't, Akibans wouldn't have had the luxury of an underground irrigation system for fresh water and wind towers to cool us down during our hottest days, both from our Persian allies, and a sewage system borrowed from the Romans. With the length of our lifetimes, if we don't adapt, my child, how would we ever survive without going mad?"

Naima couldn't argue there. Because of the knowledge of their jinn forebearers, Akiba had been far more advanced than many other nations they traded or battled with, and the human population, most of whom had only known a life in slavery before coming to Akiba, were grateful for it.

"Well, since I don't have a phone, I'll contact you the old-fashioned way." She tapped her temple.

Chirag grinned and shook his head. "If you plan to stay, which I assume you will once this is all over, you need to get with the clique as the young folks say these days."

Naima laughed. "How long have you been here?"

"Since I discovered Elise. I've been keeping an eye on her all these years just to make sure I was right about her."

"You haven't interfered in her life, have you?"

"No, other than the two encounters on Akiba, I've kept my distance. Although, her grandmother fascinates me. I haven't been drawn to a woman, let alone a human one, since your grandmother." He stroked his shorn beard in contemplation.

Naima remembered very little about her grandmother. She had been one of the jinn who helped to create Akiba but had chosen to ascend when Naima was just a young child. What she did remember was a demure blue jinn who deferred to her grandfather for every decision. Naima couldn't see Chirag and Grammy together. Knowing the feisty woman that she was, it would have to be on her terms which she couldn't imagine happening with his just as feisty and commanding nature.

"She may be human, but she's still probably quite a bit more than you can handle."

Chirag shrugged. "Only one way to find that out. Maybe you can introduce us."

"I'll think about it," Naima said in amusement. Grammy would eat her grandfather alive, especially with her intuitive abilities.

"Well, until then. I have a dinner date with a lovely American millionairess I met in the hotel lobby. She's the one who told me about those wonderfully trashy shows about housewives because she's on one of them." He looped his arm through Naima's and walked to the door with her.

"You know you can leave the same way you came," she said.

"True, but I enjoy being in human form and doing human things far too much." He gave her a wink. "When you decide to get a phone, I left my number on the coffee table for you. I will see you on Saturday." He placed a kiss on her temple before walking out the door.

Naima watched him head for the stairs instead of the elevator and shook her head. Her grandfather had always been very physically active when in human form and it seemed that hadn't changed. The white hair and aged face may have given him the appearance of a man in his seventies or eighties, but his body was always that of someone three times his junior. With his kind heart and youthful stamina, Chirag had never had to spend a night alone unless he chose to. Human and jinn females alike had swarmed to him like bees to honey. It seemed that hadn't changed either. She closed the door and walked back over to the coffee table to find a piece of paper with a phone number in his flourishing script. Naima picked it up and decided she would have to ask Elise about getting a phone. Malik had thought it amusing as well that she hadn't adapted to the cellular communication and there was no way her several-millennia-aged grandfather would be more with the times than she was.

CHAPTER EIGHT

Elise walked into her apartment to the sound of Nina Simone crooning "I Put a Spell on You," the scent of something delicious cooking, and the sight of Naima stirring something in a pot on the stove. She felt as if she'd just walked into one of her favorite daydreams of what she wanted for her life.

"Uh...hi."

Naima gazed up at her with a bright smile. "Hi. You're just in time. Dinner will be ready in about ten minutes. Why don't you go freshen up while I set the table?"

"Okay." She hung her work bag by the door then discreetly pinched herself to make sure she wasn't dreaming. Nope, not a dream. Just a fantasy come to life, she thought as she headed toward her bedroom. She gazed at herself in the bathroom mirror. "This is temporary. As soon as this curse business is over, Naima will be free to go do whatever it is jinn do when they're not granting wishes."

Happy with her much-needed reminder of reality, Elise freshened up as she was told to do, then changed out of her work clothes into a pair of sweatpants and a T-shirt, then recalled that under her June Cleaver apron, Naima wore a pair of turquoise wide-leg satin-looking pants and a matching tunic. It wasn't fancy but it was nicer than sweats and a T-shirt, so she searched her wardrobe for something more appropriate to wear for dinner with a sexy jinni. She found a black knee-length Ankara fabric tunic with long loose sleeves and turquoise, red, yellow, orange, and black Kente design bordering the neckline, sleeves, and hem. Ironically, she'd bought the tunic during her recent trip to Nosy Be from a marketplace in Madagascar while waiting for the ferry. She turned to look at herself in the mirror then frowned. She had just reminded herself that this was a temporary situation and now she was worried whether Naima would like what she was wearing. She shook her head and left her bedroom before she found herself putting on makeup.

Elise walked out to Nina Simone still crooning, but this time it was "To Love Somebody." As she looked at Naima scooping the contents of the pot into a serving bowl, the first verse of the song hit Elise squarely in her heart. Nina crooned about a certain kind of light that had never shined on her until the love she was singing about had come into her life and now she wanted to live her whole life with that person. Being on the sidelines as she watched her friends find love and start families had grown tiresome. Elise had been wondering for the past year if she would ever find somebody to love. Could Naima be the one to show her how to truly love someone heart, mind, and body? Could she show Elise what it was like to be genuinely in love? *"Not if she leaves you once you help free her"* a doubtful little voice said.

It had only been three days and Naima had somehow made Elise's home feel like a real home for the first time since she'd moved in five years ago, had made her believe in magic once again, and had found her way into her heart because Elise knew, without a doubt, that she was falling for Naima in a way that she had never fallen for any woman before. With Naima she felt her heart was home. At that realization, something deep within her shifted and began to move to the surface with more doubt and questions, but as she watched Naima puttering around the kitchen, Elise's heart warmed, and the voice abruptly went quiet.

Naima gazed up at her with that smile that made Elise want to give her the world. "I see you changed. I like it."

Elise felt her face heat in a blush. "Thank you. I thought it would be more appropriate than sweats."

Naima nodded. "I agree. Shall we eat?"

"Yes. Is there anything I can help with?"

"If you could grab the bowl of rice, we'll be good."

Elise picked up the fluffiest bowl of rice she'd ever seen and followed Naima to her dinette set off the kitchen. She couldn't remember the last time she'd used it. She usually ate at the kitchen island or on the sofa in front of the TV. Naima had formally set the table with plates, glasses of water, wine glasses, and silverware on cloth napkins Elise didn't remember ever owning. There was even a small vase of flowers in the middle of the table.

"This looks so nice. You didn't have to do all of this," she said.

"It's the least I can do. You haven't asked for any wishes other than the one your brother insisted on. I feel as if I need to earn my keep somehow. Besides, judging by what was in your refrigerator and cabinets, you obviously don't cook much." Naima gave her a teasing grin.

"Most of the time I order delivery or pick something up on the way home from work. I usually work much longer days than I did today."

Naima cocked her head to the side, gazing at her curiously. "Oh, really. What made you come home?"

Elise met her gaze and despite knowing she could lose Naima at the end of this week; she decided honesty was the best policy. "Because I knew you would be here."

Naima gave her a shy smile. "I forgot the wine. I'll be right back."

Elise liked that she could make such an indomitable woman blush. She had a feeling that in her life before the lamp, Naima was always the bold and confident one. She oversaw an entire kingdom, commanded an army, and advised a king; you couldn't be shy and meek to do that. She came back with a bottle of chardonnay that Elise recognized as the bottle she'd bought for the dinner she'd had with her last girlfriend before she'd stormed out of the apartment because Elise wouldn't give her a key despite having spent practically every weekend here. To top it off, the chardonnay had been Elise's favorite wine while her ex had preferred rosé.

"I have a bottle of cabernet sauvignon if you prefer," Elise offered, in case Naima didn't like white wine.

Naima glanced toward the coffee table then back at her with a tentative smile. "No, this is fine."

They sat down, Naima filled both of their glasses, then uncovered the dish where the delicious scent was coming from. Steam rose off its contents and Elise inhaled deeply.

"Whatever this is, it smells heavenly."

"It's a dish from Madagascar, trondro gasy. It's like a fish stew and traditionally served with rice." Naima picked up Elise's bowl and placed a scoop of rice and then a ladle full of the stew over it. Then did the same for her bowl. "I hope it's not too spicy."

Elise tasted a spoonful. "Delicious and not too spicy at all. It's perfect."

Naima looked very proud of herself. "Thank you."

They ate and Naima asked about the rest of Elise's day, but unlike earlier, she listened attentively. Then she asked about some things she'd seen on the news earlier. Elise couldn't imagine what it was like for Naima to have been out of the world for three decades and re-enter it to the mess that it currently was in. Especially in America. Naima asked great questions and even expressed how much she wished the jinn would come together and do for the world what Chirag and his tribe had done for Akiba. Elise was genuinely enjoying herself. She could get used to coming home to this every night. To an intelligent, beautiful, and caring woman waiting for her with a home-cooked meal and good conversation.

"Time for dessert," Naima said as Elise finished the last of her second helping.

"Dessert! I don't think I can eat another bite." Elise sat back and patted her full stomach.

"But I made them special for you." Naima gave her a pout.

Elise shook her head. "Well, I didn't have the rice with my second helping so maybe I can eat a little more."

Naima nodded. "Good." She picked up both of their plates and placed them on the counter then did the same with the stew and rice, went to the refrigerator, and returned with a plate of white bonbons piled in a little pyramid.

"They're called bonbon coco." She set the plate between them

Naima looked so happy Elise didn't have the heart to tell her she wasn't a fan of coconut, which she recognized as the flakes on the bonbons. She took the one off the very top, bit into it, and looked at Naima in surprise. Even with the coconut it was very good.

"These are just as good as the stew was. It tastes so decadent. What's in it?"

Naima took one as well. "It's just coconut, sugar, water, and a pinch of salt." She popped the treat into her mouth whole and chewed slowly, as if savoring every taste. "They were my favorite dessert. The cook at the palace would create a huge tower of them every year for my birthday," she said wistfully.

Elise took another off the pile. "To be made so simply they taste so bad for you."

"I could eat a dozen of them in one sitting." Naima popped another into her mouth.

Elise chuckled. She could imagine Naima as a little girl standing there piling her plate with the little desserts. "Do you have a sweet tooth or is it just this particular sweet?"

Naima grinned. "I have a bit of a sweet tooth, but mostly for chocolate and pastries."

"I guess jinn don't have to worry about gaining weight like humans."

"That's not true. In human form our bodies are subject to the same changes as a normal human. I've seen some pretty gluttonous jinn in my time." Naima looked disgusted at the thought.

"Can jinn choose any human form they like, or do they have to model themselves after someone?"

"We can do both. If we want to blend into a certain culture or region, then we model our human forms to fit the look of the people. If a jinni chooses to be more of a trickster, they may model their form to be the exact replica of someone to cause mischief in that person's life. Most jinn choose their own look based on features they've seen on humans that they like."

"What made you choose your human form?"

Naima smiled. "Like you, my human form is a mixture of my parents' human form. I could choose to change something if I like, for instance my eye color." Naima's dark eyes changed to a piercing blue and back. "My hair color." Her hair lightened to a deep burgundy and back to black. "But I like the way I look so I choose to stay this way."

"If I was as beautiful as you, I wouldn't change either."

Naima gave her a sweet smile. "Thank you."

Their gazes held, and Elise felt such a deep longing that it almost physically ached.

Naima looked down at the table. "I guess I better clean this up."

"I'll help you," Elise offered.

They cleaned up the rest of the dishes from the table and while Naima stored the leftovers in the refrigerator and wiped down the dining table and counters, Elise loaded the dishwasher. She found herself wondering what making love to a jinni was like. Was there a special way to do it? Did they use magic? She remembered a movie where a woman had fallen in love with an alien and instead of making love like two humans, the alien merged with the human to bring her pleasure. Elise shuddered in distaste at the thought of having to do that with Naima. She would prefer to touch and be touched. Then she remembered that Naima could read her thoughts and quickly tried thinking of something else like what she needed to add to her grocery list now that there were two of them in the apartment.

Just as Elise had feared, Naima had caught a glimpse of what she was thinking and felt her face heat with a blush. She couldn't remember if she'd ever blushed like this before. Elise was softening her hardened warrior shell and she didn't mind at all. While cooking for the professor had been one of many ways to thank her for sparing her having to go back into the lamp all those years, doing it for Elise was more pleasurable because she knew it would make her happy. She'd seen all the recipe books and a recipe card file she had in one of her cabinets and assumed Elise wished she had more time to cook but her busy work schedule kept her from doing so. Naima had also taken her time with her appearance tonight to look softer and more feminine to Elise with her chosen attire and allowing her hair to hang loose. She hadn't done all of that to try to seduce Elise, but knowing that she was thinking of her in such an explicit way gave her an unexpected sense of satisfaction.

"What would you like to do now?" Elise asked as she finished her task.

"What would you normally do after coming home from work?"

"Probably would've ordered something quick for dinner, then sat at the counter eating it while I worked until I was too tired to keep my eyes open."

"Do you ever take time to just relax?"

Elise quirked a brow. "Did you when you were vizier?"

Naima smiled guiltily. "Not as often as Aliya would've liked me to."

"Then why don't we do that now. Let's relax on the sofa and watch a movie or two. Something light and fun."

"Sounds like a wonderful plan to me."

They headed into the living room. Elise turned on the TV and brought up the screen that showed movie options.

"How about this one. You can't get more lighthearted than a Disney movie and I've been meaning to watch it," Elise said, choosing a cartoon titled *Soul*.

"As long as it's not that ridiculous *Aladdin* movie then it works for me." Naima's nose wrinkled in distaste.

"Wow, you really do hate that movie."

"Hate is such a strong word. I dislike it intensely." She'd read *Arabian Nights* every day for the rest of her life if it meant she would never have to watch that insulting movie ever again.

Elise chuckled. "Well, okay then."

The movie was indeed enjoyable until a hesitant soul took over the main character's body then refused to leave when it found out what it had been missing by avoiding being reborn in a human. Naima could feel just as much as she could see Elise tense up. They finished the movie, which of course had a happy ending for all, but Naima had a pretty good idea what Elise had spent the rest of the movie thinking about.

"I won't let that happen to you," Naima said as Elise turned the TV off and stared at the dark screen.

She turned to Naima with fear in her eyes. "Can you promise me it won't happen?"

Naima wasn't foolish enough to do that. "No, I can't, but I can promise that I'll do everything within my power to make sure it doesn't." She gently took Elise's face in her hands. "I care too much for you to sacrifice you for anyone's freedom. Mine or Aliya's."

"You don't even know me. How can you be willing to give up your freedom for me?"

"Because my heart recognizes yours."

The look in Elise's eyes changed from fear to sadness. She shook her head and took Naima's hands from her face. "You recognize your wife's heart."

Naima placed one of Elise's hands over her own heart. "You and Aliya may share a body, but your heart is your own." She took Elise's other hand and placed it over her heart. "My heart beats in harmony with yours. In a way it never did for Aliya. To cause you pain and heartbreak would be to do the same to me."

Elise looked from one hand to the other in amazement. "They're beating in the exact same rhythm?"

"Because you and I are matched. I felt it the moment I looked at you. I thought maybe I had recognized Aliya's soul because I had always believed she and I were soul mates. But I was wrong. It's you. It's the reason the lamp made it into your hands. My soul mate will be the one to set me free. That's you, Elise."

Elise balled her hands together in her lap looking at her in confusion. "How is that possible when I share a body with Aliya? Wouldn't that still make her your soul mate, just in a different body?"

"I can see how that would confuse you, but it is possible to have more than one soul mate. There are many soul connections a person can join with over a lifetime. We could be drawn to them and experience a connection through our thoughts, feelings, and physical attractions. The person could be entering our lives to provide insight, assist us through an emotional or spiritual transition, or provide us with unconditional love. It doesn't always end up being a lover. Whether they're just passing through or staying in your life, the bond remains forever. I will forever be connected to Aliya because we provided each other with something we needed at that time. It could have been simply to teach us how to love or to provide us with a partner that balanced us out. In the end, she is not the soul mate of my heart."

Elise's brow furrowed. She was probably trying to understand what Naima had just explained. "How do you know that I'm not just someone passing through? Just here to help you and Aliya break the spell?"

Naima took Elise's hand and pressed it above her heart again. "We are connected heart and soul. We're soul-hearted, which is a stronger spiritual connection than soul mates. I feel our bond growing stronger every day. Something I didn't feel for Aliya. I love her, but our bond was not the strength of yours and mine."

Elise looked doubtful. "How can you tell the difference?"

Naima smiled and brushed her fingers along Elise's jaw. "With you, I feel at peace. Like I can finally put Naima the soldier away and just be Naima the woman. I've become so quickly and deeply attuned to your emotions that I must forcefully block myself to keep from invading your privacy. When you touch me, even just in casual passing, it feels as if an electrical current has passed through me. Lastly, I feel deep in my soul that you're the person I'm meant to be with."

Elise gazed deeply into Naima's eyes, not turning away when she felt that hypnotic pull, and knew, in some strange way, that Naima was right. She also finally admitted to herself that everything Naima admitted to feeling, she also felt. But where Naima felt she no longer had to be a soldier, Elise felt a strong protectiveness of Naima. As if she would do anything to keep her safe. She'd never felt that for any of her past girlfriends. She leaned in toward Naima, who met her halfway, and when their lips met there were tingles throughout her whole body down to her toes. Naima seemed tentative at first, but Elise needed more so she twined her fingers in Naima's lush hair and put all her passion into the kiss.

Naima moaned against her mouth, and soon their lips and tongue performed an intimate dance that set Elise ablaze. A small pain niggled at the back of her head, but she ignored it. Her need for Naima was too strong to let anything put a stop to their passion. The kiss seemed to go on forever, but when Naima's lips left hers, Elise felt as if it had ended too soon. They gazed at each other, and the blackness of Naima's eyes was so dark nothing reflected off them and a ring of silver lit around the dark pupils.

"Tell me you don't want me, and this will never happen again," Elise said.

Naima began to speak, then seemed to change her mind. Instead, she took her hand, stood, and led her to Elise's bedroom.

"I take it that's a yes." Elise smoothed a strand of hair from Naima's face.

"Yes." Naima took Elise's hand and pressed a kiss to her palm.

The tender intimacy of her action made Elise's breath catch. They quickly undressed and Elise was almost salivating at the sight of Naima's nude form. She had to be a magical being to keep her body in such great shape for six hundred years. There wasn't an ounce of fat on her. Elise liked to think she was in shape, but Naima's tall, muscular frame reminded her of those models you saw in fitness magazines. She looked up to find Naima gazing in admiration at her and suddenly felt shy. Naima sat on the bed and reached a hand toward Elise. There was a moment of hesitation as a voice whispered "no" in her head. Elise knew whose voice it was and ignored it. She would do whatever she could to help release Aliya's soul from her curse except allowing her to take over her life. She mentally shut a door on that voice and sat beside Naima on the bed.

"Is there anything special I need to know about making love to a jinni?" Elise asked, only half joking.

Naima's brow furrowed as she tapped a slender finger on her chin in thought. "Let's see. Other than the four other arms that you'll probably feel stroking you, no, nothing special."

Elise's eyes widened as she took in Naima's serious expression until she saw the slight quiver in her lips as she tried to keep from laughing. "Oh, you got jokes?"

Naima chuckled. "My apologies, I couldn't resist. No, there is nothing special. I don't glow or turn into a wisp of smoke that needs to penetrate your body to bring pleasure. I have the same physical parts as you that work the same way as yours."

Elise felt her face heat with embarrassment. "You read my thoughts earlier?"

"It wasn't on purpose. I'm so relaxed around you that sometimes the barrier I put up to allow your thoughts to stay your own slips. It could've also been the wine." Naima winked.

Elise leaned in toward Naima until their lips barely brushed. "I relax you, huh?"

She pressed her lips against Naima's and their kiss began where the previous one ended, with heated passion. Naima's arms wrapped around Elise as she lay back on the bed. Elise laid her body along Naima's and felt herself grow even more aroused at the skin-to-skin contact. Naima may be toned and hardened muscle, but her skin was supple and soft to touch. She left Naima's lips to explore further, working her way to her neck, inhaling the wonderful scent of jasmine. For just a moment, Elise wondered how she knew the scent was specifically jasmine, then lost the thought as she reached the peak of firm breasts and Naima's fingers tangled within her hair urging her to continue. She took a hardened nipple into her mouth and was rewarded with a melodic sigh from Naima.

Elise lavished both breasts with equal loving attention until she could swear Naima's moans turned into a lyrical hum that pushed Elise's own arousal to the point that she didn't think she was going to be able to hold back much longer. She wanted to savor this moment. Bring Naima to the height of pleasure over and over before she even thought about her own release. As she ventured down Naima's sculpted abs, dipped her tongue with a quick swirl around her navel, and traced the outline of her smooth mound, she tried to think of something else to slow her excitement. Errands she needed to run, grocery list she needed to make, her schedule for work tomorrow, but nothing helped. The humming continued and seemed to be surging within her like a fire heading straight down to her sex. She followed the same path on Naima as the humming fire burning within her. When she lay between Naima's now spread legs, Elise peeked up to find Naima's head thrown back and mouth softly opened, but the only sound coming from her was panting breath. Did that mean it was coming from within Elise?

It wasn't an unpleasant sound or feeling that was brought on by it, so Elise continued. She also noticed the more aroused Naima grew, the stronger the scent of jasmine became. All of which made Elise almost dizzy with desire. She plunged her tongue between Naima's womanly lips and groaned in pleasure. It was like she'd found the sweetest of nectars and couldn't get enough as she dipped her tongue in and out and around Naima's sex so as not to miss a drop. She held on as Naima's hips writhed and her pants turned to soft mutterings in another language. Elise could barely hear her above the humming within her growing louder as her orgasm began to build. She shifted to slide a finger within Naima and suckle her clit. This seemed to be the trigger that set Naima's orgasm off as her inner walls clutched at Elise's finger and her clit hardened within Elise's mouth. Naima's orgasm set off Elise's and as she felt Naima's honeyed nectar release and bathe her finger, she felt a rush of liquid between her own legs but didn't stop as she removed her finger and caught what she could of Naima on her tongue.

Afterward, Elise lay panting with her head on Naima's thigh as the humming slowly receded. She felt as if she were boneless but managed to drag herself up to lie beside Naima. Gazing over at her, she saw a look of pure contentment on her face and felt a bit of cockiness at having been the reason for such a look.

Naima turned to her, smiling knowingly. "I've never felt such pleasure before, so you deserve those thoughts."

Elise didn't feel the least bit of embarrassment. "I've never had an orgasm while giving someone else one, so you're allowed to be just as cocky."

Naima shifted so that she was lying atop Elise. "Let's see if I can do the same." She lowered her lips to Elise's for a fiery kiss.

"It's not a competition," Elise said breathily as Naima left her lips to nibble on her earlobe.

"No, but making it one could be fun," Naima whispered in her ear, making Elise shiver with anticipation.

As Naima's mouth and fingers did things that made Elise wonder if she really did grow an extra pair of arms, the humming began again, bringing with it a hyper-awareness of every touch, lick, scrape of teeth or nails that came from Naima. She called out Naima's name as her orgasm rocked her body like never before as she felt Naima tightly grip her hips and heard her moan deeply between her legs. A moment later, like Elise had done earlier, Naima pulled herself up to lie next to Elise panting tiredly.

"Let's call it a draw," Elise said, also trying to catch her breath.

"Deal." Naima took Elise's hand.

They lay quietly for a moment, then Elise turned to face her. "Naima, did you…" She suddenly felt nervous, despite what had just happened between them.

Naima turned to face her. "Did I what?"

"It's probably nothing. Maybe it was just a song I heard recently stuck in my head."

Naima's eyes widened. "Did you hear humming as well?"

Elise almost sighed with relief. "Then it wasn't just me."

"No, I heard it both times."

"Me too."

Naima reached up and stroked Elise's cheek with her knuckles. "I think it may have to do with our bond. Our bodies are just as attuned as our hearts."

"Does that mean it will be like this every time we make love?" Elise knew that was wishful thinking that this would happen again. After all, there was no telling what would happen over the next several days.

Elise felt the soft warmth of Naima's fingers ease down her torso and sink pleasurably between her thighs. "Only one way to find out."

CHAPTER NINE

Naima watched Elise sleep and knew that she was utterly and completely in love with her. She felt as if she'd found a piece of herself that she hadn't known was missing. Her feelings for Aliya hadn't been this intense, and that frightened her because she was now more concerned with keeping Elise safe than she was with helping to free Aliya's spirit. Although Aliya hadn't come forward since Elise's regression therapy session, Naima knew with all her intuition that her wife had been responsible for Elise passing out and not remembering anything after they'd returned home from the gala the other night. Because of that, they had no choice but to free Aliya so that Elise could live her life without worrying about something like that happening again. Naima placed a soft kiss on Elise's temple, then eased out of bed. She dressed in the tunic she had been wearing and went to the kitchen.

"Grandfather...I know you can hear me. I need to speak with you," she said aloud.

A silver shimmering cloud of smoke appeared before her and quickly swirled into the regal figure of her grandfather dressed in a tuxedo, holding a glass of champagne.

"Thank goodness. I was growing rather bored." He finished the champagne in one long drink and threw the glass in the air where it disappeared before it could hit the ground. "Does our Elise still have any of that wonderful wine left?" he asked as he loosened his bowtie and took a seat at the kitchen island.

Naima shook her head. "It's nearly daybreak."

"True. But it's dinner time in Tokyo, where I was before you saved me from what was turning out to be a very boring dinner." Chirag yawned to emphasize his point.

"How about a cup of coffee instead," Naima offered, pressing the button to start the coffee maker.

Chirag pouted. "Fine."

Once the coffee was brewed, she filled two mugs and handed one to Chirag. He pulled a flask from his inside jacket pocket, poured a generous amount in his coffee, then took a long drink from his mug.

"Now that's an excellent cup of coffee."

"I see you still enjoy your libations."

Chirag shrugged. "It's the one vice I chose to keep from my previous life."

From what Naima knew about her grandfather's life as a black jinni, she was glad that was the only vice he kept. He had been very open about his life before creating Akiba to ensure that other young Akiba jinn would learn from and not repeat his life of cruelty, death, and destruction.

"What has my granddaughter up and about rather than lying in the warmth and afterglow of love?" Chirag said, grinning knowingly.

Naima felt her face heat with a blush. "I realized you were right about my connection with Elise. Now I need to know how to keep her safe while also freeing Aliya."

"Do you fear Aliya will attempt to hurt Elise?"

"I fear, after being snatched from the only life she'd ever known to be cursed with living lifetime after lifetime with no knowledge of who she is, only to be brought back and told that to be free meant she had to move on to the afterlife, may cause her to want to stay." It was the first time Naima had spoken her fear aloud, and it pained her even more to think about it.

"I see. Aliya was a gentle and kind woman, but loss and anger can change a person. Especially one with the warrior's heart that Aliya had. You witnessed it firsthand when she fought off those would-be kidnappers, and Malik and Jahir experienced it when she was able to curse them in return. Your fear is valid."

"How do I protect Elise?"

Chirag chewed on his bottom lip in contemplation, then, with a sigh, poured more whiskey in his now empty mug. "Unfortunately, if Aliya decides to take possession of Elise, it will be up to Elise to protect herself. All you can do is try to reason with Aliya to move on, but in the end, Elise is the one who'll have to reject her. Do you think she's strong enough for such a battle?"

"She's a strong, independent, and confident woman, but I haven't known her long enough to know how strong her spirit is. You've kept watch over her all these years, do you think she is?"

Chirag smiled wistfully. "She is of a strong mind and comes from a spiritually strong family. I've seen her fight off bullies who tormented her and her brother, her strength in supporting her grandmother upon her grandfather's death, and her own battle with cancer many years ago. Whether that same strength will help her against an angry soul set on revenge and making up for a lifetime taken away from her, I cannot say."

Naima's heart had skipped a beat when Chirag mentioned Elise having had cancer. "How long was she sick?"

"It was caught early but progressed quickly. Her treatment was aggressive, but it also weakened her. Her recovery was just as lengthy as her treatment. It was the one time I longed to interfere, but I knew I couldn't. If it was Aliya's time to move on to the next life, I couldn't intervene." Naima had never seen her grandfather look so sad and helpless.

She reached over and grasped his hand. "She made it through, and if she can beat such an illness her spirit is much stronger than we think."

Chirag gave her hand a squeeze and smiled. "She's also surrounded by a strong bond of love and family. That will give her much of the strength she needs for whatever fight she's in for."

Naima prayed her grandfather was right because if she lost Elise, she had a strong feeling she'd lose herself and would gladly spend the rest of the millennia in her lamp to escape the pain of her heartbreak.

Elise woke alone in bed and almost thought she'd imagined last night except for the fact that she lay naked beneath the covers and the scent of jasmine clung to the rumpled sheets. Despite the evidence, she found it unbelievable that it had happened at all. Elise normally didn't sleep with a woman until they'd been dating for at least a few weeks. Not because she was a prude but because she didn't like sharing something so intimate with someone she barely knew. It hadn't even been a week since Naima poofed into her life, and Elise had practically seduced her. Or was it the other way around? Could Naima bewitch her to get her freedom? That thought went right out of her head as intuition told her that Naima wouldn't do that. If she was that type of jinn, she could've done it that first night they kissed. Last night was different, she felt it deep within her. She and Naima had connected like the last two pieces in a complicated puzzle. A puzzle that lay on a shaky ground of magic and curses that could blow it all up any day now.

Elise rolled over, buried her face in the pillow Naima had been sleeping on, and deeply inhaled her intoxicating floral scent. Whatever this was between them, soul mates, heart mates, however Naima wanted to call it, Elise would enjoy it while she could. Even if she had to make the same wish the professor did all those years ago to give Naima some sense of freedom, she would do it. She was just about to get out of bed when the door opened, and Naima walked in carrying a tray.

"Good morning. I know you need to get up soon to go to work, but I thought breakfast in bed would be the perfect way to top off last night." Naima gave her a sexy grin.

Elise shifted over to give Naima room to sit with the tray. "You are too much. A girl could get used to this."

"I hope so. I like doing things for you." Naima leaned over and gave Elise a heated kiss before pulling away to hand her a cup of tea. "I know yesterday's breakfast was a lot, so I kept it light today. A veggie omelet, toast, and tea."

"Thank you." Elise sipped her tea and, of course, it was made just the way she liked it. "Would you like to come to work with me again?"

"No, I don't want to be a bother while you're working. I think I'll read and maybe venture around the neighborhood. I would like to ask if you happen to have another phone that I could use. I like to try and adapt to whatever modern conveniences are available if I know I'll be in a period for a lengthy amount of time."

"I don't have an extra one here, but I'm sure I can get one for you while I'm at work and have it messengered here by lunch."

"Thank you."

As they ate breakfast, Elise gave Naima a quick rundown of what was in the neighborhood. Before she left for work, she also gave her the code to get into the building and a spare key to the apartment. It wasn't until after she left that Elise had to laugh at herself as she remembered that Naima was a jinni and could pop in and out whenever she pleased. Then everything else hit her. She'd just spent a very passionate night with a sexy magical being who enjoyed making her homecooked meals and told her she was her true soul mate. She pinched herself, something she seemed to do a lot lately when it came to Naima and their situation. She tried to hold back the happy grin she felt coming remembering how they'd spent half the night before falling asleep in each other's arms long past midnight.

She was still grinning when she walked into the office and cheerfully wished Micah and Katrina, the only two in the office now, a good morning.

"Somebody had a good night after they rushed out of here yesterday," Katrina said as she followed Elise into her office.

Elise rolled her eyes. "I didn't rush out of here."

"The tread marks on the floor say otherwise, but I don't blame you. Naima is worth rushing home for." Katrina gave her a wink.

"Don't you have some work to do?" Elise said.

Katrina sat down in a guest chair. "Yes, but your life is far more interesting than floor plans."

Elise shook her head with a chuckle. "Why did I hire you again?"

Katrina gave her a cocky grin. "Because you love me and I'm good at what I do."

Elise couldn't argue that point. Katrina was like the sister she never had, and she was more than good at what she did. Her art background helped to bring Elise's visions to life on paper and through her 3D floor plan program. She also brought in some of their biggest clients because of her connections through her family's high-end real estate firm.

"I don't need to ask how you spent your night. That smile is telling enough. I've known you long enough to see that this woman is different from the others you've allowed past that jaded heart of yours. Do I detect the sound of a crack in the armor it's encased in?" Katrina held a hand to her ear.

Elise sighed in exasperation. "You're not going to let this go, are you?"

"Nope. You're my friend and I care about you. Part of our friendship is getting all up in each other's business to keep from making mistakes. Shoot, if it weren't for you, I'd have never escaped that crazy French chick before I ended up proposing to her."

"Sometimes love makes you blind to things that people on the outside have no problem seeing."

Katrina snorted. "Lust and a big ass will do the same thing."

Elise laughed. "Was that all her ass or did she buy it?"

"No, that was all hers and don't try and distract me by changing the subject. What's up with Naima?"

Elise didn't think it would work, but she had to try. She couldn't tell Katrina the truth. As much as her friend loved her, Katrina wouldn't believe a word of it. Her best strategy would be to partially tell the truth without revealing too much so she went with the story Naima had given her parents and Marcus, before he'd found out everything.

"We met while I was on vacation, happened to be on the same flight back, and she dropped by this past Friday. We spent the whole weekend together; she even came to Grammy's gala with me and met the clan. It's strange because it feels like I've known and been waiting for her all my life and now I feel like a part of me that's been broken has found its missing piece."

Katrina looked at her curiously. "You're serious?"

Elise nodded.

"Wow. And she's already met the family? How'd that go?"

"They like her."

Katrina gasped dramatically. "A unanimous like from the whole Porter clan? You better hold on to that unicorn."

"Yeah," Elise said without much confidence.

"Okay, that didn't sound very enthused. What's up?"

"Everything is moving so fast and there's a possibility that she may not be able to stay. Family obligations." Elise couldn't have chosen a better description. After all, Aliya was Naima's wife, wouldn't she have an obligation to help free her? And if she did free Aliya, as well as herself, would she want to stay?

Katrina frowned. "Oh, wow, sorry to hear that. Is there a chance that things will work themselves out?"

Elise shrugged. "Maybe. We'll find out this weekend when she speaks to them."

"Well, I'm only a phone call away if you need to talk or a shoulder to lean on," Katrina offered.

Elise smiled in appreciation. "Thanks. Now get back to work, and can you please send Micah in on your way out?"

"Yes, ma'am." Katrina saluted as she stood then marched out of the office.

A moment later, Micah entered, and they went over her schedule for the day. She had an onsite visit client meeting she'd forgotten about and realized that she might not have time to get Naima a phone.

"Micah, do we still have that extra phone that we were going to assign to the intern that never showed?"

"Yep. It's still in the box and wrapping."

"Great, I'd like to transfer it over to my personal account. My friend Naima's phone is on its last leg, and I thought I'd gift her the new one since she's going to be in town for a while. I wouldn't want her not being able to reach her family in Madagascar. And can we keep this just between the two of us?"

Micah grinned. "Sure, no problem."

"Thanks. After it's all set up, text me the number, save my number in it, and have a messenger deliver it to my apartment."

"Okay. Is that all?"

"Yes, thank you."

Micah's skill at being discreet was one of the many things Elise appreciated about him. He hated gossip and didn't believe in delving into people's business unless they chose to tell him. She could only imagine what her gifting a brand-new phone to a woman who recently entered her life must've looked like. She picked up her own phone and dialed the house number. She hadn't wanted a house phone, but Grammy insisted that there would come a day when a solar flare or some international enemy of the US would cut off access to cell phone towers and then we'd all be glad we listened to her and got landlines. She didn't know if Naima would answer it or not.

"Hello," came her sultry voice over the line bringing back memories of sexy things she'd whispered in Elise's ear last night.

"Hi, it's Elise."

"I know, it's why I answered the phone." Elise could hear the smile in her voice.

"I guess there's no way to surprise you with that intuition of yours."

"Oh, there's plenty of ways. I'll just have to show you how to block our connection."

"I don't know, I kinda like knowing we can sense each other. It's comforting."

"Really? Aliya accepted it, but it made her uncomfortable sometimes." She sounded sad.

"Well, I'm not Aliya."

"No, you're not, and I don't mind in the least."

Elise smiled broadly. "Good. I'm having a phone messengered there for you. Will you be going anywhere soon?"

"No. Probably not until after lunch. I found a few fascinating books in your collection about reincarnation, lost souls, and spirit guides. I'll probably be reading those all morning."

Elise smiled at the image of a jinni reading books about spiritualism. "Okay. The phone will come with instructions. Once you've figured it out, you'll be able to call or text me if you need to reach me. If you have any problems, feel free to call me from the house phone."

"Wonderful. I will text you once I have mastered it."

"I'll look forward to receiving my first text message from a jinni."

The sound of Naima's laughter was like an aphrodisiac. "Down, girl," she told herself. "I need to head out to a meeting. Enjoy your day of leisure."

"I shall. It will be the first one I've had in a very long time. I look forward to it." Elise could hear the excitement in her voice.

❖

As soon as Naima figured out how to use the phone, she texted and sent pictures to Elise throughout the day about all her activities. She'd discovered the Google Map feature and spent the entire afternoon at the Museum of Natural History, the Metropolitan Museum of Art and, judging by all the excited text messages she received, was like a kid in a candy store when she discovered the New York Public Library. It was charming to know such a powerful being took such pleasure in things humans tended to take for granted. She was starting to see the world in a whole new way through Naima's eyes and she had to admit that she liked it.

The rest of the week was just as eye-opening as to what she liked. Coming home to be greeted with a cup of tea, a passionate kiss, and dinner waiting. Sitting at dinner and being asked about her day with genuine interest. Cuddling up on the couch to watch TV or having Naima read out loud from one of the many books she'd checked out of the library with her brand-new library card. Ending the night wrapped in each other's arms after making slow, sensual love. Waking up to Naima's beautiful smile and being sent out the door after a homemade breakfast with a lunch bag of a delicious edible adventure, just to start the wonderful process all over again.

Elise had never imagined being with a woman who enjoyed domesticity as much as Naima. She'd always thought she would end up with a woman who was just as professionally driven as she had been before Naima began having her happily leaving work by six in the evening instead of her usual eight or nine o'clock at night and wishing she could stay abed for just one more hour in the morning.

"Do you miss being a soldier or your duties as a vizier?" Elise asked one night after a very competitive game of chess with Naima.

"Not really. The soldier's life, especially at that time, was not an easy one. Even with our magic, there are ways to hurt jinn that could end their lives or severely injure them. Hand-to-hand combat was not easy as well. Modern soldiers have the ability to keep a distance during battle, but when your weapon is a sword or knife instead of a gun, taking someone's life so up-close and personal can play havoc with your emotional well-being. With so much in-your-face violence you can either become numb to it or it can drive you mad. How wars are fought through the centuries may have changed but not their effects

ANNE SHADE

on a person's mind. It was why my grandfather walked away from the life of the black jinn. It was why I chose to be Adnan's vizier, so that I would no longer have to go into battle unless truly necessary."

Elise nodded in understanding. "My grandfather suffered from PTSD from the Vietnam War for a very long time. I remember nights when Marcus and I were little during stays with Grammy and Gramps when we'd sometimes be awakened by his screaming or crying from night terrors. It was frightening, but as we got older and learned what went on in Vietnam, we understood."

Naima gave a sad smile. "I remember that time well. I can't tell you how my lamp ended up in Vietnam, but a British soldier found it. His mother was American, and his father was from Great Britain where he was raised. When he'd found out Britain wouldn't be sending soldiers to Vietnam, he resigned and reenlisted with the United States Army. He'd been in Vietnam for almost two years when he found my lamp while digging a trench. When I appeared, he didn't seem the least bit shocked at seeing me in the middle of the night in a war-torn jungle. He thought he was hallucinating from the drugs he'd smoked just before finding the lamp. It wasn't until he made his first wish that it became real."

"What did he wish for?"

"That he'd never left the British army or his fiancée to join the war. When he woke up in his own bed, in his old life, he couldn't help but believe what he was seeing. His final two wishes were simple and more for his parents than him. Despite that, I'll never forget the haunted look in his eyes because it's the same look I'd seen in the eyes of many of Akiba's seasoned soldiers. I can only hope he found peace having returned to his pre-war life."

"We can try and find out."

Naima looked at her in confusion. "What do you mean? How?"

Elise picked up her phone. "Do you happen to remember his name?"

Surprisingly, she did. Elise ran a search of his name, and a social media account came up. She knew it had to be the right guy because he was the only one with that name living in the UK. She opened the page and turned the phone around to Naima.

"Is this him?"

Naima's eyes widened. "Older, fuller, but even with our short time together I'd never forget those piercing blue eyes. That's him." She grabbed the phone and scrolled through the page. "He's a doctor, still married to the woman he had come back to and has three children and ten grandchildren," she said happily, handing Elise her phone back.

"There's a successful magic lamp wish story." Elise was happy to have given Naima such wonderful news.

"Yes, it is. Is it possible to look up others that I've granted wishes for?" Naima asked excitedly.

Elise smiled. "Yes, but it'll probably be easier on the computer."

They spent two hours searching the names of her past lamp bearers from the modern age. All but two had benefitted successfully from their granted wishes. Families had been reunited or grown, illnesses had been cured with people going on to live long lives, and the once-impoverished were able to leave their offspring a better legacy all due to their magical benefactor. The two who hadn't done well squandered the wishes they were granted. One had served time in prison for armed robbery. The other had been in the news for a while as one of those rags to riches to rags again stories when he claimed he'd won the lottery after receiving his wished-for riches and was broke and homeless within just a couple of years.

"Thank you so much for this." Naima's eyes gleamed with unshed tears. "To know I helped so many people make the years cursed to that lamp a little more bearable."

Elise gave her an encouraging smile. "If I have anything to do about it, you won't bear that curse much longer." She pulled Naima into her arms and felt a combination of relief and fear that she knew was not her own.

Their lovemaking was slow and sweet that night. Something in Elise wanted Naima to feel loved, safe, and secure. She treated her as the rare treasure she was and dreamed of being able to do that for the rest of her life.

"NOOO!! YOU WILL NOT TAKE AWAY WHAT IS MINE!" an angry female voice screamed in Elise's head.

She opened her eyes to find herself standing amongst mounds of rubble with a woman of storybook beauty. She was a head shorter than Elise, but that didn't stop her from meeting Elise's gaze with a fiery look of anger in her golden eyes. Her hair flowed in thick, luxurious curls down to her waist, a gold chain was wrapped around the crown of her head with an egg-sized gemstone glittering in the moonlight, and she wore an elaborate sari that lent to her regal presence. Elise knew she had finally come face-to-face with Aliya, and the dark energy emanating from the princess frightened her a little, but she refused to show it.

Elise straightened to her full height and smiled down at her. "Princess Aliya, I presume." She gave a slight bow in deference to her title.

Aliya sneered at Elise. "How dare you seduce my wife! You will not claim what is rightfully mine!"

Elise shook her head. "Naima is a living being, not an object to CLAIM. She has chosen to be with me."

Aliya looked at her with disgust. "You bewitched and seduced her. She would never be unfaithful to me."

Elise couldn't help but chuckle. "Do you really think I, a human just like you, could bewitch a jinni? Especially one of Naima's powers?"

Aliya no longer looked as confident as she had when her ranting began. "I've lost everything. My kingdom, my family, my life." She turned away and looked off into the distance. "I cannot lose Naima as well."

Elise tried tamping down the bout of guilt that hit her square in the gut. None of this was Aliya's fault. Neither was it hers, but that didn't stop her from feeling like a homewrecker for her and Naima's affair.

She placed a hand on Aliya's shoulder. "I'm sorry. I didn't mean for any of this to happen. It just did."

That was obviously the wrong thing to say as Aliya jerked away from her touch and turned to her with a menacing glare. "You do not have the right to touch me," she said vehemently. "You are not worthy of that or Naima. I will do whatever it takes to get my freedom and get her back."

The momentary feeling of guilt and sympathy Elise had for Aliya melted into anger. "You do realize that freeing you doesn't mean you will suddenly be a living, breathing, being again. The body you once had is buried beneath all this." She indicated the rubble surrounding them. "You are no longer of flesh and blood, so there will be nowhere for you to go once the curse is broken."

Aliya looked her up and down then gave her a wicked grin, not quite the reaction Elise had been expecting at that hard truth.

"Enjoy your time with Naima while you can because it will be ending soon, and I will once again walk amongst the living." Aliya turned away, sauntering off toward the surrounding jungle.

"What's that supposed to mean!" Elise shouted at her retreating figure, but Aliya disappeared into the trees without responding. She wasn't sure she really wanted to know what the princess meant.

At the start of their confrontation Aliya just seemed like a spoiled princess throwing a harmless tantrum, but the way she'd looked at her in parting and the comment she made was not harmless. It was very much a threat that Elise took very seriously. If what Naima said was true that Aliya had managed to somehow curse two jinn, one a powerful black jinn, then there was no telling what she could do to her. After all, Aliya's soul was occupying her body and, once again, Elise had seen too many documentaries and movies on possession not to be afraid. She looked frantically around her, expecting to see evil spirits surrounding her from the jungle perimeter. Feeling a panic attack coming on, she closed her eyes and willed herself to wake up.

Naima could feel Elise's distress and immediately woke up. She looked over at Elise who was whimpering in her sleep. Whatever she was dreaming was frightening her terribly. Naima gently shook her and called her name, but instead of waking up, her body began to quake.

"Elise, my love, please wake up," she whispered in Elise's ear and gave her another shake.

Elise's eyes rapidly blinked open, she sat up, and then looked frantically around the room.

"It's all right. You're safe. I've got you." Naima sat up and pulled Elise into her arms. She worried when Elise's anxiety rose after awakening. "What has you so frightened?"

Elise took a deep breath, which seemed to help. "Nothing. Just a bad dream," she said unconvincingly.

"Would you like to talk about it?" Naima knew it was something more than just a nightmare, but she wouldn't push Elise, nor would she pry the information from her thoughts.

"No, just hold me. I'll be fine."

Naima did as she asked, lying down and bringing Elise with her. Elise cuddled so close it was as if she were trying to merge with Naima who held her as near and tight as she could. She could tell by Elise's breathing that she never fell back to sleep. Whatever she dreamed must have frightened her so much that she was too scared to sleep, so Naima just held her until the sun peeked through the curtains.

"How are feeling?" she asked when Elise rose to start her day.

Elise gave her a tentative smile. "I'm good. Probably just nervous about tomorrow and it manifested into my dream."

"We don't have to go." Naima's own worry that she tried tucking away about their meeting with Malik's spiritualist reared its head.

"Yes, we do." Elise placed a soft kiss on Naima's lips. "You will not see the inside of that lamp ever again if I can help it." She gave Naima a sad smile then walked into the bathroom and shut the door softly behind her.

After Elise left for work, Naima used the app Elise had uploaded to her phone to call for a car. She arrived at Jasmine's Spiritual Healing Center before they opened so she went to a Starbuck's located across the street, ordered a latte, a new favorite treat of hers, and sat by the window to wait.

"I had a feeling you'd want to visit before your appointment." Malik sat in the chair across from her and sipped at his own cup. "When was the last time the two of us just enjoyed a humanistic moment like this?"

Naima chuckled. "Without the royal twins? Never. My grandfather made sure I never forgot that I was jinn first and that my human form was just that. A form. He didn't want me getting any notions that despite my relationship with Aliya, I would always be a jinni, and to never let my guard down or the humans in our care would be the ones to pay the price."

Malik nodded. "He and the elders did their best to make sure we all followed that thinking in order to keep Akiba safe."

"But you let your guard down and allowed Jahir to enter," Naima said sadly.

Malik's smile turned to a frown. "I live with that truth and regret it every day of my existence."

Naima reached across the table and grasped his hand. "You're trying to do the right thing, that's all that matters now."

Malik smiled tentatively and gave her hand a squeeze before releasing it. "I'm assuming you're here because you have questions for Jasmine."

"Yes. I need to know that no matter what happens, Elise will be safe."

"Why don't we go chat with her. She's opened the shop now and is waiting for us." Malik stood, waiting for Naima to follow.

Jasmine's shop was small, but she managed to fill the space without overcrowding it with all manner of goods for spiritual healing. There were crystals, oils, tarot cards, books, yoga and meditation supplies, and other items Naima had seen used in various religious and spiritual ceremonies. Walking toward them from behind the counter was an attractive, petite woman with a shockingly white close-cropped haircut, smooth ebony skin, bright youthful eyes, and smile. She wore a colorful caftan, bracelets of bangles and crystals that jingled lightly as she approached, and large silver hoops in her ears.

"You must be Naima," she said, offering both of her hands.

Naima took them. "Yes, and you must be Jasmine. Malik speaks very highly of you."

Jasmine glanced at Malik with a look of pure adoration. "I think Malik is a bit biased when it comes to me. He also speaks very highly of you."

Naima looked at Malik in surprise. "Really?"

"Yes, he's told me what a good friend and brave soldier you were." She walked over to Malik and grasped his hand. "He's also told me of what he did. He's sincerely sorry not only for the loss of your home and families but also for the suffering you've endured these past centuries. I will do whatever I can to help you, Aliya, and Elise because it will help to ease his suffering as well."

Naima looked between them and saw a deep, abiding love and felt a touch of anger that while she and Aliya were suffering year after endless year without each other, he was living his life and had even found love. She could feel the air pressure in the shop change and Malik shifted Jasmine behind him, watching Naima warily. She closed her eyes and tamped down the anger rising dangerously within.

"I understand your anger and I don't blame you, but I will do whatever it takes to protect Jasmine from harm," Malik warned her.

Naima gave him a tentative smile. "I'm fine. I would never harm an innocent human."

Jasmine peeked around Malik's broad shoulders. "Now that that's settled, why don't I have my assistant cover the shop while we chat." She walked toward an open doorway in the back of the shop. "Leanne!"

Naima heard footsteps on stairs and a young pretty blonde appeared. "Yes, Ms. Jasmine."

"I need you to watch over things while I meet with a client," Jasmine said.

The young woman gazed up at Naima curiously, then back at Jasmine. "Yes, ma'am." She walked to stand behind the counter.

"Let's go to my reading room," Jasmine said.

Malik stepped aside. "After you." He inclined his head to Naima.

She followed Jasmine through the doorway and down a short hall that led to a set of stairs going to a lower level and three doors. On the doors were signs marked RESTROOM, OFFICE, and READINGS. The Readings room was at the very end of the hall. The room was softly lit with candles that smelled of sage. The furnishings consisted of a small round table and three chairs on one side of the room and a grouping of low cushioned seating on the other side. Jasmine went to the grouped seating and sat cross-legged on an ottoman. Naima and Malik joined her.

She gave Naima a sweet smile. "Now, what questions do you have for me?"

"What is it that you do?" Naima asked.

"I practice divination through reading oracle cards, numerology, astrology, and crystals, but most of my readings are done via communication with spirits. I also help lost and trapped souls move on."

"Jasmine has an online series where she works with people who are being visited, haunted, or tormented by spirits. She's encountered a few mischievous but harmless jinn in her work and handled them quite well," Malik said proudly.

"Has she had any dealings with Jahir?" Naima asked.

Malik frowned. "No. When I begin to sense his presence, I leave. We've had dealings in the past with humans who are sensitive and aware of magical beings. I don't trust that he won't harm Jasmine despite my feelings for her. He may actually hurt her because of that, especially since she's human."

Naima nodded in understanding. "His hatred toward humans is almost as deep as it is toward Chirag." Naima considered telling Malik of Chirag coming to watch over things on Saturday, but it was probably best he didn't know just in case Jahir was more aware of what was going on while he lay dormant than Malik believed him to be.

"I don't know why Malik worries so much. Don't let my stature and this white hair fool you. I've dealt with much stronger and more determined spirits than your old vengeful Jinn Jahir." Jasmine sat up straighter to make her petite frame look taller.

Malik smiled indulgently at her. "You were also half your age."

Jasmine pouted and punched Malik in the arm. "I know you are not calling me old! Especially since I've got another twenty years before I hit the century mark and you've got me beat by at least six hundred."

Malik picked up her tiny fist and placed a kiss on her knuckles. "Apologies, my dearest, I was not calling you old. I was merely stating the fact that Jahir is more powerful than any spirit or jinn you've ever dealt with. I'm just trying to keep you safe."

Jasmine looked appeased by his apology. "I know and I love how you protect me, but we both know that at some point, possibly even Saturday, we may do something to trigger Jahir's awakening. We both need to be prepared for when that happens."

Malik looked down at Jasmine. "I will stab an iron spear straight through my heart before I let him hurt you."

Jasmine looked sad. "I would prefer you not having to do that. I've liked having you around these past forty years."

Naima looked away as the couple gazed lovingly into each other's eyes. She felt like she was intruding on an intimate moment.

"Now, I have another client in an hour so let's make sure we give Naima the time she deserves to answer her concerns." Naima looked up to find her smiling at her. "Please, continue."

"I only have a couple more questions. What will you need to do, and will Elise be in any danger?"

Jasmine's brow furrowed in thought. "This is a unique situation in that the person inhabiting the spirit isn't experiencing any symptoms of possession, which is what I usually deal with. There's also the dilemma of what kind of power Aliya may possess, after all, she did manage to curse two jinn. Once I bring her forward, she may fight being released from her human form. Whether it's to seek revenge on Malik or to finally be able to live the life that was taken from her, there's the possibility of her taking Elise over."

Naima had thought about all of that but refused to let the possibilities sink in. She couldn't imagine Aliya wanting to seek revenge on anyone or hurting Elise, but she didn't know what Aliya's soul may have gone through these past six hundred years. The sweet, loving Aliya she once knew may no longer be there.

"If you see that happening. If you have the slightest inkling that Elise may be harmed or taken over, do whatever you have to do to protect her. Even if that means expelling Aliya's spirit without breaking the curse," Naima said.

Malik shook his head. "If we don't break the curse, then you'll go back to the lamp."

Naima hated the idea of having to do that, but if it meant saving Elise, she would do what had to be done. "I love her, Malik. She's what I had believed Aliya was for so long."

Malik's eyes widened. "Aliya isn't your soul mate?"

Naima smiled sadly. "No. My heart and soul belong to Elise."

Malik laughed out loud, and Naima scowled at him. "Did I say something humorous?"

"No. Don't you see what that means?"

Naima shook her head in confusion.

"Naima, if Elise is your soul mate, your one true love, she can break your curse," Malik said, smiling happily.

It took a moment for what he said to register, then Naima remembered what Malik told Aliya about the curse. *"Your dear Naima will be tied to this lamp granting wishes until she is found by her one true love. Only then, once she grants her true love's final wish, will she be free."* Elise, not Aliya, had to make the three wishes that would set her free. Her heart soared with joy. Elise had already made the one wish to prove to Marcus that she was telling the truth about Naima's identity; she only had two more wishes to make.

"I hate to be the one to point out the flaw in this, but will that also free Aliya? If not, what does that mean for her spirit and how it may affect Elise?"

Naima's bubble of happiness burst. Could she really be free knowing Aliya would continue to travel from one life to the next in search of who she thought was her one true love? What if, in any of those lives, she became aware of who she was? Would she spend that lifetime searching for Naima and the lamp not knowing that Naima could already be free?

"We have to free Aliya's soul," Naima said, already feeling guilt over having not thought of Aliya's freedom as well as her own.

Malik nodded in agreement. "I wouldn't be able to live with myself if we didn't."

"I wouldn't either but know that if I feel as if Elise is in danger, I will put a stop to it immediately," Naima said.

"Understood," Jasmine said.

Chapter Ten

Elise felt the most pleasurable sensations as a pair of soft lips on hers and gentle fingers skimming down her body eased her awake. "If this is a dream, please don't wake me up."

"If you'd like to participate, you're going to have to wake up," Naima said in a seductive tone.

"Well, in that case..." Elise blinked her eyes open to a grinning Naima.

"Good morning." Naima took one of Elise's nipples between her lips.

"Good morning," she whispered distractedly before moaning in pleasure.

There were many more moans that followed. Elise couldn't imagine a better way to wake up on a Saturday morning.

"What would you like for breakfast?" Naima asked.

"Why don't we have breakfast delivered so that we can continue this for a little while longer." She lazily ran a fingertip up and down Naima's torso.

Naima chuckled. "You are insatiable."

"And you're addictive."

"As much as I would love to spend the day making love to you, we have an appointment to keep."

Elise flopped onto her back with a sigh. "Oh yeah," she said, as if she'd forgotten, which she hadn't. It was all she'd been thinking about for the past two days.

"As I've said on several occasions—"

"I know, but we do have to do it," she said, cutting Naima off. She turned to her side and propped her head on her hand to look at Naima. "If there was another way to free you without taking the chance of being possessed by a vengeful princess, I'd jump at it but since there isn't..." She reached up and brushed a lock of hair from Naima's face. "I have no choice."

Naima looked as if she were about to say something then gave her a hesitant smile. "If there were any other way, I would tell you."

There was a niggling feeling that Naima wasn't telling her something, but Elise shrugged it off. As far as she knew, Naima had been open and honest with her from the moment she appeared. She couldn't imagine a reason for her to hold anything back now.

"Why don't I make breakfast this morning," Elise offered.

Naima's eyes widened in surprise. "Really?"

"Yes, really. Believe it or not, I can cook, I just choose not to. You go shower and poof whatever outfit you're wearing out of thin air, and I'll prepare a feast good enough for a sexy jinni."

"Poof? I don't poof anything." Naima gave her an adorable pout.

Elise chuckled then pressed a soft kiss on her lips. "My apologies."

She slipped out from under the covers, grabbed a pair of shorts and a tank top from a laundry basket of clothes on the chair, and left Naima to do her thing. An hour later, they were just sitting down to eat the breakfast she'd prepared of homemade waffles with fresh berries and cream when the intercom buzzed.

"Who could that be?" she asked as she looked at the clock on the stove. It was only a little after ten in the morning and she wasn't expecting anyone.

Elise walked over to the door to answer the call.

"Hey, sis, it's your broski and Grammy."

Elise looked at the intercom in annoyance. Their appointment with the spiritualist wasn't for another two hours and they were supposed to be meeting her and Naima there. She buzzed them up, opened the door, and waited for them to come up.

"Why am I not surprised they're here early," she said to Naima who smiled in amusement.

"Do I smell waffles?" Marcus said as he walked into the apartment.

"Kinda late in the morning for breakfast, isn't it?" Grammy said.

Elise greeted them both with hugs and kisses. "We slept in this morning."

Marcus grinned knowingly. "Must be nice. You got any waffles left?"

Elise rolled her eyes at him. "Yes, they're on the counter. Grammy, do you want anything?"

"Just my usual tea but I can make it. You go sit down and enjoy your breakfast." She walked toward Naima. "How's my favorite jinn doing?"

Naima stood and walked into her open arms. "I had no idea you knew of any others. I'm fine. How are you?"

"I'll be better when we get all this mystical baggage cleared up." Grammy gave Naima a pat on the cheek before heading into the kitchen to make her tea.

"Speaking of that, why are you guys here? I thought you were meeting us at the shop?" Elise asked as she sat back down with Naima to eat.

Marcus joined them with his plate piled high with the rest of the waffles she'd made. "Grammy thought it might be a good idea to get together beforehand to strategize."

"What's there to strategize about? This spiritualist is going to bring forth Aliya's spirit so that she can connect with Naima, make her three wishes, and free them both. Hopefully, all without a fight from the princess," Elise said, despite knowing it probably wasn't going to be that simple, but she couldn't bear to think about the *what-ifs*.

What if the woman couldn't bring Aliya forward? What if Aliya didn't want to leave? What if she followed through on the threat that she was intimating in Elise's dream the other night? Thinking about all of that only brought on her anxiety so she tried NOT to think about it.

Grammy sat in the last chair at the table. "Marcus, tell them what you told me last night."

Elise looked at Marcus whose usually jovial expression had turned serious. He pushed his plate away as if he'd suddenly lost his appetite. "I had a vision last night. I was talking to you, but you weren't you. You looked the same and sounded the same, but you had no memories of our childhood, or anything that happened in your life prior to that moment, and when I looked into your eyes, it was someone else looking out at me. You were in there somewhere, but it was as if you were trapped behind a door and couldn't get out." Marcus shivered. "It was creepy as hell."

Elise suddenly lost her appetite as well. "Do you sense something wrong? Should we not go to the spiritualist?"

"No, I don't sense danger, but I do sense trouble. I also feel as if we need do this now. If we don't, things could get dangerous for you and Naima the longer we wait."

Elise looked from Marcus to Naima then to Grammy. "Are you sensing anything?"

Grammy took a slow sip of her tea. "Nothing I can put my finger on, but I do have a sense of foreboding."

Elise looked at Naima again. "What are your jinn senses telling you?"

"To be cautious," Naima said, her waffles sitting on her plate barely touched as well. All that hard work to make breakfast was going to be wasted.

"Okay then, since I'm the only one without some kind of Spidey sense to tell me what to do, how do you all suggest we approach this?" Elise asked.

"Unfortunately, this is a wait and see situation. You could have the same issue you had during your session with Maureen where it was too difficult for you to bring Aliya forward, or this spiritualist may have a better technique since she's dealt with possessions and trapped souls before," Grammy said.

Elise looked at her in surprise. "How do you know that?"

Grammy snorted. "Did you really think I was going to agree with sending you to some fortune teller without looking her up? It seems this Ms. Jasmine is no joke. I watched all her videos on her YouTube channel. You didn't do the same?"

Elise shrugged. "I didn't feel the need to. Naima visited her the other day and believes she's the real deal. I chose to take her word for it."

"You did some reconnaissance? You can take the soldier out of the uniform, but you can't make the soldier stop soldiering," Marcus said with a teasing grin.

Elise chuckled. "I don't think that's quite how the saying goes, Marcus."

"Hey, I tailored it for the situation." He turned back to Naima. "Anything we need to know before we go in?"

All eyes turned toward Naima expectantly.

Naima felt like a cornered mouse. She'd rather be relegated back to her lamp than lie to these people who she honestly felt she could call friends. Maybe, someday, even family. When Jasmine brought up the idea of still working to free Aliya's spirit even though not doing so would have no effect on freeing her from the lamp, Naima had decided that she wouldn't tell Elise because she didn't want her to have to make the decision whether to let Aliya continue to suffer or free them both. If she continued to believe that one was connected to the other, then she'd be spared from that decision.

"Nothing worth mentioning other than Malik will be there, as well as my grandfather, Chirag." Guilt ate away at her for not being completely honest.

Elise looked at her in surprise. "He's here? In America?"

Naima nodded. "He came to me the day after the gala. As you know from your brief encounters with him in Nosy Be, he's been trying to help with our situation."

"What are you two talking about? There's another jinn mixed up in this?" Grammy asked.

"Remember the old man I told you about who gave me both the toy lamp my first trip to Nosy Be and then Naima's on my last trip? It turns out that he's Naima's grandfather," Elise explained.

"The original jinn who created Akiba and is pretty much the whole reason for Jahir cursing everyone and their mother?" Grammy said with a look of disbelief.

"So that would make him like thousands of years old," Marcus said. "This whole thing gets more unbelievable each day."

"Is it really smart for him to be anywhere near Malik and Jahir? I don't want to be in the middle of some magical battle between ancient jinn," Elise said.

"He will be nearby just in case he's needed. As long as Jahir remains dormant within Malik then we should be fine," Naima said with an encouragement she didn't quite feel.

Elise looked at her knowingly. "Okay," she said skeptically.

"Do you doubt my ability to protect you all?" her grandfather said before a silver cloud of smoke appeared in the middle of the kitchen and reshaped into Chirag dressed in a track suit and sneakers.

"What the fuck!" Marcus said, practically knocking his chair over as he stood and lifted his fists ready for a fight.

With a look of amusement, Chirag quirked a brow at Marcus. "What a brave young man you are. That's good. Your sister will need that bravery for what's ahead."

Grammy stood, walked up to Marcus, and touched his arm. He lowered his fists but still looked wary. "Chirag, I presume," she said.

Chirag grinned charmingly, stepped forward, took Grammy's hand, and bowed at the waist. "At your service, lovely lady." He placed a kiss on her knuckle before releasing her hand.

Naima was surprised at the shy smile Grammy gave him, as well as the way her grandfather's eyes brightened looking at her.

Naima walked up to him and placed an affectionate kiss on his cheek. "Grandfather, you have to stop just popping in like this. You don't know who could've been here."

Chirag waved a hand dismissively. "I peeked in before appearing. Since everyone here knows all, I didn't see any reason not to."

"So, this copper-toned tanned version of Santa Clause is your grandfather? And I thought Black don't crack. You jinn got us beat by a landslide." Marcus held out a hand in greeting. "Marcus Porter."

Chirag smiled and shook Marcus's hand. "Yes, I know who you all are. I've watched you since the day you were born."

Marcus's eyes widened. "Seriously?"

"Seriously. I've known of Elise's predicament since I first found out that she and Aliya's spirit were intertwined," Chirag said, gazing over at Elise.

Elise walked directly up to Chirag, hands on her hips with an angry glare. "Wait, so you've known my entire life that this was going to happen?"

"Yes," Chirag answered matter-of-factly.

"When we met during my first visit to Nosy Be you knew?"

"Yes."

"And instead of warning me you decided it would be a good idea to sell me a stupid toy lamp?" Elise's voice rose and Naima could feel the anger rolling off her.

Chirag looked unsure of himself under her glare. Something Naima had never seen from him, and she found it almost amusing when he took a step back from her.

"We could've taken care of this years ago instead of making Naima suffer more time in that lamp at the command of others."

"Would you have believed me? You were but a child who couldn't possibly understand the seriousness of the situation. I was not going to leave the fate of my granddaughter in the hands of a child whose mind probably couldn't handle a process such as the one you'll be going through today." Chirag straightened to his full height in an attempt to intimidate Elise.

It didn't work, Elise still skewered him with her dark glare. "You don't know what I could've handled considering what I felt being on that island. Or should I say what Aliya felt. I was drawn to it because she was, and that would've been the perfect opportunity to tell me the truth. You would think that your time living amongst the humans of Akiba who accepted you and your jinn tribe would have taught you not to underestimate them, but I guess that only goes for the jinn who grew up among them like Naima. You robbed the princess and Naima of their freedom just as Jahir had done because your God-like ego couldn't imagine being vulnerable to possibly failing."

Naima shifted so that she stood partially blocking Elise. She looked at Chirag expecting to see his own dark anger lighting his eyes at Elise's words, but she only saw sadness and regret. Chirag sighed heavily and sat on one of the stools at the island.

"My dear Elise, you have wounded me with the truth. My ego was the reason I waited," he said with a sardonic smile. "I wanted to be able to confront Jahir and knew that wouldn't happen for some time, so I waited until Malik made his way to America seeking out whoever carried Aliya's spirit. I learned that Malik had tracked each lifetime her soul had gone through, and when you came along, I knew it was the right time. I sought out Naima's lamp and bided my time for you to become a woman so that your role as her soul mate would make it easier for all of this to happen."

Naima frowned. "You used us to get close to Jahir? You're no different than he was when he used us to seek his revenge for what you did to him."

"Not completely. I was attempting to hit two birds with one stone. Free you and make Jahir pay for destroying Akiba." The look in his eyes was a plea for understanding.

Naima shook her head. "Hasn't there been enough pain and destruction from seeking revenge? First Jahir, then Malik, even Aliya somehow managing to curse them both, and nothing has been solved from it. I won't allow you to put Elise and her family in the middle of a war, Chirag. I'd rather return to the lamp than watch you destroy more lives."

Their gazes locked. Both were determined to do what they thought was best. In the end, her grandfather must have seen her reasoning and nodded. "You're right. The only thing that matters is freeing you and Aliya's spirit. Akiba is gone and nothing I can do will bring it back." He looked heartbroken.

She understood his pain. Akiba had been his sanctuary. His redemption for all the death, pain, and destruction he'd caused in his life prior to creating the island and his tribe of reformed and battle-weary jinn. He thought he'd left the island in good hands, but not even his powers gave him the foresight to see what was coming. Naima approached him and wrapped her arms around his shoulders. His came tentatively up around her waist and he squeezed her tight with a shuddering sigh.

"You are all I have left, granddaughter. I cannot bear to lose you if Jahir's need for revenge still runs hot," Chirag said.

"I may only be blue jinn, which leaves other jinn underestimating my power, but I am the granddaughter of the great Jinni Chirag and more powerful than many expect. Once this curse has been broken, the bindings hindering my magic will be as well. If Jahir is still itching for a fight, I will be by your side," Naima proclaimed.

Chirag took her face in his hands and placed a kiss on her forehead. "Still the bravest warrior in all worlds, I see."

Naima smiled. Unlike her brother who was a powerful jinn in his own right but preferred the knowledge of combat to magic, Naima showed equal interest in both as soon as she could walk. Chirag took her under his wing and taught her everything he knew of magic apart from the dark arts. He refused to put that temptation in front of her as her powers grew beyond what was expected of blue jinn. Under her grandfather's tutelage, her magic combined with her warrior training made her into a fearsome jinn soldier. Unfortunately, the bindings of the curse Jahir had put on her subdued her magic so that she couldn't use it to escape the lamp. But once free of that godforsaken prison, and joining forces with Chirag, she would be able to protect Elise and her family from any harm Jahir might send their way.

"As much as I appreciate a heartwarming family reunion, can we please focus back on Elise and how we're going to keep her from turning into that girl from *The Exorcist*?" Grammy said from behind her.

Chirag chuckled. "I knew I liked her." He gave Naima a conspiratorial wink.

She shook her head at Chirag's obvious fascination with Grammy, then stepped back to stand beside Elise again.

Chirag directed one of his charming smiles at Grammy. "Of course, you are correct, lovely lady, we should be focusing on keeping Elise safe. I doubt very much she'll be spewing green vomit or that her head will be spinning on her neck, but she could have a mental and spiritual fight on her hands if Aliya refuses to let go."

"Are you seriously flirting with our grandmother?" Marcus asked, looking more amused than angry.

Grammy punched him in the arm. "I doubt it and if he is it's none of your beeswax," she said, blushing as she directed a shy gaze at Chirag. "Is there anything we can do to protect her if that happens?"

Chirag walked over to Grammy, towering over her despite her height. He took her hands in his and gazed down into her eyes. "You all have the most important job of all. Surrounding Elise with your love so that she knows what she has here. You will be her tether to reality and her shield against whatever tricks the princess may have up her sleeve."

Grammy seemed mesmerized under his gaze. Both Elise and Marcus watched her in amazement.

"Wow, I need some of whatever he's got. Do you know how many ladies I'd be snagging with all that magical charm?" Marcus said.

This time Elise punched him in the arm. "Shut up. Since you all are choosing to discuss me as if I'm not here I'm going to shower and get dressed. Feel free to continue to plan my life for me while I'm gone," she said in annoyance as she left.

Elise sat with Naima in the back seat of Marcus's car while Grammy sat up front with him. Chirag decided it would be best for him to stay out of sight and monitor the situation from afar so his presence wouldn't trigger Jahir's awakening. She was still annoyed that they had all been discussing what could happen and the best way to handle it without even including her in the conversation. After all, it was happening to her. They were all pretty much just observers. The only two people who could be truly affected by the outcome of this situation would be her and Naima, but mostly her since the stubborn princess was inhabiting her body and had pretty much threatened not to leave it.

After Marcus told her about his dream, which scared the crap out of her, Elise considered telling them about her own dream, but that scared her even more because she really didn't think it was just a dream. She had a feeling Aliya had found a way to communicate with her and was actually in her head. Channeling through her the way she had those few times that first day of Naima's appearance was frightening enough, but to be able to manipulate her consciousness that way was some *Creepshow* thriller shit that she wasn't sure she was ready for.

Naima took her hand. "You know we didn't mean to exclude you the way we did. We're just all concerned about your welfare."

"Well, you're not the only one," Elise said in annoyance. "I'm scared and I don't like to be scared unless I can control it. I have no control over what could happen. This isn't a situation where I can just walk out or close my eyes. I'm actively participating in what could be my own demise." She felt her heart beginning to pound rapidly and tried taking slow, easy breaths to calm down.

"That's it. Just breathe," Naima said, rubbing her hands, which had grown cold.

Elise closed her eyes and focused on Naima's touch. That seemed to calm her better than her breathing exercise was doing. When she felt her heart beating normally again and felt warmth seeping back into her fingers, she opened her eyes. Naima was fully facing her with a worried expression.

Elise gave her a smile to reassure her. "I'm good. Thank you."

Naima began to speak, and Elise shook her head. "Please don't say it. We have to do this. I care about you too much to send you back to that prison. Whether you choose to stay with me or move on with your life, I want you to be free to make that decision without worrying about how much time you have before you're once again summoned at someone else's bidding."

Naima's eyes glittered with unshed tears. "Thank you." She leaned forward and pressed a soft kiss on Elise's lips.

"Hey, hey, you two. No making out in my back seat. You can get a room when this is all over," Marcus said, catching Elise's gaze with a mock frown in the rearview mirror.

Elise couldn't help but smile. Marcus had always been the only one who could make Elise smile when she was feeling low or calm her down when she had one of her panic attacks. They were like two halves of a whole. She was usually serious and focused, while he was jovial and casual. Chirag had said Marcus and Grammy would be her tether to reality. She looked from one to the other and couldn't imagine having two stronger connections than them to keep her in the real world.

They arrived at the spiritualist's shop right on time. Marcus opened the door to allow the ladies to enter first. Elise hesitated on the threshold and felt a warm hand grasp hers.

"We got you, sis. We're right here behind you," Marcus said.

She'd never seen him look so serious. In an odd way, it comforted her more than his jokes and sarcasm did. She nodded and walked into the bright shop.

"Marcus, you and Elise go on in. Naima and I will be there in just a moment," Grammy said.

Elise gazed back at them. "Is everything all right?"

Grammy smiled. "It's fine, honey, I just need to talk to Naima really quick. It'll only be a minute."

Elise looked at Naima who smiled as well, but she could feel her nervousness. She felt like she didn't want to be a part of whatever discussion they were about to have. She had enough to think about. "Okay." She heard the door close behind Marcus.

"What aren't you telling us?" Grammy asked, her hands on her hips and her gaze practically piercing through Naima's soul. "And don't lie to me. I knew back at the apartment that you were holding something back when we asked if there was anything else we needed to know. I figured if you hadn't told Elise, then it's something that could hurt or scare her. Out with it."

Naima should've known she wouldn't be able to keep anything from the clairvoyant woman. She ran her hand through her hair with a frustrated sigh then told Grammy the truth about Elise being the one to break the curse, not Aliya, and why she kept that information from Elise.

Grammy nodded. "I understand why you did it, but I don't think you're giving Elise enough credit. She's stronger than you think. The decision should be hers to make."

Naima chewed her bottom lip in thought. "I guess you're right. I'll tell her before the session starts."

Grammy took her hand. "That's a good idea. Now, let's go before they think we left them to fend for themselves."

They walked into the shop to find Marcus talking to the young woman Naima had seen when she visited the other day and Elise looking at a display of gem and crystal jewelry.

"Jasmine is finishing with a client," Elise said.

"Malik isn't here?" Naima asked the salesclerk. She hesitantly looked away from Marcus. "He'll join you as soon as Ms. Jasmine is finished with her client," she said, leaning on the glass counter, looking dreamily back at Marcus.

Grammy chuckled. "That boy doesn't need anything your grandfather has. He's a born charmer, he's just picky as hell when it comes to staying with a woman. Almost as bad as his sister." She grinned at Naima. "Well, she was until you poofed into her life."

Naima rolled her eyes. "I do not poof."

Grammy chuckled again and joined Elise at the jewelry display.

A moment later, Jasmine walked out of the back area with a balding middle-aged man who looked nervously at their group.

"Leanne, would you please ring up Mr. Singleton's usual while I take my next clients in the back?"

Leanne quickly stood and looked away from Marcus as if she'd been caught with her hand in the cookie jar. "Yes, ma'am." She gave Marcus a nervous glance then walked over to take charge of Mr. Singleton.

Jasmine walked toward them, holding her hands out to Naima. "Naima, it's a pleasure to see you again."

Naima gave a respectful bow at the waist. "It's good to see you as well." She introduced Grammy, Marcus, and Elise.

Jasmine grasped Elise's hands and closed her eyes for a moment. She opened them again with a smile. "You have strong energy within and around you. Tap into that if you feel yourself getting lost." She released Elise and nodded. "Come, Malik should be finished cleansing the room," she said as they walked along the hallway toward her reading room.

She opened the door, and they were met with the fragrant scent of freshly burned sage. Malik stood in the middle of the room looking remarkably nervous as Elise walked into the room. He was dressed in jeans, canvas shoes, and a pullover sweater. He still maintained his gray hair and beard.

"Hello, Malik," Naima said in greeting, trying not to take pleasure in his discomfort. He might have been the catalyst for all of this, but he was trying to fix it which was admirable.

"Can I get anyone anything? Water, tea, a plate of high tea lemon cookies from a recipe handed down for generations in my family?" Jasmine asked pleasantly.

"Tea and lemon cookies sound lovely," Grammy said.

Jasmine nodded. "Please, make yourselves comfortable. We'll be using the seating area as it's less formal than the table." She gave Malik's back a quick rub and a smile of encouragement before she left them alone.

"So, you're Malik?" Elise asked, her head tilted as she looked him over curiously. "You look older than I expected. I assumed you and Naima were the same age when everything happened."

He gave her a tentative smile. "This is for Jasmine's benefit. So that we can walk down the street without drawing attention because of the appearance of our age difference. Would you be more comfortable if I looked as I truly am?"

Elise crossed her arms and looked him straight in the eye. "Yes, I'd like to see the true face of the jinni who paved the road to the pain Naima and Aliya endured and which I may end up enduring trying to free them."

Naima watched Malik's Adam's apple bob nervously as he attempted to swallow some courage in the face of his truth.

"Very well. As you wish." His hair darkened and lengthened to just past his shoulders, his beard darkened but stayed the length it was, and most of the wrinkles on his face smoothed to a more youthful look. He could pass for a man in his mid-thirties to early forties. "Is that better?"

"Yes," Elise said, taking a seat on the low sofa.

Marcus walked up to Malik eyeing him with a narrowed gaze. They were the same height. "I see you, but I also feel a darkness close to the surface that I don't like. I'm watching you," he said before taking a seat beside Elise and placing a protective arm around her shoulder.

Grammy was the last to speak to him. "I don't know how much Naima may have told you about me but know that if I sense an inkling of deceit or danger coming from you, Aliya's curse will be nothing compared to what I'll do. I don't care how powerful a jinn you are."

She gave him a very intimidating stare down before turning and sitting on the other side of Elise.

Jasmine walked in rolling a cart with a plate of cookies, an electric tea kettle, cups, and all the fixings for a proper cup of tea. The warm smile she came in wearing slid from her face when she looked at Malik. "What did I miss?"

Malik gave her a nervous smile. "I've been sufficiently and deservedly warned."

Jasmine looked from Malik to the trio sitting on the sofa with Grammy and Marcus looking every bit like Elise's very own dangerous bodyguards. She ducked her head and continued into the room but not before Naima saw the amused grin on her face. Naima sat on a cushion across from the family, Jasmine sat beside her, and Malik grabbed a chair from the table and sat as far away from the group as the room would allow. Naima could feel the fear and nervousness rolling off him. While they enjoyed their refreshments, Jasmine asked Elise questions about her life, her everyday activities and any occurrences that happened over the years that may have given her a clue as to Aliya's presence.

"I just need to know how ingrained in your soul Aliya might be. If there were signs that she may have tried coming through prior to Naima's arrival, then calling her forward may be easier than expected," Jasmine explained.

Elise chewed her bottom lip as she considered what Jasmine said, then shook her head. "Nothing that I can remember other than when we went to Nosy Be."

"What made your family decide to vacation there?" Jasmine asked.

Naima leaned forward in anticipation of Elise's answer. She had wondered the same thing but never thought to ask her about it.

Elise's brow furrowed. "You know, I don't remember. My parents had been planning to take us to Africa for years, but our stay at Nosy Be during that trip was a last-minute decision."

"You honestly don't remember?" Marcus asked.

"No, should I?"

Marcus looked surprised. "Yes, because you suggested it. Dad had been considering spending a week of our vacation in Madagascar, and as we looked at a map of the area you pointed to Nosy Be and said you wanted to stay there. Mom and Dad didn't even know if there were hotels or anything on the island until you brought it to their attention. We changed our whole trip because you were so excited to go to Nosy Be and got Mom all excited about the spa resort. Instead of two weeks at the safari resort, it was a week of safari and a week in Nosy Be."

"I don't remember that," Elise said in confusion.

"Could seeing the map of Madagascar and the island have triggered Aliya?" Naima asked.

"It could have," Jasmine said, then directed her attention to Marcus. "Do you remember your sister exhibiting any other strange behavior when you were children?"

"You mean other than her usual strangeness?" Marcus said, chuckling.

Elise punched him in the arm.

"OW!" He rubbed his arm. "Actually, yes, there was something. She used to talk in her sleep when we were in elementary school. It usually happened when she was stressing out about a test or when she was getting picked on."

"I did?" Elise said.

"Yeah, but I always thought it was gibberish because I could never understand what you were saying."

Jasmine looked at Naima. "I'm assuming Aliya spoke Arabic."

Naima gazed at Elise in amazement. To hear that Aliya may have tried to come through when Elise was so young meant the princess's spirit was much stronger than she thought. "Yes, she actually spoke Arabic, French, Malagasy, and English."

"It could've been Arabic. I remembered hearing something similar while we were in Nosy Be," Marcus said.

Elise shook her head. "No, I don't even know any Arabic. I barely remember the French I learned in high school. The only other language I can speak fluently is Spanish and that's because most of the contractors I work with speak it."

Naima felt Elise's unease at her brother's revelations. She couldn't bear putting her through any more of this.

"Elise, if this is all too much—" Naima said.

Elise cut her off. "I'm fine, really," she said unconvincingly.

"I'm sure you are, but there's something you need to know—"

Naima was cut off again but this time by Grammy. "She knows all she needs to do what needs to be done. Prolonging it won't make it easier." She gave Naima a look of warning.

"Grammy is right. There's nothing else you can tell me that will make me change my mind. I want to do this for you, for Aliya." Elise gave Naima a tender smile. "For us."

Naima swallowed what she was about to admit. Even with all her knowledge and power she felt completely helpless.

"No need to worry, granddaughter, I'm here. I will not allow Elise to come to any danger." She heard Chirag's comforting voice in her head.

She took a deep breath and gave Elise a smile and a nod.

Chapter Eleven

Elise was a ball of nervousness that seemed to not only come from her own worries but everyone else's as well. She didn't need to have psychic or intuitive abilities to know that both Grammy and Marcus were just as nervous as she was. She could tell by the way Grammy gripped her hands tightly together in her lap despite her smile and the way Marcus chewed on his bottom lip. She could feel Naima's nerves through their bond and see the way Malik's leg bounced as he tried to sit inconspicuously on the other side of the room. The only person who looked calm and collected was Jasmine as she cleared away their teacups and plates and lit an incense stick that sat on the low table in the middle of the seating area.

"This is rosemary. The scent can be used to attract spiritual beings," she said, then took her seat again and focused her attention on Elise. "I want you to close your eyes and take a few deep breaths of the scent."

Elise did as she was told, wondering if this was going to be another hypnosis thing. With her first breath, the rosemary tickled her nose, and she wiggled it to avoid a sneeze. With her next two breaths she didn't inhale as deeply and just let the scent flow through her.

"Good, now I want you to focus your thoughts on Aliya, as if you're searching for her."

Elise thought of the woman who'd come to her in her sleep the other night. She envisioned her dressed just as she'd been in her dream. Her image was fuzzy at first, but the more Elise focused on it the clearer it became until Aliya was standing before her with a curious gaze. Elise worried that it had been too easy to call her forward.

"She's there, isn't she?" Elise heard Jasmine say.

"Yes."

"She's stronger than I expected to have been dormant for as long as she was." Elise didn't like the note of worry in Jasmine's tone.

"So, you've come looking for me now?" Aliya asked.

They were once again standing amongst the ruins of Akiba. Elise thought it was so weird, as if she were in a waking dream. A little like what she felt during hypnosis but more aware of what was going on around her than she was then. She could feel the heat coming from Grammy and Marcus sitting on either side of her, smell the incense burning, and feel Naima's comforting presence.

"Yes, I want to help you," Elise said.

"Do you?" Aliya looked amused. "And how would you go about doing that? The only way you can help me is to free me of this prison. To let me live the life I was denied."

Elise heard Jasmine calling her name, but she found she couldn't respond. "I can help free you but not the way you would like. You can move on the way your soul should've been allowed to do centuries ago."

"You're offering to help me die, is that what you're saying?" Aliya looked as if Elise was telling her an amusing story.

"I don't understand why you seem to find this so amusing. Aren't you tired of going from life to life with nothing but a few moments of awareness of what's going on? You're Buddhist, wouldn't you rather be released from this to be reborn in a more natural way?" Elise hoped using spiritual logic would convince her to not do what she was so afraid Aliya would do.

Aliya smiled knowingly and that's when Elise remembered that since she was in her head, she probably could tell what her thoughts were.

"What do I have to do to obtain this wonderful freedom you speak of?" Sarcasm was obvious in Aliya's tone.

Elise chose to ignore it. "Give Naima her freedom. Acknowledge her and make the wishes that would set her free."

Aliya gave a loud bitter laugh, and before Elise could blink, the princess was on her, grabbing her wrist, and standing so close Elise could smell the sweet scent of mint on her breath.

"Why should I free Naima? So that you can have her all to yourself? You are not worthy of replacing me in her heart. I am her one true love, not you. You're just a pretty distraction until I can be with her again." Aliya's face contorted into an ugly sneer.

All traces of the soft and beautiful storybook princess was gone and replaced by something dark and evil. Elise tried snatching her wrist away, but Aliya's grip was like a vise holding her in place.

"ELISE!" She heard Marcus's deep voice shouting and looked toward the direction it came from. There was nothing but darkness beyond the thick foliage.

"Do you know how long I've waited for a moment like this? For one of these pitiful lives to offer me an escape that would allow me to finally live my life. Oh, there were plenty with weak minds that I could manipulate to my will but none with lives that were worthy of me choosing to live."

"ELISE!" This time it sounded like Grammy.

Elise knew from the panic she heard in Grammy's voice that something was wrong, and she needed to get out of there, but Aliya had a hold on her that she couldn't break free of.

"Let me go," she said, trying to stay calm.

Aliya's gaze narrowed into an angry glare. "I will not be denied the life I deserved."

She stepped so close that their faces were mere inches from each other. Then, to Elise's utter horror, Aliya stepped *into* her. She could feel the princess spreading and stretching into her body and limbs to fit into Elise's as if she were simply putting on a full-length body suit, then Elise was alone with the eerie darkness of the surrounding forest creeping in on her.

Naima knelt in front of Elise whose eyes stared blankly ahead trying to warm her cold hands with her own. When Elise had stopped responding to Jasmine, she, Marcus, and Grammy all tried to wake her from whatever trance she was in. When their coaxing and desperate pleas didn't work Naima tried reaching out to her through their bond and was met with a steel wall that she could feel nothing of Elise through.

"Please, Elise, come back to us," Naima urged her gently, kissing her knuckles, and holding her hands against her chest hoping that the feel of her beating heart would get through to her.

Something dark passed across Elise's eyes and she rapidly blinked them before focusing on Naima. Her eyes widened and she pulled her hands out of Naima's grasp and placed them on her cheeks.

"My love," Elise said in Arabic.

"Lord, child, you had us worried," Grammy said, rubbing Elise's back.

Naima removed Elise's hands from her face and sat back on her heels. "It's not Elise."

"What do you mean it's not Elise?" Grammy said.

Out of the corner of her eye, Naima had noticed Marcus put some distance between him and his sister at the same time she realized what was happening. His connection with his twin must have told him something was wrong as well.

"Are you not happy to see me?" Aliya said, still speaking in Arabic.

Naima gave her a tentative smile. "Of course, I am. I'm also concerned about Elise. Where is she?"

Elise's full lips turned down into a pout. "We've been separated for six hundred years and you're more worried about your little plaything than me?"

Naima tried to look happier but her concern for Elise was overwhelming any other emotions. "I'm just worried about her on her family's behalf," she said, indicating Grammy and Marcus who watched Elise—rather Aliya—warily. "They came here to help keep her safe."

Aliya turned first to Grammy then Marcus with a pleasant smile. "Safe from me? What could I possibly do to harm her? She has allowed me to come through so that I may do what must be done to free us." She now spoke in English.

"She's lying," Grammy said angrily.

Aliya turned back to Grammy, her face a mask of haughty anger. "How dare you accuse me of lying. Do you know who I am?"

Grammy met Aliya's glare with her own. "I do know and don't care. You just better release my granddaughter."

"Your granddaughter is fine and safely tucked away until I've finished what I came here to do."

Naima didn't like the tone in Aliya's words. "What is it that you came to do?" Naima said, pulling her attention away from Grammy's combatant gaze.

Aliya smiled sweetly at Naima. "To be with you, my love. I'll make my wishes which will free both of us and then we can finally be together again." She looked down at Elise's body then shrugged. "She's a bit too tall and less curvy than I like, but you seem to like her so I can live with it."

Naima's blood turned cold. "You cannot stay once we're free, Aliya. You must release Elise and let her live her own life." She spoke as gently and reasonably as possible as she felt that Aliya's curse had changed her. She no longer seemed like the gentle and loving woman she once was.

Aliya continued smiling, sat back, crossed her legs and arms, and quirked a brow at Naima. "No."

"What do you mean, no?" Marcus said, looking angrily at the woman who resembled his sister but wasn't.

"You do not belong in this world," Jasmine said from behind Naima.

Aliya gazed around at the spiritualist curiously. "Who might you be?"

Jasmine didn't have the same worried expressions as everyone else did. "I'm a spiritual guide to help you move on to your next life." She spoke calmly and serenely.

Aliya chuckled. "Isn't that sweet. Well, you're not needed. I deserve to be here just as much as any of you. I was the one who had her life snatched away at the petty whim of a jinni. Elise has lived hers. It's my time again."

Naima sat back on the ottoman at a loss for words at Aliya acting the petty spoiled princess she spent her whole life trying to avoid becoming.

"You can't just take over someone's life. You've lived yours as well and it ended when it was supposed to end. Release Elise to the lifetime she is meant to live and allow your soul the freedom it deserves," Jasmine said.

"Do you think you and your little spirit guide are going to stop me with some candles and chants? I've waited six hundred years to find my way to the one lifetime that was worthy. I've found it and I'm not going anywhere." Aliya looked from Jasmine to Naima with a smug grin.

"That's all well and good, Aliya, but if you decide to stay, your curse will never be broken," Malik spoke up.

All eyes turned in the direction he'd been sitting the entire time. Naima noticed he'd hidden himself in shadows that were slowly dissipating. He must have done it when Aliya came through to keep her from noticing him. He stood and walked toward the group. Naima looked back at Aliya whose eyes had widened in shock then narrowed in anger.

"You," she whispered vehemently as she also stood.

"Greetings, Princess." Malik gave a bow in deference to her title.

Aliya looked back at Naima. "Why is he here? Hasn't he caused enough heartache?"

"He's here to help us. To right the wrongs that were done," Naima explained.

Aliya looked back at Malik. "Can you bring my brother back? Can you turn back time and revive the rubble that was once our kingdom?"

Malik stood before Aliya but kept his distance. He was afraid of her. "No, but with Jasmine's help I was able to go back and free the souls of all those who suffered and were trapped there, including Adnan's."

Aliya cocked her head to the side looking at Malik curiously. "You freed Adnan?"

Malik smiled. "Yes. He suffers no more and has joined the rest of your family and our people in the afterlife. Allow Jasmine to do the same for you."

Something shifted across Aliya's face. "Our people?" She slowly walked toward Malik who flinched under her dark countenance. "They stopped being your people the day you brought that jinni amongst us."

The temperature in the room dropped enough for everyone to notice and look at each other nervously.

Jasmine raised up to stand beside Malik and took his hand. "Malik has regretted that decision and suffered for it every day since. He's trying to help you now. Please listen to what he has to say."

Aliya raked her gaze over Jasmine and stopped at their clasped hands. She gave him a sardonic grin. "So, you've found another human to take my place in your heart. And look how wonderfully she comes to your defense. I may only be a spirit, but I've learned things over the centuries that have enlightened me to a power that lay dormant within me. I just needed the right vessel to hold it."

The room felt as if someone had turned the air conditioner that hummed in the background on full blast.

Naima walked over to Aliya and took her hand. "Aliya, please, this is not you."

Aliya turned to Naima with a sad smile. "This has always been me; you were just too busy to see it. Weapons training wasn't the only thing I was learning while you were off soldiering and helping Adnan run the country. Did you know we had a practicing witch living in Akiba? She lived among the mountain tribes and offered me a reading to thank me for my kindnesses. I went to see her once while you and Adnan were away on some mission or other and she told me that I hold a power that only humans with jinn blood held."

Naima shook her head. "That's impossible. None of the royal family took a jinn as a mate. You were the first."

"That's what I thought until I looked through the family archives and found some missing information. The first Adnan's son's wife had a jinn mother who left shortly after she was born. Chirag brought them to Akiba to protect them and she was raised by her human father never knowing who her mother was. The truth was buried within the archives until I stumbled upon it and asked the Akiba historian about it. Of course, he claimed that there were no jinn in the royal family until you, but after a few drops of a serum the witch gave me, he revealed the whole story. He had a terrible headache when he awoke the next day but was none the wiser of having told me anything. Because she didn't know of her mother's identity, she never used her magic. She was rumored to be an intuitive, like dear Grammy." She gave Grammy a wink and received a scowl in return. "But her magic lay dormant growing weaker and weaker with each generation of Fadels."

Naima couldn't believe what she was hearing. *"Is it true?"* she telepathically asked Chirag who she hoped was still nearby.

"Yes, it's true," he said without further explanation.

Naima brought her attention back to Aliya.

"While you and Adnan were busy, I had the witch brought to the palace regularly over the years to show me how to use my power. It wasn't strong enough to do much more than a few parlor tricks, but with the help of some incantations she taught me and a spell book she gifted me with, I was able to do more."

"That's how you were able to curse me," Malik said, a bit of admiration in his voice.

Aliya glared at him. "You're fortunate that was all I was able to do."

Grammy stood and joined them followed by Marcus who hovered near her protectively as he eyed Aliya suspiciously.

"You said you waited for a lifetime that was worthy of you. Have you been aware of the people your soul has been reborn to all this time?" Grammy asked.

"Yes. It took a few lifetimes with flashes of clarity before I became fully aware and none of them were harmed. They may have experienced some momentary memory loss when I stepped forward to do what I needed, but they were still able to function and live their lives normally," Aliya said without the least bit of regret or concern for those people.

"This is the woman you've been pining away for the past six hundred years?" Marcus looked at Aliya with disgust. "Release your hold on my sister."

Aliya quirked a brow at him. "When I'm ready, I shall. Until then, she'll be fine."

"You need to release her, Aliya," Malik said. "Neither you nor Naima will be free if you continue on this path."

"Shall I remind you of Jahir's words about the curse? Naima will be tied to the lamp granting wishes until she is found by her one true love. Only then, once she grants her true love's final wish will she be free. Well, here I am." She spread her arms as if they needed reminding that she was there.

"But you are not Naima's one true love." Malik gave her a smug grin.

Aliya laughed aloud. "If it's not me then who? We've known since we were children that we were meant to be together, which we happily were before your interference."

"It's true, you were meant to be together, but that doesn't mean you are her one true love. It's Elise. It's the reason she ended up with the lamp and your soul. She's the key to breaking the curses, not you."

Naima noticed Malik no longer cowered or gave off any fear of Aliya. He grinned cockily and she could feel something different in the air around him.

"He's coming, be prepared. I'm physically keeping my distance so as not to antagonize him, but I will not hesitate to come if I feel he's about to do harm," Chirag said.

Naima brushed her hand against Jasmine's to get her attention. When she looked away from Malik there was concern in her eyes. She must have felt it as well from her bond with him. She gazed over at Marcus and Grammy and thankfully saw they had distanced themselves from the group with Marcus placing Grammy protectively behind them. Their intuition had also warned them that something was wrong.

"LIAR!" Aliya screamed, the temperature in the room dropping again.

"What would we have to gain by lying? We want this curse broken just as much as you do. We are weary of this fleshy form and these tiresome humans," Malik said, sneering down at his body.

Jasmine grasped Malik's hand. "Malik, if you can hear me, please, fight it. Don't let him take over. You're stronger than you think."

Malik ignored her, continuing to pin Aliya with a hard stare.

Aliya looked at Jasmine in confusion then at Malik. Her face lit up with the realization of what was happening, but instead of backing away she stood taller and met his gaze.

"So, you are still in there? I wondered how well my parting gift had worked. The look on your face before you expelled my soul from my body was truly priceless."

"We should have snapped your neck as we did your dearly departed Adnan," Malik said.

Aliya raised her hand and slapped Malik across his cheek so quickly and hard he stumbled back from the power of it, Jasmine was dragged back with him since she was holding his hand and tumbled over an ottoman onto her backside.

"Don't you ever speak his name. He loved Malik like a brother. Stood beside him in battle. Even fought for him before the jinn counsel to bring him home, and how was he repaid? By being killed and having his soul damned to purgatory for your entertainment." Aliya's chest rose with angry breaths and her eyes shone with rage and unshed tears.

Malik ignored Aliya this time as he helped Jasmine up and took her face in his hands. "Are you hurt?" he asked.

"No, what about you?" Jasmine touched his cheek where Aliya's hand had landed.

"I'm fine for now. The slap surprised him, giving me a chance to step forward while he was caught off guard, but it won't last." Malik turned back to Aliya. "Among the many things I regret, Adnan's death is greatest, but we don't have time to argue over it. You need to let Elise come forward and break the curse. I've been able to keep Jahir tamed because nothing has happened to make him want to stay, but your return has piqued his interest and need for a challenge. If we don't break all three curses now, neither I nor Chirag will be able to protect any one of us from his wrath."

Naima should have known Malik would know Chirag was nearby. He'd told her when they first spoke earlier that week that he could sense when there were jinn nearby. If he could sense Chirag's presence, so could Jahir.

"If you're going to help—" Naima said to Chirag.

He cut her off with, *"I'm here,"* then appeared by her side with little smoke and fanfare.

Before anyone had time to acknowledge his appearance, he grasped Aliya's face and surrounded them in an invisible bubble that brushed up against Naima as it formed and nudged her away from the pair. She tried using her magic to breach it, but Chirag's was too powerful. She could only watch as Aliya went limp in his grasp.

❖

When the darkness began closing in, Elise just knew this was it. Her life as she knew it was over and Aliya was making her a real-life victim of all those paranormal shows and horror stories she'd seen. Then she remembered that this was her mind and she still had control over it. She closed her eyes and envisioned the throne room the way she had seen it when Malik came to her in her sleep. At this point, she wouldn't be surprised if she ended up with insomnia once this was over. When Elise opened her eyes, the rubble was replaced by the finery of Akiba's throne room. Thunder and lightning raged outside, but the darkness no longer creeped in on her. She tried reaching out to Naima but was met by a dark wall. She was a prisoner in her own head unless she could figure out how to reach Naima or even Aliya to somehow convince or trick her into releasing her.

Suddenly, there was a rumble of thunder so strong it shook the palace, then there was a flash of blinding lightning right in the middle of the throne room. When Elise's vision cleared of the spots the bright light caused, she saw two people standing in the scorch mark of the bolt. It was Chirag and Aliya.

"What have you done?" Aliya asked as she looked frantically around the room before her confused gaze landed on Elise. "No, I can't stay here, I need to be free!" she shouted.

The fear in her voice almost broke Elise's heart…almost. Chirag ignored her tantrum and came to Elise.

"Are you well?" he asked in concern.

"Yes, but how did you get here?"

"I used Aliya's connection to bring us here. We must hurry. Malik won't be able to hold Jahir off much longer."

Aliya ran up and pummeled his back with her tiny fists acting more the spoiled child than the sophisticated princess. "I will not allow you to ignore me!"

Chirag closed his eyes and shook his head looking every bit the impatient parent. "You must take control. You can do it. I feel your family's and Naima's strength surrounding you. Use it to strengthen your own resolve and come back so that we may end this."

Elise closed her eyes and thought of Grammy, Marcus, and Naima. She felt the depth of their love as well as their fear and resolved that she would not allow Aliya to take them away from her. She opened her eyes to find Chirag smiling down at her as he kept Aliya from scratching her eyes out.

"I will not allow you to take what isn't yours. This is my life. It's time for you to move on," Elise said, feeling a strange calm wash over her.

She also noticed that the storm had subsided, and blue sky and bright sunshine shone brightly into the throne room making the marble floor and gold filigree on the doors sparkle. She looked back at Aliya who'd stopped struggling and stood looking oddly subdued.

"Naima was right. This is not who I am. I'm sorry if I've caused you any pain. It's just been so long, and I've felt so lost never knowing when I'd be free of this curse." Tears slipped from her long lashes and plopped onto the floor. "Once you've made your wishes, the curse will be broken, and I won't bedevil you any longer. I'll finally be reunited with my family."

Elise studied Aliya's beautiful face for any deception but only saw sadness and regret. She looked at Chirag who also watched Aliya skeptically then looked at her and shrugged.

"Come, we have to go now," Chirag said, offering her his hand.

Elise took it and was instantly swept up into darkness. She almost panicked until she heard Chirag say her name. She blinked her eyes open to find herself on his lap on the floor of the reading room.

"What happened? What's going on?" Elise heard Marcus say. He sounded as if he were speaking to her from the other side of a door.

She looked around and found everyone staring down at them but not approaching. She didn't realize why until Marcus raised his hand and pressed it against an invisible barrier. Elise gazed curiously back up at Chirag.

"I had to contain Aliya in order to reach you without interference," he explained.

Her ears popped and sound came rushing back in as Naima appeared in front of her and Marcus beside her.

"Elise?" Marcus said.

"Yes?" she answered.

He looked as if he was about to cry with relief. He placed a gentle kiss on her forehead. "I thought we'd lost you."

Elise rubbed his cheek. "You can't get rid of me that easily."

"Are you truly all right?" Naima asked, looking just as relieved as her brother.

"Yes. I'll be even better once I'm off your giant of a grandfather's lap. I feel like I'm five years old sitting on Santa's lap at the mall."

Marcus offered his hand and pulled her up. She turned back to Chirag. "Thank you for coming after me."

He gave her an elegant bow. "My pleasure."

"Do you feel as if she gave up too easily?" Elise asked him.

His brow furrowed in thought. "Yes, but I didn't feel any animosity from her. She seemed sincere."

Elise was no spirit or jinn expert so she would have to take his word for it, but something felt off about Aliya's sudden change of heart.

"We must do this now. I can't hold him back much longer." Malik looked as if he were in pain. His forehead was covered in beads of sweat as he leaned his tall frame on petite Jasmine's for support.

Elise didn't know what happened while she was trapped in her own head, but obviously whatever Aliya had been doing had not been good. "But don't we need Aliya?" As much as she hated risking her taking over again, Aliya had to be there to make her wishes for the curse to be broken.

Naima touched her arm to get her attention then took her hands. Elise had never seen her look so serious before. "What's wrong?" she asked.

Naima seemed to take a breath then gave Elise a tentative smile. "Aliya cannot break the curse. She's not my one true love...you are."

Elise looked at her in confusion. "Wait...what?"

"You are the only one who can break the curses set upon all of us. Aliya never would have been able to break it, even if we had found our way to each other before now. You are my heart. The one I truly love with every beat of it."

Naima leaned forward and brushed her lips softly against Elise's, then gazed at her with eyes so full of love Elise could feel it wrapping around her own heart like a comforting and safe blanket. She knew, deep down, that what Naima said was true. She knew it days ago but was too afraid to believe it.

Naima looked at her as if she knew the moment Elise accepted the truth. "You've already made one wish. You only have two to go."

Elise's heart beat rapidly as she thought about the responsibility she held. With two simple wishes she could free Naima, release Aliya's spirit, and hopefully break the curse she'd placed on Malik and Jahir. She gazed over at Malik who gave her a weary smile and nod. Then she turned to look at Grammy and Marcus standing nearby.

"Look at that, you always felt somewhat cheated that you didn't get any of the family's little gifts and it turns out you got the best one of all. The power to free jinn from curses," Marcus said with amusement.

Grammy walked up to her and gently clasped her cheeks. "The decision is completely yours. Don't let any of us pressure you to do anything you aren't ready for."

Elise felt her heartbeat slow down and the rising anxiety fade away at her grandmother's words. She nodded and turned back to Naima who watched her patiently. Whether she'd known all along or just figured it out recently, she never once pressured Elise to do anything. She had been willing to sacrifice her own freedom to keep Elise safe. Her feelings for Naima had been a surprise and had grown quickly but felt right. Like she'd waited her whole life for just this woman and this moment, and she didn't want to mess it up.

"There is no rush," Naima said, probably having read Elise's emotions through their bond.

"By the looks of Malik over there, I'd say there is," Marcus said.

"Shut up, boy," Grammy said before Elise heard Marcus grunt, probably due to a punch from Grammy.

Elise gazed over at Malik again.

"She's right, there's no rush. I'm fine," he said, despite a sudden flinch and pained expression.

She knew enough about Jahir to not want to have to face him, so she decided what to do. She took Naima's hands. "What is the one wish you've always wanted besides to be free?" she asked.

Naima looked surprised by the question. "I never thought about it. Being free and with Aliya is all I ever focused on." Her brow furrowed in thought. "Right now, all I want is to be with you. To spend what lifetime we have left together."

"And after my lifetime is over, what do you want for yourself? You're jinn, you'll outlive me for many more centuries."

"This isn't about me, Elise. They're your wishes."

Elise just looked at her. What she wanted to wish for she couldn't do without knowing what Naima wanted.

"You're my life so anything after that would feel empty, but I would have to go on. Whether we get fifty years, or you wish for immortality, and we have a millennium, I just want to spend it with you."

Elise would have never thought to wish for immortality. Probably because the thought of outliving her entire family, having to watch them all grow older and pass on made it a very unappealing way to live. Then she thought about what Naima said about what her life would be like once Elise's lifetime had passed and she wondered if that was her way of answering Elise's unasked question. She met Naima's dark gaze, loving the swirling galaxy within them and trying to read what she wasn't saying.

Naima gave her a grin. "You don't need to read my mind. The answer is yes."

Elise's heart soared with joy. She thought of the perfect wish that she hoped covered both of her last two wishes.

"Are you sure about this, granddaughter?" Chirag asked.

Elise assumed he must have read both of their minds.

Naima nodded. "I'm tired, Chirag."

He nodded in understanding and Naima turned back to Elise.

"Are you ready?" she asked.

Elise nodded. "I wish for you, Naima, to have the life you've always wanted and deserved and that we share that life together."

Elise didn't know if that would mean Naima would become human or that she would become somewhat immortal like Naima, but she figured Naima would know how to grant it since she knew what was in Elise's heart.

Naima began to glow with a lavender light that turned into the same swirling purple cloud she had appeared out of the lamp from. She released Elise's hands and stepped back as the cloud enveloped her. At the same time Malik began to laugh in a voice that echoed throughout the room and was also enveloped in a black cloud of his own. Chirag grabbed Jasmine and placed her behind him, and Elise was torn between watching Naima's purple cloud and Malik's black one. She felt someone grab her hand and turned to find Marcus pulling her back toward him and Grammy to distance her from both jinn. Elise almost fought him until a boom of thunder rumbled through the room and the lights flickered on then off. Chirag backed Jasmine up into Elise's group and all the noise in the room became muffled.

"I think he placed us in one of his protective bubbles," Marcus said.

Elise walked forward and met with an invisible wall. Jasmine came up beside her. They gazed at each other with concern.

"He's yours, isn't he?" Elise asked.

"Yes," Jasmine said.

They both turned to look back out at the two swirling masses that began rising off the ground and Chirag standing as if ready for battle.

CHAPTER TWELVE

Naima evaporated into the cloud, becoming a part of it. She could see everything going on in the room, including what was happening to Malik. Malik's powers were always represented by a charcoal gray cloud, so she knew the black one that enveloped him was Jahir's. It either meant Elise's wishes worked and he was separating from Malik's human form, or he had managed to take Malik over again. Chirag stood guard in front of Elise, her family, and Jasmine, watching Jahir's black cloud carefully. She felt a pop within her as her human form assembled and began to lower to the floor. She knelt there feeling as if every bone and muscle in her body ached.

"Naima! Get up! NOW!" Chirag said.

She struggled to stand but collapsed and felt herself being lifted and hurtling toward Elise and her group and placed within Chirag's protective shield. She slid down the invisible wall into a sitting position and Elise knelt in front of her.

"Are you okay?" Elise asked in concern.

Naima nodded. "I think so. Everything aches."

"Welcome to the world of being a human," Jasmine said.

Elise looked at Jasmine then back at Naima in wide-eyed amazement. "It worked?"

Naima cocked her head to the side, listening to her own internal workings. She didn't feel the heaviness of her powers, she couldn't even sense the power of the other jinn, and it took her a moment to realize that she didn't feel the pull of the lamp. No matter how far she'd traveled from it she could always feel its tug like a magical umbilical cord.

She gave Elise a huge smile. "It did. The curse is broken."

"Uh, guys, you might want to see this," Marcus said, not giving them any time to celebrate.

She could feel her strength coming back, but Naima was still appreciative of Elise assisting her to stand. They turned toward the activity going on outside Chirag's shield, and what Naima witnessed turned her blood cold. Malik lay unconscious on the floor as the black cloud poured out of him, forming into who Naima assumed was the real Jahir, which meant Elise had managed to break Aliya's curse as well. He stood twice as tall and wide as Chirag, with dark ebony skin, a lush black beard that reached his belly, a thick mass of curls on his head that went past his shoulders, a broad nose, full lips, and bright eyes with pupils that resembled a flickering flame.

"I am free!" his voice reverberated through the room, even clearly penetrating Chirag's shield.

"Malik?" Jasmine cried, drawing Jahir's attention.

He gazed down in disgust at Malik's still form. "He lives…for now."

Jasmine covered her mouth and whimpered. Grammy put an arm around her shoulders in comfort. Jahir turned his attention to Chirag. Naima feared for her grandfather despite how powerful she knew he was.

"Chirag," Jahir growled, his form now fully solid and growing so tall his head skimmed the ceiling as he slowly approached Chirag.

Chirag stood his ground against the giant jinni. "Jahir," he said, meeting his fiery gaze.

"I was told you had ascended," Jahir said.

Chirag shrugged. "Rumors of my ascension have been greatly exaggerated. As you can see, I am still among the living and quite enjoying it."

Jahir bent toward Chirag, his face hovering just inches from Naima's grandfather's. "I could make the rumors true," he said menacingly.

"I have no doubt that you could."

Jahir looked at him suspiciously. "Then why are you not begging for your life?"

"Because somewhere, amongst all that dark anger, is the man who Fatima once loved. Who I once loved."

Naima couldn't see his face, but she could hear the sincerity in his tone.

"They were lovers?" Elise asked.

"Yes," Naima said.

"We were more than lovers," Chirag said. "Jahir, Fatima, and I were life mates."

Jahir's face contorted in anger. "You speak of love, yet you left me behind and turned me away for your little island utopia. We were gods! We were worshipped by humans and jinn alike!" His voice began to reverberate again, causing the ceiling light to shudder and flicker.

"I asked you to come with me. It was what you, Fatima, and I had talked about. Finding a peaceful place for us to live out our existence. You chose to stay behind," Chirag said sadly.

"I chose to avenge Fatima's death while you chose to run and hide. You dishonored her by making her death meaningless." Jahir's tone was more bitter than angry now.

"I chose to honor her final request. She asked us not to avenge her. She didn't want her death causing more death. She wanted us to continue with her plans. It pained me to walk away from you." Chirag reached up to stroke Jahir's cheek. His hand looked like a child's on the giant jinni's face. "I begged you not to continue on your path, Jahir, but you called me a coward and broke my heart."

Jahir looked unsure and his form began to shrink until he and Chirag were eye to eye. "Then why did you banish me from Akiba? To break my heart in return?"

"That's the last thing I would ever want to do to you, my love, but you would've made a mockery of the peace I had created in Fatima's memory. Akiba wasn't just an island made of earth and rocks. It was an extension of Fatima herself."

Jahir looked confused then his eyes widened in realization. "You took her heart," he said quietly.

Chirag nodded. "It was her final wish. Akiba is literally the heart and soul of Fatima. The mountains, the trees, the land, the very crops which the humans of Akiba survived on for centuries before you destroyed it all grew from Fatima's heart. I couldn't let you destroy that, so I had to turn you away." Chirag's voice broke and he took his hand from Jahir's cheek to ball into a fist at his side. "It nearly destroyed me."

"Why didn't you tell me?"

"Because the only way for you to stay on Akiba was to accept what we were doing there, but you were blinded by your anger and superiority. I realized you had only agreed to our plan because of Fatima, and without Fatima you would never find peace. It was obvious that my love for you wasn't enough to make you want it. Look at what you did despite it. I knew your anger would bring you back for revenge. I thought that leaving Akiba would keep them safe, but I was wrong." Chirag turned toward Naima and the group, raised his hand, and dispersed the protective bubble.

Jasmine ran from Grammy over to Malik who was beginning to stir. Naima looked over at her grandfather and her heart broke at the heartbreak she saw in his eyes. He turned back to Jahir.

"If you still want revenge for the hurt that I caused you, here I am. But I will die trying to destroy you before I let you harm anyone else here. Just as Akiba was an extension of Fatima, so are they. You've caused enough destruction to her legacy," Chirag said.

Jahir looked back at Malik lying on the floor with his head in Jasmine's lap as she ran her fingers through his hair, then toward Naima and Elise. Out of habit, Naima moved to partially block Elise from any harm, then she remembered she no longer had her power.

"Did you truly free me of that prison?" Jahir asked Elise, pointing toward Malik.

"I think so," Elise answered.

"Is that witch of a princess truly gone?"

"I think so."

He nodded. "Then you have nothing to fear from me." He turned back to Malik who was slowly standing up with Jasmine's assistance. "You, on the other hand, may still be on borrowed time."

Malik stood straight to face off with Jahir. "I did what I had to do to break the curse you created that got us into this situation. If you want to kill me for giving you your life back, there's nothing I can do to fight it."

Jahir didn't look as if he liked that answer, especially since Malik was right. He was no longer trapped within Malik's human form. "It is only because of that that I'll let you live," he said, scowling.

Malik collapsed on a nearby ottoman in relief. Jahir turned back to Chirag. "I still cannot forgive you for deserting me, but you're right. After Fatima's death, a life of peace no longer appealed to me. I was jealous that you seemed to love that damned island more than me. Now I understand why. If you had only told me that our beloved's heart was there..." Jahir grew quiet.

It looked to Naima as if he were trying to get his emotions in check. He looked full of regret. To see Jahir and Chirag, two of the most powerful jinn she knew, look so vulnerable was strange.

Chirag gave him a tender smile. "Your destruction of Akiba did not destroy the entire island. Under the care of the keepers, Fatima's heart beats strongly."

"Keepers?" Naima said.

Chirag turned to her. "Yes, I and two of the original jinn of Akiba who survived Jahir's attack. We've nurtured the island back to life and turned it over to the environmentalists that are the current caretakers, but we continue to watch over it. It's still our home." He turned back to Jahir and offered his hand. "You are welcome to return with me, my love."

Jahir looked at Chirag's hand and back at him in confusion. "You still want me after everything I did? The lives I destroyed." Jahir shook his head. "You've always been a romantic fool, Chirag."

"You acted out in pain and have suffered mightily for it these past six hundred years. Allow my forgiveness to ease that pain. It's what Fatima would have wanted. What her heart still aches for. Come home, Jahir." Chirag still held his hand out, patiently waiting for Jahir to take it.

Naima would never forget what he'd done to Adnan, their people, and their home but Chirag was right. Jahir had been just as much a prisoner of his revenge as she and Aliya had. Maybe he deserved to have peace as well.

Jahir once again looked unsure of himself. He raised his hand, lowered it, frowned at it, closed his eyes, and after a few moments, breathed a weary sigh before finally accepting Chirag's hand. "I don't deserve your forgiveness and love or Fatima's heart."

Chirag pulled him close, wrapping his arms around him. "She loved me, but her heart always beat strongest for you. If you don't deserve it, then who does?"

Jahir's arms tightened around Chirag, and just before a shimmering silver cloud enveloped them, she saw a single tear drop from the corner of his eye, then they were gone without even a wave of farewell.

"Well, that was anticlimactic," Marcus said.

Elise shook her head. "Only you could ruin such a beautiful moment."

"Sorry, I just expected to be a witness to a dramatic battle between two powerful beings, not the end of some real-life romance novel."

Naima smiled, because she agreed, but she was also relieved that it hadn't ended that way. There was no telling what destruction would've come of such a battle.

"I, for one, am glad Chirag was able to talk Jahir down," Malik said, looking fully recovered as he stood and wrapped an arm around Jasmine's waist. She did the same and laid her head on his shoulder.

Naima turned to Elise and noticed her brow furrowed in thought. "Is something wrong?"

She hesitated in answering, then gave Naima a smile and shook her head. "It's nothing. I just can't believe all of this is over."

"Yes, can we go home now? My old heart can't take much more excitement," Grammy said.

After Jasmine did a cleansing for Malik and Elise to insure there were no remnants of Jahir's dark magic and Aliya's presence, they all left the shop in much better spirits than when they arrived.

Elise looked down at Naima cuddled into her side as they watched a marathon of one of the Housewives shows that had become Naima's obsession. It had been a few months since the curse had been broken and Naima had adapted to being a human quite well. Elise could tell she sometimes missed the convenience of her magic, but she had been so fascinated with doing human things prior to losing it that it made the transition much easier. Elise was still treated to breakfast every morning, dinner ready when she arrived home, and wonderful nights of passion.

While Elise was at work, Naima spent her days learning the city, until several days ago when she announced she wanted to find a job. Elise encouraged her, even tried to help her figure out what she would like to do. They narrowed her choices down to chef or librarian, but after a visit to the Museum of Natural History, Naima found her calling. Having pretty much been a witness to so many major events in history, she became a docent. It was unpaid, but Elise was doing well enough to support them and if Naima was happy, so was she.

She still found everything that happened unbelievable. One day, she'd been cleaning a lamp, and Naima swept into her life in a whirlwind of mysticism and magic. Now she was living a life she'd never imagined happening with a woman she'd never imagined loving. It was all too good to be true and sometimes, late at night, while she watched Naima sleep beside her, a little voice in Elise's head would tell her that what she had wouldn't last.

If she didn't know any better, she would've sworn it was Aliya trying to mess with her head, but there had been no sign of the princess since the day the curse was broken. Elise just chalked it up to the years she spent swearing she would never find the true love everyone craved because she was incapable of romantic love. Now that she had, her subconscious still hadn't caught up with her heart.

After the show was over, they were getting ready for bed when Elise's cell phone rang. "Who could that be calling this late?" She picked her phone up off the nightstand and was surprised to see her brother's name. "Marcus? What's up? Is everyone okay?"

"Hey, sis, yes, we're all fine. I was calling to see if you were okay." He sounded relieved to hear her voice.

"Yeah, I'm good. Why? Are you feeling something?"

"Yeah, something's been off all day. Then I felt the need to call you, so I figured it had to be something going on with you."

Elise didn't like that one bit. Marcus's intuition had never been wrong. Naima watched her with concern. Despite the loss of her jinn magic, she and Elise were still just as sensitive to what the other was feeling as they were before. Elise tried to give her an encouraging smile so she wouldn't worry but knew it would be pointless.

"Do you know what it might be?" Elise asked Marcus.

"No. I called Grammy just in case and she's also felt off today regarding you. She didn't want to worry you until she was sure what it was. Do you want me to come by?"

"No, it's too late for you to be driving in from Brooklyn. I'm fine. If anything is wrong, Naima knows how to reach you all."

"Are you sure? Whatever is coming feels very wrong." Elise didn't like the fear in his tone, but there was nothing she could do about it. Even when they were kids, she couldn't ease his worry when his premonitions kicked in.

"Positive. Just keep your phone on in case we need to call you, okay?"

"Okay," he said hesitantly. "Love you, sis."

"Love you too, broski."

"What did he say? Is everything okay?" Naima asked.

"I'm sure it will be. If nothing's happened yet, it probably won't." Elise wasn't sure if she was trying to convince Naima or herself.

They climbed into bed, Naima pulled Elise protectively within the circle of her arms, and the warmth of her body quickly lulled Elise to sleep.

Naima was awakened by Elise's hand inching its way up her leg beneath her nightgown and her teeth nibbling gently at her earlobe. The room was still dark with only the streetlamps dimly shining through the window. She smiled, loving being awakened by Elise so pleasurably no matter what time of night or day it was.

"And here I thought you were asleep," Naima said, helping Elise by pulling her nightgown completely off and tossing it aside.

Elise sat up, gave her a sexy smile, and pulled her nightgown over her head to join Naima's on the floor. She then straddled Naima's hips and lowered her head for a kiss. The immediacy and depth of her desire for Elise always surprised Naima. The passion of their kiss went from zero to sixty in a matter of seconds. When Naima reached up to touch Elise, she captured Naima's hands and pressed them down on either side of her head. Naima looked at her curiously. Elise shook her head with a mischievous smile and lowered it again until their lips met. Her grip on Naima's wrists was strong, almost painful. Her kiss even became rough when she bit Naima's lip.

"Elise, you're hurting me." She attempted to pull her wrists free, causing Elise's hold to tighten even more.

Elise hovered above her, their faces just inches from each other. "Has becoming human made you weak, my love? I remember you used to enjoy a little rough play every now and then."

Naima looked into Elise's eyes and didn't recognize the darkness that loomed there. She didn't need her powers to feel the evil coming off her.

"Aliya?"

"Aww, were you expecting someone else?" Aliya said with a pout.

Naima struggled in earnest now to no avail. Aliya's grip was like bands of steel. "How? What have you done with Elise?"

Aliya laughed. "Did you all really think it would be that easy to get rid of me? I've had six hundred years to prepare for this moment."

"Chirag and Elise said you had accepted your fate. That you were ready to move on." Fear and desperation like she'd never known surged through Naima as she realized she was completely defenseless without her powers. It was the first time since giving them up that she'd regretted doing so.

Aliya laughed. "Chirag had no idea who he was dealing with and that amateur spiritualist of yours was clueless. I never left. I had sunk so deep down into Elise's subconscious that she didn't even know it was me sending up doubts about your love since that day." She frowned. "Unfortunately, it didn't work. It seems you two really are heart mates. No doubts I buried in her head stuck long enough to take root and influence her feelings for you. Which is why I had to take a more proactive approach."

"What did you do with her!" Naima shouted angrily.

"Ah, there's that fire I remember so well. Too bad it's wasted on the concern of someone else. Don't worry, she's tucked safely away unaware of what's going on. It was always much easier to subdue her while she's asleep than when she's awake and aware of what's happening." Aliya released her grip on Naima's wrist and sat up, still straddling her waist.

"What happened to you, Aliya? What's made you so cruel and heartless?" Naima asked.

Aliya gave a bitter laugh. "You mean other than being trapped in countless lifetimes of people who had no appreciation for the gift of life they were given? Let's see, a family who kept me trapped like a prized pet because they underestimated my ability to keep myself safe, my wife spending more time by my brother's side than with me, a man we treated like family brought death and destruction to our home, and when I'm finally reunited with the love of my life, I find that she has set me aside and is in love with someone else. That about covers it, don't you think?"

After hearing it directly from Aliya, Naima couldn't blame her for being angry, but for her to have such an extreme personality change made her wonder if such darkness had always been within Aliya and she had been too blind by love to notice.

Aliya gave her a sympathetic frown. "Poor Naima. Not quite the reunion either of us expected after so long, is it?" She shifted off Naima's lap and hopped off the bed. "I'm hungry."

Aliya didn't even bother putting clothes on as she strolled out of the bedroom. Naima quickly got up, picked up the closest nightgown off the floor, not caring if it was hers or Elise's, and followed her. It seemed Aliya must have been seeing things through Elise's consciousness because she knew exactly where to go. Naima found her rummaging through the refrigerator. She squealed with delight as she held up a container of dates Naima had just bought Elise that morning. She popped one in her mouth, closed her eyes, and chewed slowly, as if savoring the taste.

Naima sat at the island. "What are your plans, Aliya?"

Aliya looked annoyed at being interrupted. "To live the life that I was denied."

"And how do you plan to do that? Elise has a family, a business, a whole life of her own. Do you really think no one is going to try and stop you?"

Aliya waved her hand dismissively. "A minor issue that will not be a concern once I'm gone." She put the dates back in the refrigerator and went back to the bedroom.

Naima stayed close on her heels. "What do you mean once you're gone?"

Aliya turned and looked at Naima as if she were a silly child. "Did you really think I would stay here? I had hoped that you and I would travel the world together as we once dreamed, but now that you no longer love me and you've given up your powers, there's nothing here for me." She walked over to Elise's closet, pulled a suitcase out, and began searching through her clothes.

Naima couldn't let her leave. Once she did there was no way for her to save Elise. She grabbed Aliya's arm. "I won't let you leave here with Elise."

With the same inhuman strength that she'd held Naima down on the bed, Aliya shoved her across the room into the wall. Naima gasped for the breath that was knocked out of her as she struggled to stand.

"In spite of your betrayal, I don't want to hurt you, Naima, but I will if you try to stop me," Aliya said before returning to her packing.

The apartment's alarm screamed, then quickly chirped off.

"Naima! Elise!" she heard a male voice call.

"In the bedroom!" Naima answered as she watched Aliya look from the doorway to her with a scowl.

Within seconds, Marcus and Grammy stood in the doorway.

"Good. You're okay." Marcus said as he walked toward Aliya.

"STOP! It's not Elise!" Naima said.

Marcus halted halfway into the room, then looked at Naima and back at Aliya in confusion.

"Isn't it ironic that we both had twin brothers?" Aliya walked up to him and stroked his cheek. She cocked her head to the side and gazed at Marcus curiously. "I wonder if I could bring Adnan back through you? I do know a few resurrection spells."

Marcus's eyes widened in horror, and he backed away. "I thought you were gone."

"You thought wrong," Aliya said with a grin. She looked at Naima. "So, you called for backup? Do you really think you three could stop me?"

"No, but we know a few people who can," Grammy said with a grin as three clouds of silver, black, and gray swirled around Aliya, effectively trapping her in place.

Elise lounged in her own personal cabana on a white sand beach with water so clear and blue it was like looking through tinted glass. This was one of the many reasons she loved coming back to Nosy Be. It felt like her own personal island paradise. Like she was home. A feeling that something wasn't right came over her and she gazed up and down the beach, surprised not to see any other people. The resort was never really crowded, but there were usually at least a dozen or so other guests enjoying the quiet and seclusion. Curious, she left her cabana and walked back toward the main building. She passed a few staff who greeted her with a smile and a nod but no other guests. When she stopped at the front desk, there was no clerk, and no one responded when she called out. Elise looked around the lobby…she was alone.

She began to panic, then a little voice in her head told her, *"Just breathe. You're probably just tired from all the sun and need a nap."* She suddenly felt very tired and went to her room to do just that.

When Elise woke up it was dark, and she heard music. A familiar melody she remembered being played on a flute by the man who sold her a plastic lamp during her first trip to Nosy Be with her family. It called to her as if it were whispering her name beneath the soft notes.

She still wore her bathing suit from earlier and changed into a sundress and sandals before heading out of her room through the private patio doors that lead right out onto the beach. Just a few feet from her patio sat two men, one with dark hair and an ebony complexion and the other with white hair and a golden complexion. Like yin and yang, they were opposites of the other but somehow belonged together. The darker one played a lyre harp while the other played a wood flute. They sat upon cushions on a large Turkish rug and a third cushion sat vacant between them. Elise had a feeling that the third seat was meant for her, so she sat down as they continued to play for a few more minutes. Elise felt soothed by the music and the men's presence. As if she had been in danger before and didn't know it until she entered the safety of their little gathering.

"I know you, don't I?" she asked the white-bearded man when their music ended. "You sold me a toy lamp when I was younger."

He gave her a kind smile. "Yes. I'm Chirag and this is my friend Jahir."

Elise gave both a smile and a nod. "It's nice to meet you. Are you guests here?"

"Not really, but we're here to take you home," Chirag said.

"But I just got here...I think." Elise gazed at him in confusion.

"Do you remember how you got here?" Jahir asked.

Elise turned to him. His smile was kind as well, but there was something about him that seemed familiar enough for her not to trust him. Like he'd lied or done something wrong to her, but she couldn't remember what it was.

"By the ferry from the mainland, like I always do," Elise said.

"Do you know how long you've been here?" Chirag asked.

Elise began to answer, then realized she honestly didn't know. "Why are you asking me all these questions?" She stood, ready to run if needed.

"We are not going to hurt you, Elise. We're here to help you escape," Chirag said, his understanding and patient gaze just like the mall Santa during her and Marcus's first visit and she wouldn't leave her mother's side out of fear of the bearded stranger.

"Escape? I'm on vacation, why would I need to escape?"

As soon as she said the words a wariness came over her as she remembered how empty the resort was of other guests. The handful of staff she'd seen whose faces all resembled different versions of the same person. She gazed around her and noticed they were the only people on the beach and the resort building was now dark. Not even the tiki torches along the patios of the guest rooms were lit.

"This isn't right?" she said, looking down at Chirag.

He stood and grasped her hands. "Remember, Elise." His voice was calm and soothing.

He'd said they were there to take her home, to rescue her. From what? Then it all came rushing back to her. She'd been in bed with Naima one minute and was on the beach in Nosy Be the next. How was that possible? Did Naima still have powers and brought them here? If she had, then wouldn't she be with her? Then Elise remembered the few resort staff and who they resembled. Aliya. Even the men had her regal and dark features but in male form.

"Aliya is still here?" she asked Chirag, trying to keep the rising panic from taking over.

"Yes. It seems she was much stronger than we anticipated," Chirag said with a regretful smile.

"You think?" Elise said sarcastically, allowing anger to replace her fear.

"That's it. Let your anger strengthen you. You'll need it for the fight ahead," Jahir said as he stood and walked to stand near Chirag.

Elise eyed him warily. "Why are you here? You caused all this trouble in the first place."

"I like her. She's feisty," Jahir said with a playful wink.

"He's here to help. Aliya has experience with dark magic, and Jahir is a very powerful black jinn. I'm a bit out of practice in that department," Chirag admitted.

"We don't have much time." Jahir's head was cocked to the side as if he were listening for something.

Elise noticed the sound of the waves crashing on the shore was louder than before. She looked out toward the water and saw the white foam caps churning in the darkness. "She's coming, isn't she?"

Jahir nodded.

"Is Naima safe?" she asked Chirag.

"Worried about you but other than that, she's fine," he said.

Elise nodded. She was tired of Aliya and all her drama. She just wanted to live her life in peace without worrying one day to the next about the soul of some vengeful long-gone princess completely taking over her body and life. Elise felt the heat from the small fire they had been sitting around grow more intense. She looked at both Chirag and Jahir, then all three turned toward the fire. The flames grew higher, and the heat had them backing away to keep from being scorched. A feminine form appeared in the flames and Aliya walked out dressed in all the finery your typical storybook Arabian princess would wear. Silk and satin from head to toe, jewels and gems from the tiara on her head to the toe rings on her bare feet. She also shone with an unearthly glow that wasn't from the fire which had died down once she stepped from it.

"She definitely knows how to make an entrance," Jahir said, more sarcasm than admiration in his tone.

"Did you really think trying this little trick would work again?" she asked Chirag in amusement.

"Not alone, which is why I brought a little help."

Aliya gave Jahir a look of disgust. "Neither of you holds any power here."

Jahir grinned at Aliya. "You're right, but we can put our power behind the one who does." He and Chirag turned to look at Elise.

"Despite her presence, ultimately this is your domain, Elise. You must be the one to expel her and take back your mind and body," Jahir explained.

"I guess there's no wishing this away," Elise said to the two jinn.

"Unfortunately, no. But as the kids say, you got this," Chirag said. He and Jahir gave her an encouraging smile.

Elise almost chuckled, but the ominous presence standing nearby still lit from the fire's glow she'd walked out of dimmed the humor from the moment. She took a deep breath and turned to Aliya. "Let's do this."

CHAPTER THIRTEEN

Aliya quirked a brow and smiled in amusement at Elise. "Yes, let's do this. You know it doesn't have to be this way. Just let go and I can make all your fantasies real."

Elise glared at Aliya. "About as real as this moment is now? You want to trap me in my own head while you traipse around in my body like it's a coat for you to wear? No, not happening. You need to go," she said angrily. She was tired of Aliya's games and just wanted her life back.

Aliya slowly sauntered toward her, stopping within half a step from Elise. "I just need your body. The shelter and fantasy world I've been offering you has been a courtesy." The look in her eyes and her wicked smile promised she would no longer offer such niceties.

Elise was frightened but it wasn't of Aliya. It was of losing herself to the determined princess. Despite that fear, she met Aliya's cold eyes without hesitation. "This is MY body, MY mind, and MY soul. I refuse to let some spoiled, irrelevant princess take any of that away from me."

A breeze kicked up, ruffling Aliya's long hair and silks, her eyes began to glow with an unearthly light, and if looks could kill, Elise would probably have been burned alive. She stood her ground, even as Aliya began to hover a few inches above it.

"You dare speak to me that way? You took the woman of my heart and tried to relegate me to the afterlife before I'd even had a chance to truly live my life! I'm done playing games with you, Elise! I'm taking what I'm rightfully due!" Aliya's voice reverberated around them.

A pain so sharp it felt as if someone had shoved a hot poker into her head had Elise gasping for breath and collapsing to her knees. She felt two sets of strong hands lift and hold her up. Elise could feel Chirag's and Jahir's strength seeping into her like the sun's warmth against her skin earlier.

"*We're here, honey,*" she heard Grammy's voice in her head.

"*I got you, sis!*" followed Marcus's declaration.

She didn't know how they knew she needed them, but she was comforted and strengthened by their presence as well.

"*I love you, Elise,*" Naima's voice said softly.

As softly as it was spoken, it seemed to reverberate just as loudly as Aliya's voice had, but instead of causing more pain, it soothed the one she was suffering. Elise took in all the love that was offered to her and collected it around her like a cloak of armor. She stood, gathered her strength, and stepped away from Chirag and Jahir. She gazed up at Aliya, who now levitated at least two feet off the sand and was beautifully magnificent in her fury and not looking at all like the gentle, loving, kind princess Naima had described her to be. Elise had the feeling this was the true Aliya. The one she'd kept hidden from those she loved. Aliya grinned as if she knew what Elise had been thinking which, considering they were in her head, she probably did.

"You're correct," Aliya said, confirming she'd read Elise's thoughts. "Naima knew but she refused to see the truth. I truly did love her, but I let her continue to believe what she wanted about me. My family had no idea. Not even Adnan could see me as anything other than his intelligent but equally frivolous and silly younger sister, which was fine for my purposes. I could've been co-ruler, but I wanted my freedom too much. I wanted to travel the world fighting my own battles. Sitting on the throne would take that all away. Unfortunately, I did too good a job because no one wanted to risk the life of the Heart of Akiba, which they'd begun to call me."

"So let me get this straight. You grew up in a palace with servants at your beck and call, a whole island of people practically worshiping the ground you walk on, and were surrounded by people who loved and adored you so much they would do anything to keep you safe, and you're angry about that? Maybe you do fit in this century after all," Elise said sarcastically.

Aliya's anger literally glowed like the fire she'd walked out of. "Are you trying to get yourself placed into a living hell in your own mind? If so, you're doing an excellent job," Jahir whispered harshly.

Elise ignored him. She was just as angry as Aliya and no longer cared about trying to appeal to the kind heart everyone believed she had. She stalked up to Aliya's floating form, grabbed her leg, and yanked her down. The princess seemed caught off guard by the physical attack and landed with a thud on the sandy ground. The impact caused the scenery around them to wobble like a curtain disturbed by a breeze. Elise didn't give Aliya time to recover. She continued her physical attack by grabbing her by her luxurious hair and dragging her toward the shoreline, which flickered from a watery horizon to the rubble of Akiba and back. Aliya squirmed, cursed, and screamed trying to escape Elise's grasp, but she was at least a foot taller than the petite princess and worked out regularly. It was a fight, but she managed to drag Aliya far enough out into the water to shove her head beneath the waves.

Unfortunately, the time it took Elise to do that gave Aliya time to recover enough to gather her own strength. With an ear-piercing scream, she used whatever powers she had to toss Elise a good twenty feet back onto the beach, but as her body twisted and turned mid-flight, she realized the beach was no longer there. In its place was the rubble of Akiba and she was heading for a large, jagged block of stone that was going to go straight through her chest once she landed.

"This is my head. I control what happens," she said to herself, then screamed, "STOP STOP STOP!"

It took a moment for her to realize she'd stopped moving and that she wasn't impaled on the stone but hovering mere inches above it. Elise closed her eyes with a sigh of relief. "Okay, girl, she only has power because you're allowing her to have it. Take back control." She gave herself a little pep talk as she felt her feet touch the ground.

Aliya stood across the clearing from her, her hair a wet, tangled mess, clothes dripping and hanging off her. They faced each other like two prize fighters sizing the other up. Elise couldn't see them, but she knew Chirag and Jahir were nearby.

"How many others have you done this to?" Elise asked.

"Too many to count over the centuries. Some were clueless, others fought it, and then there were those who broke much sooner than I expected," Aliya said coldly.

The rubble began to shift and move until they were standing in the throne room as if it had never fallen and sunlight shone on the marble floors from the windows and balcony. Elise held back a smug grin as a flicker of surprise registered on Aliya's face. This was not the time to get cocky and underestimate what Aliya could do. Naima had told her that Aliya had jinn heritage as well as knowledge of witchcraft and black magic. Since she didn't have that advantage, Elise chose another route. She was connected to Aliya just as much as Aliya was connected to her, which meant that if Aliya could delve into and use her memories of the resort in Nosy Be to control her, then she could do the same with Aliya's memories.

Elise closed her eyes and focused her thoughts on Aliya and Akiba. The memory of the day all their lives changed came quickly to mind. She snagged one memory from that day then opened her eyes to find the throne room shifting around them. They stood on the edge of the very moment Naima and Adnan had appeared before Jahir had used Malik to destroy their world. Elise gazed over at Aliya who looked at the scene, frozen in time, in disbelief.

"How?" she asked.

"Turnabout is fair play. This is my mind and you're an unwanted guest in it. I may not have your magical knowledge, but I also won't make it easy for you to just take over." Elise began the scene just the way she remembered seeing it while she was under hypnosis and had been brought back to this memory by Aliya's connection.

"NOOO!" Aliya screamed just as Malik picked up Adnan by his neck.

Elise felt no pleasure at the pain in Aliya's eyes as she prepared to watch the moment her brother died. She couldn't imagine having to endure watching the same thing happen to Marcus. She hit a mental pause button on the scene and walked toward Aliya until she stood directly in front of her, blocking the tragedy from view.

"I don't want to hurt you, Aliya. I only want to free us both from this back and forth because I swear to you, if you continue to attempt to take over my life, I will continue to fight you, to bring you back here, to this moment, repeatedly. I don't care if it drives us both mad, you will not enjoy the life you steal from me." Elise stepped aside and restarted the moment. She stood beside Aliya, watching it all play out.

Aliya screamed again and quickly levitated off the floor mumbling and moving her hands as if she were writing in the air. Elise could see symbols she didn't recognize but knew had to have been some type of spells lighting up and the scene begin to fade away. She knew Aliya was trying to stop it, but Elise was determined. She didn't know witchcraft or spells, but she wanted to survive, to live, to be with her family and Naima again. She reached out for their love and strength, for Chirag's and Jahir's magic, closed her eyes and focused on the memory, rewinding it each time Aliya tried to make it go away. After several attempts of this going back and forth, Elise began to grow tired, and her head ached. She looked at Aliya and noticed that she no longer levitated and the spells she was still attempting to draw were fading. She covered her eyes as Adnan's death, no longer paused by her attempts, played out. The sound of his neck snapping reverberated around the room and Elise felt sick at the sound. Then something unexpected happened. Shortly after Adnan's body fell lifeless to the ground, the scene shimmered away and he stood, alone in the middle of the room, looking sadly toward Aliya.

"Aliya," Elise said warily. She didn't respond; she just stood, covering her eyes and weeping. Elise tried again. "Aliya, you might want to look."

"No, please, no more," she whimpered pitifully.

Elise could only watch as Adnan walked toward Aliya, gently grasped her hands, and pulled them away from her face. "My beloved sister, look at me."

Elise had no idea what was going on because this wasn't her doing. She gazed around the room and saw Chirag and Jahir standing near the throne looking just as bewildered. When they met her gaze they shook their heads, answering her unasked question. This wasn't their doing either. Then, for just a moment, she humorously wondered if her head would explode from overcrowding with her, Aliya, the larger-than-life jinn lovers, and now a long dead king.

Aliya gazed up at Adnan in confusion then looked at Elise who shook her head in denial of having anything to do with his presence.

Adnan gazed lovingly down at Aliya. "You brought me here, sister. I've always been near, right here." He placed his hand over her heart. "Your pain is my pain, and for so many years I've felt you struggle from one life to the next not being able to do anything about it because I was also trapped. But then Malik and his friend freed me from the hell he had unwittingly sent me to and now I'm here to free you from yours."

"But I don't want to go. There's so much that was stolen from me that I deserve to get back," Aliya said bitterly.

Adnan gave Aliya a patient smile. "You can have all of that back. Your family, your people, they're all awaiting you in the afterlife. Your time here is over. You were freed when the spell was broken yet you ignored our call when we came for you. You've always been the more headstrong of the two of us so I knew bringing you home wouldn't be easy, which is why I'm here."

"You're here to escort me to the afterlife?" Aliya asked.

Adnan nodded.

She shook her head and pulled her hand from Adnan's grasp. "No, I won't go. I'm owed a lifetime!"

"Aliya, you lived your lifetime. This one is not yours to take."

"You can't make me go," Aliya said like a petulant child.

"You're right, I can't. You can stay here, battling for a life that isn't yours with a woman whose spirit and will is much stronger than you think, or you can come with me and be with the people who love you and see the world not as a malevolent spirit but as one free of the bitterness and resentment that has darkened you for so long."

Aliya looked as if his words were getting through, and Elise felt a flicker of hope but didn't want to feed too much stock in it in case she was wrong.

"Yes, see the world as a free spirit not bound by time and space or hindered by a body that will grow old and brittle over time," Adnan said.

Elise was a bit insulted by the old and brittle comment, but she kept it to herself. The best thing for her to do was not draw any attention to herself while Aliya was struggling with what to do. As if she'd read Elise's mind, which, once again, they were in it so it wouldn't be a surprise, she gazed over at her as if seeing her for the first time. Elise felt self-conscious at the way Aliya looked her up and down, frowning in distaste as if she could see Elise's body growing old and brittle before her eyes. Elise stood a little straighter and taller and Aliya grinned knowingly before looking back at Adnan.

"There is a darkness within me, Adnan, that pulls me in a direction I find too tempting to let go. I don't know if I ever can," Aliya said.

Adnan offered her his hand. "Take my hand, beloved sister, and we will find a way to heal you together."

Aliya looked from his offered hand to Elise, who felt like a tempting treat under her dark gaze.

"I will fight you every step of the way," Elise reminded her, just in case she was leaning toward staying.

"Such a tempting offer," Aliya said with a wicked grin. Then a look of sadness came over her. "Will you please tell Naima that I have, and always will, love her. That I hope she lives a happy life?"

Elise nodded. "I'll tell her. I'll also do my best to make her happy."

"You better or I will return and make your life a living hell," Aliya said with a serious expression.

"I don't doubt it," Elise said, just a little worried she meant what she said.

Aliya reached for Adnan's hand, then stopped and turned toward Chirag and Jahir. "I'm also watching you, jinni. From this moment on, if I learn of just one life you have used your evil to manipulate, I will come for you with a vengeance you have never known."

Elise assumed she'd directed her threat at Jahir because his eyes widened fearfully, and his face paled noticeably.

"You were always one for the dramatics, sister," Adnan said humorously.

Aliya gave him a wink and took his hand. They walked toward the balcony and disappeared in the rays of sun shining through the open door. Elise watched for a moment, just to make sure this wasn't a trick, but something deep within her told her Aliya was finally gone. She sighed with relief and met Chirag and Jahir halfway across the room as they walked toward her.

"Can we go home now?" she asked.

Chirag smiled happily and offered his hand. Jahir still looked shaken by Aliya's threat, but he offered his hand as well. Elise placed her hands in theirs and the palace faded away as darkness surrounded them.

❖

"I think she's waking up," a familiar voice said.

Elise's head felt like it did after a night of too much wine. She groaned and slowly blinked her eyes open to find she was lying in bed with Naima sitting on one side of her, Grammy on the other, Marcus standing near Grammy grinning happily, and Chirag, Jahir, Malik, and Jasmine crowded around the foot of her bed. She felt like Dorothy at the end of *The Wizard of Oz*.

"How are you, honey?" Grammy asked. Elise realized it had been her voice she'd first heard upon waking up.

"Like I just had a battle for my very soul." Elise flinched from the pain in her head when she tried to chuckle at her own joke. "How long have I been out?"

"Almost a whole day. We wanted to take you to the hospital, but Jinn One and Jinn Two over there," Marcus pointed his thumb at Chirag and Jahir, "put up one of their invisible shields to keep us out. They didn't let us near you until an hour ago."

"It was to protect you in case anything went wrong," Chirag said, meeting Marcus's annoyed expression with a grin.

Looking at Chirag and Jahir together, Elise found it hard to believe that Chirag had been an evil jinni once. The few times she'd been around him he'd been so jovial while Jahir seemed to have a permanently dark, brooding face. She looked at Naima whose eyes were bloodshot and tired.

"I'm so sorry I couldn't help. If I hadn't given up my magic, I would've sensed what was going on and been able to stop her," Naima said, tears gathering in her eyes.

Elise cupped her cheek and wiped away a fallen tear. "Don't blame yourself for this. I thought she was gone, let my guard down, and she took advantage of it. Besides, in the end, it was always up to me to be the one to stop her. There was nothing you could've done."

Naima leaned forward and pressed her lips to Elise's. The kiss was soft and brief. "I love you," she whispered against Elise's lips.

The words trickled softly between her lips, down her throat and filled her with a comforting warmth. "I love you too," she whispered in return.

"Jeez, could you two at least wait for us to leave?" Marcus said, making a gagging noise.

Elise and Naima chuckled. She turned to Grammy and Marcus. "I felt your presence while I was stuck in my head. Thanks for listening to your intuition and not me when I told you everything was fine."

Grammy held Elise's hand and brushed a stray curl away from her face. "We may not be powerful jinn, but our family has the power of love. As long as we have that, we'll always be here when you need us."

Marcus sat on the bed next to Grammy and placed his hand on top of theirs. "I know I joke a lot, but there's nothing funny about how much I love you and how far I'll go to protect you, sis."

"Same here, broski." They knew how they truly felt about each other and rarely considered the need to express it in words, which made moments like this more special. Elise looked toward the end of the bed and smiled in appreciation at Jasmine. "I'm assuming I have you to thank for Adnan's presence?"

Jasmine took Malik's hand and smiled up at him before looking back at Elise. "With a little help."

"Thank you both." She looked back at Chirag and Jahir. "I also can't thank you two enough. Without you I would've never known there was something wrong and been trapped in my own fantasy for a long time. How did you know what was happening?" She looked at Naima. "Are you still able to communicate with your grandfather?"

"No, I was just as surprised to see them as you probably were," Naima said.

Everyone turned to look at the two jinn. Chirag was smiling broadly and Jahir looked bored with the whole thing.

"Jahir sensed there was something off, so we kept an eye on you just in case," Chirag explained.

"You've been watching us? Like the WHOLE time?" Elise said, her face burning remembering the very intimate moments she and Naima have shared.

Chirag chuckled. "We were not physically watching you. We just kept in tune to what was going on. Naima may no longer be a jinn, but she is still my granddaughter, which is a bond that will never break. If she's in distress then I'll know it, which is how we knew something was wrong and arrived to find Aliya attacking her."

Elise looked at Naima in concern. "She used me to hurt you?"

Naima gave her a reassuring smile. "It was nothing. I'm fine and it wasn't your fault."

Elise couldn't help but feel it was her fault since she foolishly believed Aliya would just leave and that it was her hands that may have hurt Naima. She had become very protective of her since she'd given up her powers to become human and to know that she could've seriously hurt Naima, whether she was in control or not, was devastating.

"No use getting yourself worked up over something you had no control over," Grammy said. "You're both safe now and the catalyst for all your troubles is gone." She quirked a brow. "She is gone, right?"

Elise gave her a reassuring smile. "Yes, she's gone."

"You're sure? She lied the first time, what makes you think she hasn't again?" Marcus asked.

She understood their doubt. She would be skeptical as well if she didn't feel deep down within her soul that Aliya had moved on. "This time I can feel it. There's always been a strange heaviness deep within me that I never told anyone about. I no longer feel it."

"Well, we'll keep an eye on you for any strange behavior just in case," Grammy said.

"We've also got the jinn crew on speed dial," Marcus said in amusement.

Elise felt a little bad for Chirag and Jahir. She knew her brother well enough to imagine him prank calling two of the most powerful jinn in the world.

"Well, now that all that drama has ended, I say we celebrate." Elise sat up in bed, only now realizing she was wearing a pair of silk pajamas she'd never seen before, which wasn't what she'd worn to bed. She looked at Naima in confusion.

Naima's face darkened with a blush. "I'll explain later."

Elise shook her head. "You know what, it doesn't matter. The only thing that matters is that it's over, you're free and we're all together.

Chirag insisted on providing a feast, but it wasn't quite what Elise would've expected from the jinni. Like his granddaughter, Chirag loved to cook. He wasn't thrilled about grocery shopping, so he did use his magic to shop out of thin air and he and Naima whipped up an American and Moroccan fusion brunch that would put a restaurant to shame. Elise's apartment was filled with more people than she'd ever had there. Grammy, Marcus, Naima, Jasmine, Malik, Chirag, and Jahir were gathered around her small dinette set and in the living room enjoying a meal, talking and laughing as if half the group weren't from a magical realm and that the past months' unbelievable events hadn't happened. Even Jahir's brooding expression finally collapsed as he let loose a guffaw at something Grammy said.

Marcus, who was sitting beside her, moved his chair closer. "So, has my little sis finally found love?"

Elise gazed across the table at Naima who seemed to be in a deep conversation with Malik. "Yes, I think I have."

"I'm relieved to hear you're not the aromantic you thought you were. Gives me hope that maybe there's someone out there for me. They wouldn't need to be a magical being like the love of your life, but I wouldn't turn them away if they were, so if Naima happens to know someone…" he said, grinning.

"Broski, I think you might be even more than a jinni could handle," Elise said in amusement.

"Only one way to find out," he gave Elise a wink. "Hey, Jahir, you got any more of those magic lamps?"

Elise chuckled and gazed over at Naima again who was watching her with such a tender look that it made her heart skip a beat. She could only hope Marcus would be lucky enough to find a love as magical and real as she found with her own personal jinni.

Epilogue

Naima awakened to the warmth of the sun shining through the open patio doors of their suite of rooms. She eased out of bed so as not to wake Elise and padded quietly out onto the patio which looked out over a beautiful garden, a large infinity pool, and the lush forest of Nosy Be. She could see the white stones of what was left of the Akiban kingdom's palace in the distance and felt at peace knowing that the last of the souls left from its destruction were now also resting at peace thanks to Malik and Jasmine. Jahir and Chirag had also asked forgiveness and made peace with the ancestors of Akiba and had become the official keepers of the enchanted island and the heart of their beloved whose magic and spirit kept it thriving.

This was her first time back to the island since she'd been cursed to the lamp. She and Elise had just arrived the day before and were staying at Chirag and Jahir's home, which Elise had called a mini palace because of its grand scale. They had been given a whole suite of rooms on the third floor consisting of a large bedroom, living area, and a bathroom with a bathing pool instead of tub and a shower big enough to fit their whole bathroom from home in. Chirag and Jahir had the entire second floor for their private rooms and there were smaller guest rooms on the first floor. The house was built into a cliffside and practically blended into the landscape. It reminded Naima of the ancestral Puebloan cliff dwellings in the American Southwest, but with modern and luxurious amenities. Perfect for two over-the-top jinn.

Naima heard rustling behind her, and a moment later a pair of arms were wrapped around her waist and a soft kiss was placed on the nape of her neck.

"Good morning," Elise whispered in her ear.

Naima smiled. "Good morning, my love."

"I couldn't decide which view was more beautiful, my bride-to-be's bare backside or the colorful sunrise, so I thought I'd enjoy a close-up of both." Elise reached down and cupped one of Naima's butt cheeks.

Even after a year together their passion hadn't waned in the least. Naima sighed in pleasure, arched her back to give Elise more to grasp, and was rewarded with Elise's long fingers sliding down the cleft of her behind and dipping into her sex, which had begun gathering moisture the moment she'd heard Elise getting up.

"I like how you're always ready for me," Elise said as she slowly delved her fingers in and out of Naima's inner lips.

Naima whimpered in pleasure and almost cried out when Elise tweaked her nipple with her other hand.

"Will you come for me, Naima?" Elise asked.

"Yes," Naima said breathlessly.

"Turn around. I want to see your beautiful face."

Naima did as she was told and turned in Elise's arms. She felt a momentary sense of loss when Elise's fingers stopped their intimate caress, but she didn't have to wait long for their return. Elise leaned forward and took a nipple into her mouth as her fingers thrust deeper within Naima's sex and slowly withdrew. She repeated the thrust and slow withdrawal until Naima could feel her inner walls convulse hungrily around Elise's fingers. She tried to prolong her orgasm, but Elise played her like a fine-tuned instrument. She knew just the right chord to stroke to make Naima sing her joy to the heavens. Afterward, her legs began to give out, but Elise was there to hold her up and lead her to a nearby divan where they cuddled together as the sun continued its ascent.

Since their first days together after Naima had been summoned from the lamp, her role as a warrior and protector had given way to something softer, feminine, and vulnerable. She enjoyed not having to worry about when the next battle might happen, or what the next crisis might be. Surprisingly, even during her time in the lamp, she held on to that mentality doing her best to protect and advise her summoners just as she protected Akiba and advised Adnan. She would still not hesitate to put her life on the line for Elise, and she knew the feeling was mutual. She and Elise were equals. Wanting to be seen as equals was her main reason for choosing to become human, the other was not wanting to watch Elise grow older while she slowly aged then spent the rest of the millennia without her once she passed on.

"You're awfully quiet. Penny for your thoughts?" Elise asked.

"Just thinking about the future. Something I despaired doing for so long while I was trapped in that lamp."

"Do those thoughts include how to get your grandfather to promise not to use any magic while my parents are here for the wedding?"

Since Naima was now human, Elise insisted her parents didn't need to know the true nature of how they met or about her coming from a family of jinn. They'd managed to keep them clueless of the truth until their engagement dinner. Chirag and Jahir attended, and when Chirag got annoyed by their waiter's attitude, he turned him into a toad right in front of Elise's family and friends. Elise had been horrified as the room full of people stared in open-mouthed shock at Chirag and the huge warty toad sitting at his feet. Fortunately, since they were in a private dining room and the group was small, he was able to wipe the incident from their memories, but it hadn't made Elise any less paranoid about their wedding next week. Especially since it was taking place here at Chirag's home where even some of the staff were jinn.

Naima smiled. "I think Grammy will be able to keep him in check."

"I still can't believe she accepted Chirag's proposal to be his and Jahir's mate. My grandmother in a polygamous relationship is not something I could've ever imagined."

"Does your mother know about that yet?"

Elise snorted. "Of course not! My mother is far from being a prude, but even she may have a tough time accepting that. Grammy's plan is to wait until after the wedding to tell her."

"I think it's nice. I've never seen my grandfather this happy, and from what I knew of Jahir, I didn't think it was possible for him to smile, let alone laugh, but Grammy has seemed to soften him up."

"Or she's the only human not the least bit afraid of him. She says he gives the appearance of being dark and moody but he's really a sweet and kind man."

It was Naima's turn to snort. "Jahir sweet and kind? I still find that unbelievable."

Elise shifted to look at Naima. "Well, he did help to bring me back, and with Grammy's intuition, I can't imagine she's wrong about him, so there's gotta be some good in him."

Naima cupped Elise's cheek. "I guess you're right. It's still a little difficult to equate the jinni that left a trail of destruction and heartbreak behind him with the one you all see. I haven't quite forgiven him for that or the curse."

Elise gave her an understanding smile. "That's fair and I'm sorry for the loss of your home and people, but I'm also thankful for the curse that brought you into my life. Jahir's actions gave me something that I never thought I'd find, a true love that I couldn't imagine living my life without." She brushed her lips across Naima's for a soft kiss.

"I guess I should thank him for that," Naima said petulantly.

Elise gazed at her curiously. "Do you ever regret giving up your powers?"

"No, not at all," Naima answered without hesitation. "There are times I miss the convenience of being able to conjure something out of thin air or use magic to travel from place to place, but none of that is worth spending a life without you. I love you with every fiber of my being, Elise Lynn Porter.

"If I had only been granted one wish it would've been to be with you like this for the rest of our days. I love you too, Jinn Naima of Akiba."

The End

About the Author

Anne Shade indulges in her passion for writing from the idyllic suburb of West Orange, New Jersey, and is the author of *Femme Tales: A Modern Fairytale Trilogy*, *Masquerade*, *Love and Lotus Blossoms*, *Her Heart's Desire*, and *Securing Ava*. Anne has also collaborated on two Bold Strokes Books anthologies, *In Our Words: Queer Stories from Black, Indigenous and People of Color Writers* and *My Secret Valentine: 3 Romance Novellas*. Her other passions include planning dream weddings and making plans for her future bed and breakfast where she plans to spend her days writing and hosting old, new, and future friends and family.

Books Available from Bold Strokes Books

Broken Fences by Jo Hemmingwood. Former army sergeant Seneca Twist has difficulty adjusting to civilian life until she meets psychologist Robyn Mason and has a place to call home. (978-1-63679-414-3)

Never Kiss a Cowgirl by Ali Vali. Asher Evans dreams of winning the National Finals Rodeo in Vegas, and Reagan Wilson wants no part of something that brings back the memory of what killed her father. (978-1-63679-106-7)

Pantheon Girls by Jean Copeland. Cassie Burke never anticipated the detour life was about to take when a meeting with a prospective client reunites her with a past love and reignites the star-crossed passion they shared twenty years earlier. (978-1-63679-337-5)

Roux for Two by Aurora Rey. For TV chef Chelsea Boudreaux and hometown boy Bryce Cormier, love proves as tricky as making a good pot of gumbo. (978-1-63679-376-4)

Starting Over by Nance Sparks. Jennifer has no idea if she can mend Sam's broken soul after the sudden loss of her wife, but it's never too late for starting over. (978-1-63679-409-9)

The Accidental Bride by Jane Walsh. Spinsters Miss Grace Linfield and Miss Thea Martin travel to Gretna Green to prevent a wedding, only to discover a scandalous passion—for each other. (978-1-63679-345-0)

Three Wishes by Anne Shade. A magic lamp, a beautiful Jinni, and a cursed princess make for one unbelievable story. (978-1-63679-349-8)

Undiscovered Treasures by MJ Williamz. For Cyl and her friends Luna and Martinique, life's best treasures often appear when you're not looking. (978-1-63679-449-5)

Curse of the Gorgon by Tanai Walker. Cass will do anything to ensure Elle's safety, but is she willing to embrace the curse of the Gorgon? (978-1-63679-395-5)

Dance with Me by Georgia Beers. Scottie Templeton mixes it up on and off the dance floor with sexy salsa instructor Marisa Reyes. But can Scottie get past Marisa's connection to her ex? (978-1-63679-359-7)

Gin and Bear It by Joy Argento. Opposites really can attract, and as Kelly and Logan work together to create a loving home for rescue cat Bear, they just might find one for themselves as well. (978-1-63679-351-1)

Harvest Dreams by Jacqueline Fein-Zachary. Planting the vineyard of their dreams, Kate Bauer and Sydney Barrett must resist their attraction while battling nature and their families, who oppose both the venture and their relationship. (978-1-63679-380-1)

The No Kiss Contract by Nan Campbell. Workaholic Davy believes she can get the top spot at her firm if the senior partners think she's settling down and about to start a family, but she needs the delightful yet dubious Anna to help by pretending to be her fiancée. (978-1-63679-372-6)

Outside the Lines by Melissa Sky. If you had the chance to live forever, would you take it? Amara Rodriguez did, and it sets her on a journey to find her missing mother and unravel the mystery of her own heart. (978-1-63679-403-7)

The Value of Sylver and Gold by Michelle Larkin. When word gets out that former Boston homicide detective Reid Sylver can talk to the dead, the FBI solicits her help on a serial murder case, prompting Reid to assemble forces once again with Detective London Gold. (978-1-63679-093-0)

When It Feels Right by Tagan Shepard. Freshly out of the closet Marlene hasn't been lucky in love, but when it comes to her quirky new roommate Abby, everything just feels right. (978-1-63679-367-2)

Lucky in Lace by Melissa Brayden. Straitlaced stationery store owner Juliette Jennings's predictable life unravels when a sexy lingerie shop and its alluring owner move in next door. (978-1-63679-434-1)

Made for Her by Carsen Taite. Neal Walsh is a newly made member of the Mancuso crime family, but will her undeniable attraction to Anastasia Petrov, the wife of her boss's sworn enemy, be the ultimate test of her loyalty? (978-1-63679-265-1)

Off the Menu by Alaina Erdell. Reality TV sensation Restaurant Redo and its gorgeous host Erin Rasmussen will arrive to film in chef Taylor Mobley's kitchen. As the cameras roll, will they make the jump from enemies to lovers? (978-1-63679-295-8)

Pack of Her Own by Elena Abbott. When things heat up in a small town, steamy secrets are revealed between Alpha werewolf Wren Carne and her human mate, Natalie Donovan. (978-1-63679-370-2)

Return to McCall by Patricia Evans. Lily isn't looking for romance—not until she meets Alex, the gorgeous Cuban dance instructor at La Haven, a newly opened lesbian retreat. (978-1-63679-386-3)

So It Went Like This by C. Spencer. A candid and deeply personal exploration of fate, chosen family, and the vulnerability intrinsic in life's uncertainties. (978-1-63555-971-2)

Stolen Kiss by Spencer Greene. Anna and Louise share a stolen kiss, only to discover that Louise is dating Anna's brother. Surely, one kiss can't change everything…Can it? (978-1-63679-364-1)

The Fall Line by Kelly Wacker. When Jordan Burroughs arrives in the Deep South to paint a local endangered aquatic flower, she doesn't expect to become friends with a mischievous gin-drinking ghost who complicates her budding romance and leads her to an awful discovery and danger. (978-1-63679-205-7)

To Meet Again by Kadyan. When the stark reality of WW II separates cabaret singer Evelyn and Australian doctor Joan in Singapore, they must overcome all odds to find one another again. (978-1-63679-398-6)

Before She Was Mine by Emma L McGeown. When Dani and Lucy are thrust together to sort out their children's playground squabble, sparks fly leaving both of them willing to risk it all for each other. (978-1-63679-315-3)

Chasing Cypress by Ana Hartnett Reichardt. Maggie Hyde wants to find a partner to settle down with and help her run the family farm, but instead she ends up chasing Cypress. Olivia Cypress. (978-1-63679-323-8)

Dark Truths by Sandra Barret. When Jade's ex-girlfriend and vampire maker barges back into her life, can Jade satisfy her ex's demands, keep Beth safe, and keep everyone's secrets...secret? (978-1-63679-369-6)

Desires Unleashed by Renee Roman. Kell Murphy and Taylor Simpson didn't go looking for love, but as they explore their desires unleashed, their hearts lead them on an unexpected journey. (978-1-63679-327-6)

Maybe, Probably by Amanda Radley. Set against the backdrop of a viral pandemic, Gina and Eleanor are about to discover that loving another person is complicated when you're desperately searching for yourself. (978-1-63679-284-2)

The One by C.A. Popovich. Jody Acosta doesn't know what makes her more furious, that the wealthy Bergeron family refuses to be held accountable for her father's wrongful death, or that she can't ignore her knee-weakening attraction to Nicole Bergeron. (978-1-63679-318-4)

The Speed of Slow Changes by Sander Santiago. As Al and Lucas navigate the ups and downs of their polyamorous relationship, only one thing is certain: romance has never been so crowded. (978-1-63679-329-0)

Tides of Love by Kimberly Cooper Griffin. Falling in love is the last thing on either of their minds, but when Mikayla and Gem meet, sparks of possibility begin to shine, revealing a future neither expected. (978-1-63679-319-1)

BOLDSTROKESBOOKS.COM

Looking for your next great read?

Visit BOLDSTROKESBOOKS.COM
to browse our entire catalog of paperbacks, ebooks,
and audiobooks.

Want the first word on what's new?
Visit our website for event info,
author interviews, and blogs.

Subscribe to our free newsletter for sneak peeks,
new releases, plus first notice of promos
and daily bargains.

SIGN UP AT
BOLDSTROKESBOOKS.COM/signup

Bold Strokes Books
Quality and Diversity in LGBTQ Literature

*Bold Strokes Books is an award-winning publisher
committed to quality and diversity in LGBTQ fiction.*